GOR SAGA

Maureen Duffy

THE VIKING PRESS   NEW YORK

LIBRARY OF CONGRESS CATALOGING IN PUBLICATION DATA
Duffy, Maureen.
Gor saga.
I. Title.
PR6054.U4G6   1982   823'.914   81-69974
ISBN 0-670-34655-1   AACR2

Printed in the United States of America
Set in Caslon

'A faire felde ful of folke fonde I there bitwene,
Of alle maner of men, the mene and the riche,
Working and wandring as the worlde asketh.'

William Langland

I
THE BIRTH
OF GOR

He never really knew his mother. He was taken away from her as soon as it became clear that to Mary the child was just another toy, to be cuddled and crooned over when that mood was on her but in danger of having his brains dashed out when he screamed or she simply became bored with him.

'She doesn't seem to have much maternal instinct, sir,' Knott said.

'I never thought she would.' Forester knocked out his empty pipe in the palm of his hand. 'Not Mary. She's always been too self-centred.'

'Mary want Micky,' she signed at him now through the glass.

'Who's Micky?'

'The cat, sir.'

Knott always sirred him. Secretly Forester found it easier to handle than the informality of Christian names, as he still mentally called them in his old-fashioned way, would have been. It allowed him to use 'Knott' as a kind of symbol and it fitted the man perfectly, his kind of negative durability, a tight-grained nodule turned in on itself.

'Mary got baby,' he signed back at her.

'Baby no good. Baby dirty. Baby loud.' She dangled it by an ankle with its head an inch from the cage floor. She had recognized his interest in it and the gesture was half in blackmail, half in jealousy.

Forester sighed. It would all be so much easier if the animals were less acute socially, less quick to pick up every emotional nuance, and to exploit their own moods as if they knew how ex-

9

pensive and irreplaceable they were. It had taken nine years to train Mary and now she had the temperament of the most difficult *prima donna*.

'You'd better take it away. Though what to do with it . . .?'

'The wife will have it, sir. She's got nothing on hand at the moment.'

'I'd be most grateful to Mrs Knott. You can indent for its upkeep as usual. Then we'll see how it goes. Perhaps it won't survive.'

Indeed it was in danger of a very early extinction. Mary was bumping it along the ground like a wheeled toy on a string.

'Mary give me baby. I give Mary Micky.'

'I'll fetch the cat, sir.'

Forester and Mary stared each other down through the glass wall while Knott fetched the black and white cat in its carrier. Mary had learned by a combination of Micky's own claws, sharp mother-of-pearl rose thorns, and the knowledge that he would be taken away from her if she was too rough with him, to treat the cat gently. Forester wished she could have felt the same about the child whose screams had subsided into a weary grizzle.

'It's a chubby little thing, Knott said when they had made the substitution. 'Not much hair either.'

'Perhaps Mary's been pulling it out.'

Knott shook his head. 'Something not quite right with it. I'll tell the wife not to get too attached to it in case it doesn't live. Always dodgy, these externals.'

Forester kept down an impulse to snap. Knott was one of the old school that still liked everything to be as natural as possible even against the highly artificial nature of the Institute. Mary had firmly resisted all attempts to mate her. Bad mother, she had been a more than indifferent lover, driving off the wretched Jo-Jo, her selected husband, so often and fiercely that he eventually sat in a corner rocking himself in misery with his arms over his head.

Even artificial insemination had failed. Forester had felt a quickly suppressed tremor of excitement as he had pushed the inseminator between the bright pink buttocks which he'd expected to find repulsive, and pressed down the plunger. Perhaps it was the knowledge that Mary had always been a little in love with him, which was partly why she had treated Jo-Jo so badly, calling him 'Dirty monkey', that made Forester

10

feel that she might have accepted his attentions even without the general anaesthetic Knott had given her. For a moment he had almost felt tenderness for the inert form.

The operation itself had been a failure. Mary's body rejected the intruding sperm as she had rejected Jo-Jo. It gave Forester the legitimate chance to try an *in vitro* fertilization, replanting the fecund egg back in her body. This time the enveloping tissues accepted the stranger and carried it the full term before ejaculating it into the common day out of her warm blind dark. The birth had been hard and bloody and Mary had screamed with pain and rage. Once again she had been sedated while the torn flesh was stitched. No wonder the child was doubly unwelcome.

Knott had been his helper when he had taken the egg from her and again when he had put it back. He had watched as Forester had placed it in the culture dish of prepared clear liquid and added the droplets of cloudy seed, exuding a disapproval as palpable as a film of sweat. 'If she wanted to be an old maid why couldn't she have been let,' he argued later with his wife.

'Perhaps she didn't,' she had said then. 'After all, a lot of women have had children the same sort of way.' But when she heard of Mary's unmotherly behaviour she had been less sure. 'Maybe you were right.' She knew the conversation was really about their own childlessness and that they were walking on opposite sides of a crevasse with the tips of their fingers barely touching across the gap.

Now she looked at the down-darkened head on the blanket, at the bundle of a small body snuggled against the hot water bottle Knott had given it for comfort on the journey to their bungalow in the assistants' quarters, and the thin pink fingers curled fiercely round one of her husband's own, and felt a contraction, or an expansion, she couldn't tell which, in her breasts.

'I'll make it a bottle.'

'Don't get too stuck on it, Nance; it mayn't survive.'

'If I could feed it myself . . .'

'You couldn't.'

'I could. After all, you put cow's milk in your tea. There's no difference.'

'What's it to be called, sir?' Knott had asked Forester and he had answered at once.

11

'Gordon.' Knott had entered it in the file with the date of birth, Mary's name, the batch number of the sperm, and the infant's weight.

'Bring it back in a fortnight for a check-up if it lasts that long,' Forester had said.

Nancy had once nursed an orphaned colobus monkey and in her own childhood she had helped with the motherless lambs her father sometimes brought in from the hills. Now she thrust the rubber teat between the red lips and watched the small hands grip on the bottle, and asked its name as her husband had done.

'You'd better get it some clothes if it's still alive in a day or two.'

'It'll need a nappy before then,' she laughed, lifting up the blanket. 'I didn't know they were like this when they were little, so like a human I mean.'

'See them before they're born and they're exactly like, at least the chimps are.' Knott had been shocked one morning to find Sally crooning over her lifeless and miscarried baby. He had only been able to get it away from her after a day of grief when she was finally prepared to admit that it was dead.

'Even so . . .' Nancy looked doubtfully at the small dark pink limbs and dusky belly where the first hair had rubbed away in patches.

'I see what you mean. Maybe it'll get more normal as it gets older.' The baby opened its mouth to belch, dropping the empty bottle and falling asleep all in one go.

'That baby gorilla, sir,' Knott said a few days later.

'Oh yes, how's it doing?' Forester looked up carefully.

'Fine. The wife sees to that. Proper spoils it. But it's not that.'

'Oh?' Forester made the sound of traditional polite unconcern, keeping the file card he had been studying poised as if he had only a moment's attention to spare.

'Yes. I reckon it's a bit of a freak.'

'"Freak" isn't a very scientific term. Is there anything wrong with it?'

'Well yes and no. It's got all its bits and pieces. It's just that it isn't very like any baby chimp or gorilla I've ever had to do with.'

'That's interesting.' Forester put down the card. 'Perhaps we've got a mutation of some sort.'

12

'Yes sir, that's what I think.'

'Well let's hope Mrs Knott can keep it alive for us. Let me know how it goes on. I'd like you to keep a full record of development and I'll come along and see it in a week or two.' He had been afraid his hand might shake visibly as he picked up the card again in a gesture of dismissal. He wanted to shout and laugh and instead he had to stay absolutely calm and pretend to no more interest than Knott's words would be expected to provoke in a person of his known character.

He had done it. While all the rest were speculating about the possibility he had quite simply pulled it off. Even the Russians who had been rumoured to have been trying since the early seventies hadn't made it yet or word would have got out. He had been monitoring the journals very carefully and there had been no breath of success.

But he would keep it quiet for a while yet and there, when he had thought about the problem of secrecy, the Knotts had presented themselves as providing the perfect hide-out. Knott himself didn't mix with the other attendants so there would be no gossip, and his wife was a proven nurse. Forester had to admit that Knott was sometimes right in his preference for the natural over the artificial. Primates throve best with living foster mothers if they couldn't have their own. Kept in incubators, even though fed and warm and given a cloth figure to cling to, they pined mysteriously, almost perversely. Its best chance of survival was with Mrs Knott and the smother love she would give it. He had manoeuvred carefully to bring this about.

He couldn't tell yet, of course, what he had created. It might be mad, monstrous, sterile. He would watch and wait. Meanwhile he had taken out a patent on the chemical process he had disguised from Knott. It was the infant's only birth certificate, Forester reflected. If it perished only Knott and his wife, apart from himself, would know it had ever been. The card could be removed from the file and destroyed. Mary's antipathy for it would provide an explanation of its death.

Forester didn't think that Gordon would die, not deep down in the marrow of his brain, although he tried to guard against disappointment by mentally crossing his fingers in doubt. When Knott had gone he sat on at the white plastic table that served him for a desk, waiting for his pulse to slow and the hum in his ears, as if his head was connected to his body only by a

13

flow of energy, not flesh and bone, to die away. It was like his first lust for Ann over again.

Gor didn't think that he would die either or at least his tissues didn't. His brain wasn't capable yet of thought. It responded automatically to the messages the senses brought it and made his mouth open in a yell when it received tokens of hunger or discomfort, wind or wet. He was a small world with its own weathers.

Nancy had clothed him now and the clothes had rubbed away more of the baby hair so that he was bald almost all over. Already his near black eyes followed her comings and goings and his hands grabbed at her clothes as she lifted him up. 'You sure he's a monkey?' she asked Knott one evening.

'Ape.'

'Ape then.'

'The professor says he could be a mutation.'

'What's that?'

'Well, not quite right.'

The changeling looked up at them from his cot and at the slowly turning mobile of coloured plastic balls Nancy had hung above it.

'He's bright enough anyway. Them little boot-buttons follow me everywhere.'

'Boot-buttons? Boots don't have buttons.'

'It's a saying for eyes when they're sharp and round and bright like his.'

Nancy had a store of such sayings. Knott had found them endearing at first but now they only emphasized the difference between them, as if they indeed spoke two languages which had once been the same until driven apart by distance and time. Against all his warnings she had become bound to the infant so tightly that he felt that if circumstances, or Knott himself, were to prise them apart some of her body might be torn away in the rending.

As promised, Forester called on the Knotts at the end of a fortnight when Nancy was bathing the baby. Forester frightened her, with the effect always of making her seem almost insolent. Now she was afraid that he had come to take Gor away and the terror filled her throat like bile so that she seemed to be choking while she made useless gestures of appeasement, offering him tea and biscuits which he didn't want and then instant coffine.

14

'Thank you, I won't. I've just come for a little check on progress. If you could just turn it over.'

Nancy obediently put Gor face down. There was still some hair down his back and the backs of his legs. Forester took a tape measure from his pocket and measured the small skull at its widest point. Like all babies Gor had no neck and his legs were still permanently bent. Forester sensed Knott's wife flinch as he extended a leg and then an arm. It was strange how the maternal instinct could be transferred on to almost any infantile form while still being inconsistent enough to allow some mothers to batter their own babies. Well, its strength in Knott's wife suited his purpose now. Later it might become a nuisance.

There seemed to be an even blend of characteristics, with the human well advanced although it was difficult to tell at this stage and he mustn't be unscientific in his desire to applaud his own achievement, his little Caliban. 'You're doing extremely well.' He pressed the catch on the tape measure that caused the length of tape to whirl back onto the spool. Gor showed his gums and clenched and unclenched his fists towards the noise.

'He's very knowing,' Nancy proffered. She had realized with a great swell of relief, as if the bubble of fear had burst inside her leaving her head singing, that Forester wasn't going to take Gor away, not this time at least.

'All mammals tend to be at that age.' She mustn't be allowed to find Gor too exceptional. 'Think of kittens.' And then to Knott, 'Your wife's doing a splendid job. It looks much stronger now than when I last saw it. If you can keep it a bit longer. . .' He let the words trail so that she would run after them.

'Oh he's no trouble. I like having him. Gives me something to do.'

As Forester drove away from the assistants' quarters rain lashed at the windscreen and flattened like magnified cells against the glass. Needing the drive, he turned towards the northern perimeter. The barrier lifted when the scanner had identified his identity card and he drove out onto the road past the sign which warned against trespass with the acronym MOD. '"Mad" it should read,' Ann always said.

He took the road through the downs that were the colour of wet tweed under the falling sky. A band of lemon lit by an invisible sun was taped between earth and cloud to keep them apart and Forester drove till he came to the highest point on the road where he could pull off on to a flat of sodden verge. Ignoring the rain he got out and stood looking across at the black henge blocked in against the pale strip of sky. He had done something as great as that. He gulped in wind and rain until the high crown of exaltation passed and he became aware of runlets trickling down his face and dripping unheroically from the end of his nose. He got back into the car, found the tissues he always kept in the glove compartment and mopped at his hair and face until the cellulose paper began to disintegrate. For a moment he thought of throwing the soggy mess out of the window. After all he had the right now, an almost divine right to do anything. Nature wept violated over him. Forester recalled from somewhere, though he couldn't track down where, a picture of the rape of Lucrece, as English had made the Roman matron: the parting thighs and lips, the eyes between sparkle and horror at the complicity of her own lust, Tarquin's raised dagger. Forester had taken a scalpel to her and she had given herself up to him.

He put the tissues into the ashtray and started the engine. It was almost dark by the time he reached home. The lights were on here and there, making amber patches in the black bulk of the house. Forester had decided from the beginning that he would live outside, not over the shop, and he was senior enough to achieve this. Now he was doubly glad of the separation. This was another reality that would help him steady himself.

He had bought an old farmhouse. Ann believed of course that they had bought it together and he let her think so. They had looked at several which had given her the illusion of choice. He didn't care, once he had established the principle, which particular assembly of bricks and mortar it took form in and anyway she was better at both the practical and the aesthetic aspects of life. Women's minds generally, he believed, were more fitted for that sort of thing while men's were better at abstraction, logic, pure science. Among even the best of his female colleagues, and there were one or two, there was a tendency to trivialize by too great attention to detail, to the practical. They saw problems not solutions. Forester let himself into the warmth of the house.

'Is that you, darling?' Ann called from the kitchen. As a rule it annoyed him and he had once asked what reply she thought she would get from a burglar or rapist, but this evening he merely called back the required answer: 'It's me!'

He was still, three years into marriage, able to be surprised by her appearance at the kitchen door, that this strange person should be there at all and that she should be so remarkably beautiful. Since he had never been in love with her there had never been any heat of physical passion to fuse them together and they therefore remained strangers, at least in Forester's mind.

Ann's feelings were less consistent. She sometimes experienced a surge of panic when she looked at Norman across the table and wondered who he was and what she was doing sitting there opposite him. Then she would feel guilty, speak quickly, foolishly to have the reassurance of his voice. 'I do love him,' she would say to herself. At other times she would see them both out walking together down some damp hazed autumn lane over a carpet of deep chestnut leafmeal between stripped hedges and think, 'There's Norman and Ann Forester, husband and wife.'

Today there wasn't any room for doubt any more. The test had been positive and she had to tell Norman before the others arrived. 'You're soaked,' she said, going up and touching his coat which had begun to give off its smell of damp wool in the warmth of the hall.

'I went over to see Knott and got wet getting back to the car. Have I got time for a bath before they're all upon us?'

'Only if you let me wash your back.' They played a game of constant pseudo eroticism, pretending to desire to cover its real lack, but today Forester felt a quick response in himself.

'Okay,' he said. 'I'll take you up on that.' He stripped off his wet top coat and made for the stairs, beginning to undo his tie and shirt. Ann followed. She hadn't really meant to be bounced into her offer but she had to talk to him. 'Run the bath for me, darling.' He vanished into the bedroom as she bent over the console that controlled water and foam. Suddenly she felt him behind her thrusting at the back of her long evening skirt.

'How about that?'

She turned and saw the full erection under the open towelling dressing-gown and she was moved by tenderness and pride towards it. 'Norman, I'm pregnant.'

'Christ! Are you sure? You know last time . . .'

17

'The test results came this morning. I sent away when I thought I might be. I didn't want to go to old Stammers and make a fool of myself again.'

'You used a testing service? They're for the nons.'

'Not only, and anyway it seemed better just in case I was wrong.' The humiliation of her interview with Dr Stammers when he had implied that she had brought on a false hysterical pregnancy still pained her.

The erection sunk to a slight flatulence now, Norman climbed into the bath. Well, there was no harm in it and it would increase his status. The next time he was asked to lecture in the States his faculty card would read with more health, 'married to Ann, one son', or 'daughter.' It might even be useful in other ways though he couldn't see how at the moment.

'I hope it won't always have that effect on you,' Ann laughed.

'Well, it is a bit of a blow, not a bad one, but even a good one knocks you off your feet rather.'

She wanted to ask if he was glad but was suddenly afraid of the answer. 'I'd better get back to the kitchen. Darling . . . ?'

'Uh?'

'I'd rather we didn't tell anyone yet.'

'Okay, if you say so.' Left alone, he soaped his armpits and lay back in the suds, cupping the weight of his genitals comfortingly in one palm and resting his head and neck against the end of the bath. He could easily lie here for hours, fall asleep even in a cocoon of foam bath and achievement.

Downstairs Ann stirred the vegetables in the wok with a wooden spoon. She had got it said and it hadn't been so bad. She didn't know why she had been so frightened; well, not frightened, just a bit worried in case she was making a fool of herself. But Norman had believed her. He'd been a bit put out about her using a pregnancy testing service and it was true that people of their status usually went to their personal physician for that sort of thing. But the testing services were reliable. They had to be because their certificates of pregnancy entitled you to the free government vitamins and things, so the government inspectors made sure they were efficient to keep down fraud.

Ann couldn't bring herself to use the word 'nons' as Norman and many others of their friends did and it left her at a loss for a descriptive term. In the end she had settled for 'ordinary people' when to her they were completely extraordinary. She thought it was partly the difference in their backgrounds. Norman had been the clever child of a word processer in local government who had passed his selection and been aided for a good school and then to Cambridge.

'Word processer' was just the polite term for a machine minder, Norman said, and in that sense he had come from the nons and was proud of it, proud to have left them behind. He knew what they were really like whereas Ann knew nothing about them. Her father had been a don. That was how she had met Norman. Professor Briles had believed in inviting his brighter students home for tea, particularly if they needed the social corners knocked off a bit. The civilizing presence of Mrs Briles's thin sandwiches and rock cakes could be very good for aided boys. Curiously the girls never seemed to need it. They acquired the right camouflage much more easily. Which was just as well. He didn't know how Ann and her elder sister, Fanny, would have responded to his bringing young girls home, let alone his wife, whereas she was devoted to the boys because, he supposed, they had no son of their own or because the students were always so attentive to her.

Thank God that phase when the young had got so out of hand and above themselves was long behind. They knew their manners today. Not that Norman Forester would have been his first choice for Ann, even though he was one of the brightest students ever to pass through Briles's hands. He would have preferred someone of their own status, with the extra social facility that would have meant, but he had to admit that Forester had been a quick learner in every way. Now you would hardly guess his origins. A lot of that was Ann's doing of course. Marriage to her had given him the final polish. But the education system had done its job remarkably well too and Briles was proud to be part of it.

He wondered if Norman had ever had an accent. Lower clerical usually carried a sort of nasal twang with it: 'Slough deferential', a colleague in linguistics had defined it as. Norman's accent was carefully neutral.

Sometimes when Ann caught the sound of her own voice she was irritated by its girlishness but there was nothing she could do about it and she supposed that even when she was sixty it would still be the same, as the colour of her eyes would never

19

alter either. Fanny had the same intonation even though she was five years older than Ann, and in half an hour they would be chiming together and she would catch a quickly wiped away half smile on Norman's face that she had sometimes thought patronizing. She didn't care, not today, and if she surprised it there she would read it as affectionate rather than sardonic. All must go well today and her own thoughts not be allowed to sour the air. She scraped chopped onion and green pepper into the bowl of saffron rice and mixed them with a wooden spoon.

She wouldn't tell even Fanny yet until she felt more sure of the baby inside her, though she told her sister almost everything, except those doubts about Norman's identity which seemed to hover on the edge of lunacy.

Fanny had married Charles Widdington whom she had met not under her father's aegis, for he was in a different department, but because he rode. Norman didn't ride and it was another mark of his 'ordinary' background. He had first decided to marry Ann when he had seen the sisters and his future brother-in-law walking their horses into the paddock that lay beyond the garden of the Briles house and they had seemed, in winter sunlight against an uncharacteristically blue English sky, like a cavalcade from childhood, a combination of princeliness and power that he intended to be part of.

His now brother-in-law had been in the sparks department of the engineering faculty. He had gone into a computer firm after Cambridge and had then struck out on his own, setting up a small factory to design and produce hardware gadgets of his own invention which interested him more than turnover and profit figures, though these seemed to grow spontaneously even without his interest.

Professor Briles had been sorry to see his son-in-law go into industry and thought him a bit of a buffoon while admitting that academic posts weren't easily come by and that they were all dependent on the firms for funding. But what Charles did was more like a mechanic's job. Briles suspected that he might even sometimes use a screwdriver or press the buttons which automated the robots that welded or painted. Still, he provided well for Fanny and their three children and was easygoing enough never to assert himself in either the Briles home or his own detached colonial-style house in Andover.

Forester stood up in the bath, pushed the plug release with his big toe and reached for a warmed towelling robe to wrap

20

himself in, a more solid extension of the foam bath, while he applied the electric toothbrush to his rather small teeth. On the whole he was glad that the Widdingtons were coming. He would be able to half-listen and smile, and any silences on his part would be covered by Fanny who always had a lot to tell her sister, not as information but as a form of affection, the spreading of a shawl of words round Ann's more vulnerable shoulders.

The love between Ann and Fanny constantly surprised him. Although their voices, and to some extent their features, shadowed each other, they were temperamentally very different. Fanny was robust and secure in herself; Ann's was a more fluid, almost tremulous, personality which suited Forester very well. He was constantly surprised too by his brother-in-law's ability to soak up his wife's assertiveness like a boxer taking body blows seemingly without injury.

There was a crunch of tyres on gravel, the slamming of doors and then the chimes of the doorbell. Voices drifted up from the hall as Forester finished dressing: Charles's baritone, strong and confident, and the two soprano sisters, Fanny's a little louder on the hard palate.

'How're your pensioners, Ann?' Charles was asking as Forester entered the drawing-room. 'Hallo, Norman.'

'You're looking very radiant, Norman.' Fanny offered him a still chilled cheek to kiss, smelling of night air and *Cajoler*.

'Well scrubbed. Twice in fact: once by the rain, once by me. What's everyone drinking?' He knew the answers but it was form to ask. Charles would have malt whisky; Fanny would have a dry vermouth and Ann a gin and tonic, in reversal of what might have been expected of them.

'So what's new down at the mill?' he asked his brother-in-law as he handed him a half-filled glass of liquid topaz.

'Charlie's dreamt up a new gidget that'll make more pots of lovely loot. It's called "Printin". It does away with all those vast sheets of paper and smudgy newsprint.'

'It'll save trees,' Charles said. 'Cheers!'

'Will it?' Ann asked. 'That's marvellous. I've always hated the thought of all the tall beautiful trees sawn and battered to a pulp to make paper, even though I love paper itself.'

'You'll still be able to have it as a luxury item for personal stationery.' Charles rolled the highlight from the chandelier round in his glass.

21

'How does it work?'

'Two versions: a mini reader or an input to the telly screen. It's a variation of microfiche but very cheap to produce. There's a pocket-size push button for train reading, a slightly bigger home or office job and then the telly printin that can also translate to cassette. Build your own library of *The Times* with no storage problems.'

'Don't make it sound too attractive or Ann'll be after one each for all her pensioners and the house'll be nothing but a continuous bring-and-buy sale.' Norman laughed, pulling on his own whisky.

Ann's pensioners were a family joke. She collected books from everywhere she could and ferried them in a van to outlying villages where she set up her library stall in the church or some suitable hall or hut. They could be borrowed for a small fee. Many of them had been read so often that there were pages missing and these were catalogued at the front of the book. Often she would go into Salisbury to get pages machine copied from the city library to insert in her own tatterdemalions. She wondered at people's ingenuity in piecing together a plot where crucial elements might be missing, but again and again her customers chose the most depleted texts, believing that where so many had read it must be worth a follow, however you had to leap from narrative stepping stone to stone. Surprisingly, none ever reneged, except by death or long sickness, on their unwritten contract with Ann to bring back the books. Norman said it was because they were responsible to her personally. How could they fail? How would they ever face her or each other again?

She had no training for this self-elected job. When Norman had first met her she was studying music and had eventually taken her degree but from there on she hadn't known where to go. To hustle was outside her nature. Competition was fierce for places in groups, let alone orchestras. Ann's taste and technique were for older music and for preference she played the viola, d'amore or da gamba. Here she was at the further disadvantage of having to compete with friends and those whose work she respected, and which her low assessment of her own abilities caused her to constantly overvalue. In a way, Norman had been her rescue. She had no longer had to try.

'But I must do something, darling,' she had said, 'otherwise you'll get bored with me.' And so the pensioners' library had been born. Ann would have been the first, and indeed the only one, to admit that she did it for the good that was done to her. It brought her the contact with those 'ordinary' people whom she had never learned to call 'nons'. At first she had been very frightened. What would she say to them or they to her? Would she be repelled by them? Suppose they were hostile? In the beginning she had nearly made mistakes in her nervousness.

In spite of the label 'Ann's pensioners' they weren't all old. Some were quite young, disabled or unemployed, young mothers with children under six, though it had been the elderly who had come first. The others had drifted in almost surreptitiously later, almost indeed expecting to be turned away. Sometimes a child came on behalf of parent or grandparent. Her stock was small and they had often to take what was left if they were late. Something they had to have, to bear home 'for a read'. For a heart-sinking moment she wondered whether Charlie's new 'gidget' would do away with books altogether in time. What would she bring them then? Guiltily she caught herself beginning the thought: 'I'll have the baby.'

Forester was glad of her pensioners. It gave them something to talk about or rather it gave Ann something to tell him when he came home, an offering of words that covered his own lack of any such gift. It also gave him something to trade with colleagues in return for their bits of mingled gossip and shop, which were the mirrors and beads of social intercourse at the Institute. With the latest saying of one of the pensioners to offer he had no need to tell them about his work and he was able to bask in some of Ann's reflected altruism as well.

'Country people are so much nicer than the city nons,' Fanny was saying.

'There was rioting again in Bradford on the tellynews.'

'When isn't there?' Charles offered.

Ann had switched on while she waited for Norman and prepared the wok. There had been the usual angry faces with noises over though Ann knew that these were often dubbed in from stock. Sometimes she had the heretical notion that the 'rentacrowd', as it was called, was hired out not by the opposition but by the media or even by the government to keep the Home Counties complacent. She had shocked herself with this thought and she had tried to dismiss it but couldn't. It was there like an unfilled cavity in a tooth.

'Things are pretty awful in the cities,' Fanny was saying. 'I mean, thank heavens we don't have to live there.'

'If you did you'd soon get something organized. Instead of just lying down under fate, I'm sure you'd do something to change it.' Forester had always admired his sister-in-law's drive, although knowing it would have been a frightening force if it had ever been directed against him, if, for instance, he had seemed to be hurting Ann.

'I wonder. With three kids like we've got it wouldn't be easy.'

'That's why they're discouraged from having more than two, why the government downgrades the family supplement after that.'

'While it's our duty to have as many as we can afford. Well, that's why I don't really want Charlie to make much more money or I shall feel like nothing but a breeding sow,' Fanny laughed.

Ann had come in from the kitchen at the end of this remark. She wanted to say, 'Norman and I are . . .' but instead it came out as 'If you'd like to come through . . .'

She was less nervous than usual because this was a family party and Fanny was there. Any failure on her part would be seen through the prism of affection not criticism. Even so she found it hard to concentrate on the flow of talk. Her mind slipped sideways out of a backdoor into a garden where she sat with a child whose sex she couldn't yet divine. She would have more to talk about in future. She would be able to join in the child gossip of other women, the complaints that were actually boasts about demands on their time and money.

'Thank heavens for automation,' Fanny was saying. 'I don't know how women used to manage.'

'They had servants,' her brother-in-law said.

'Oh I don't mean then. That was fifty years ago. I mean in the period between then and about ten years ago when people of our status just had perhaps some old duck who came in to clean once a week, and they did all the cooking and the rest of the cleaning themselves. And you had to remember to shop and get the laundry ready on the right day, which was never really the right day because they could never keep to schedule. And you had to talk to the cleaning woman so that her feelings weren't hurt and have all sorts of peripheral meaningless relationships with people who were nothing to you except that you were dependent on them.'

24

'Ann would have liked that.'

'Oh no . . .' she began in protest.

But Fanny interrupted, 'Oh yes you would because you do it now. What else are your pensioners?'

'And you cook,' said Charles, 'and I have to admit it does taste better than even the most exotic of the frozdishes.'

Ann felt the beginnings of a blush which she tried to control because it was ridiculous to be blushing still when you were only a couple of years off thirty. Charlie was really rather a dear. She supposed that was why Fanny seemed so aggressively content.

'I cook too. You don't starve,' Fanny protested.

'You fling a pack into the heater and set the dial. Then you take it out when the bell rings.'

'That way you get three meals a day, all four of you.'

Ann smiled. She was glad Fanny was happy, glad they were so fond of each other that it could show itself in this kind of bantering which she realized was a variety of sex play.

'Suppose,' Norman was saying, 'you could have a species of animate robot to do these things for you. Then you might get the best of both worlds.'

'The trouble with robots,' said Charles, scenting one of his favourite discussions, 'is that no one has yet been able to simulate the senses of a human being to make aesthetic choices. For that you seem to need old-fashioned flesh and blood, even if it's only a non.'

'That's what I mean.' Forester was almost angry with himself for introducing the theme yet part of him enjoyed the danger and he felt almost giddy. Perhaps he was drinking his wine too fast. 'Suppose you were able to have intelligent subhumans?'

'But where would be the difference,' Ann asked, 'from the old-style servants?'

'All the difference.'

'Not to Ann,' said Fanny. 'You remember Willie?'

Ann did. For a moment she felt she might begin to weep again even after all these years. Though in theory the family cat, Willie's relationship with Ann had been much stronger than with any other human. Professor Briles had thought him a nuisance but tolerated him and Willie had managed to stay out of his way as he did with Mrs Briles who complained that he 'left hairs everywhere'. Fanny he treated as a lesser equal but

25

Ann he adored, sleeping on her bed at night and even accompanying her to the lavatory where he waited outside. So much of a person was he to Ann that she would no more have allowed him inside than she would anyone else. When she went away to school he became subdued and distant until she was home again when he rejoiced loudly, gambolled, purred and followed her about. If he fell asleep and Ann left him, when he awoke he would begin to call her, stalking from room to room in search, until he was able to wind and rewind himself about her legs. He had been run over in term time by a passing car. When she had heard, Ann had become ill with grief and had to be sent home from school. Only Fanny, out of her own deep love for her sister, had half understood.

'But you don't really like horses,' Charles said.

'What's that got to do with it?' asked his wife.

'I know what Charlie means,' Ann said, 'but it's because they're so much people. It isn't that I don't like them, it's that I don't see why they should carry me about and that makes me frightened because I know they need to be told and guided if they're to do the right thing and I can't see why they should take that from me.'

Her fundamental dislike of riding had secretly angered Forester at first and he had felt somehow cheated as if the antique silver he had bought had suddenly revealed itself as electroplate.

'The line must be blurred sometimes with your monkeys, Norman,' Charles said.

'Apes,' said Ann. 'You're not allowed to call them monkeys, it's unscientific.'

Charles was unabashed. 'Well, apes, but anyway there can't be much difference between them and some of the subier nons one sees about.'

'Ann doesn't like us to call them "nons". They're "ordinary people".'

'There seems to be a lot about me and my views this evening,' she said, laughing a little.

Fanny had been growing disquieted and ready to jump to her sister's defence or change the subject but for once Ann didn't seem upset by this constant verbal attention. Indeed she almost seemed to be enjoying it. Was it the wine? Fanny wondered. She was a little flushed and almost, well, hectic.

'What else can one call them?' Charles asked. 'C, D and E is

26

too long. It's better than "proles" or "trogs".'

'What does it really mean?' Ann asked.

'Non-achievers,' her brother-in-law answered, forking up the last of his plateful.

'Or Non-U,' offered Fanny. 'It's marvellous how that show keeps running. Charlie and I go every couple of years to see how they've updated it.'

'Nonentity: that's what it stands for,' said Forester fiercely. 'Have some more wine, Fanny.'

'Hey, careful.' Charles pushed his own glass forward. 'Remember you're the driver.'

'Oh, I'll put her on automatic.'

'You're the only one I know who can override the computer by an exercise of will.' Charles himself still liked to drive part manually though there were only a few systems you could cut out altogether. The anti-collider and the centreline scanner for instance were always in operation. Fanny and he drove over so often to see Ann and Norman that they had taped the journey and fed it into the memory circuit so that there was no need to do anything except keep your hands on the steering wheel which served as a dead man's handle when the car was on full automatic.

Forester was relieved now that the conversation had swung away. He was surprised that he had made such a dangerous game for himself. He must be more careful in future, particularly at the Institute.

'Wake up, Norman,' Fanny said. 'You've gone off.' She had made a family joke of his habit of ignoring the company for his own thoughts, a joke which, although it irritated him, Forester sometimes found useful. The image of him as a harmless boffin whose eccentricities had to be humoured covered his own personality with a softening gauze.

'I was saying,' Fanny went on, 'that I don't know what I'll do when Harriet goes to school, what I'll do all day I mean.'

'You could start a book round like Ann,' Norman offered.

'Oh, I haven't her patience with the pensioners. Besides I like to see some real return to me and mine. I might get a couple more horses and give lessons to children. That would make me some rag money and keep me from getting bored.'

'It would be nice to have more horses about the place,' Charles said.

For a moment Ann had a return of her earlier hallucination

of the child whose sex she didn't know, but laughing down at her now from ponyback. She could know of course in a few weeks if she wanted to. But did she? Did Norman? What did he want anyway? She realized she had no idea. The ambisexual child looked down at her very seriously, its smile stilled.

'Honestly, Ann, you're as bad as Norman.'

'Sorry.' She jumped guiltily.

'No one listens to me and my problems. They just think, "Old Fanny will cope. No need to bother seriously about her. She'll get through."'

'And so you will,' her husband smiled.

'I think the horses are a very good idea,' Ann said, getting up and beginning to remove the remains of the meal. She had made individual crèmes brûlées for pudding. For a moment the pattern of the four dishes, with their part glazed, part crystalline treacle-brown spheres against the pale yellow pine of the table, held her mesmerized in a second's perception of them as painted there without depth or being of their own. 'I am Ann Forester married to Norman and I'm going to have a baby,' she had to say to herself before she could put out a hand to pick each one up in turn and place it on an ultramarine glass tray, the colour, Ann had often thought, of the sea gazed down on from the deck of the Greek liner plying between the islands where she and Norman had honeymooned. Perhaps that was why she had bought it.

'Are we going to have a tune?' asked Fanny.

'If you like.' Surprisingly to those who knew her and thought her a mouse, a beautiful mouse, Ann didn't mind playing in public or the semi-public of the family. She had trained for it and in any case when she played the audience fell away from her and she was playing alone to herself.

Forester hadn't known at first how to take this strange accomplishment in the girl he had decided to marry. It had embarrassed him quite as much as if she hadn't known how to dress or whistled in public. But then it had appeared that it added cachet to his acquisition. Once again it was something to offer in conversation. He noticed that colleagues who invited them to dinner at their homes were intrigued when they heard and when ritually invited back, eager for the plates to be removed, the liqueurs brought out and for Ann to come forward and sit quite unselfconsciously in the middle of the room to play, making a study of such charm that Norman had considered having her painted, as the fashion now was.

Ann had rejected the idea, somehow conveying that she found it vulgar. It seemed to her odd that his colleagues' wives should want their own faces to peer down, glossily stylized as in a magazine advertisement and reconstructed from a photograph by a hack painter, from the walls of their own homes. It would have made her feel that she was already dead or else that the portrait was to remind her how far she was from the accepted ideal, of what she ought to be if she really tried.

Now she moved forward the green velvet-covered chair on which she usually sat to play and opened the case to take out the viola d'amore. The blindfold infant cupid carved on its pegbox, Ann thought, smiled at her knowingly as her hands positioned the instrument, a trick of the shower dazzle of light from the chandelier under whose fountain she sat.

She chose music that Cromwell might have heard in his Protector's palace at Hampton Court made by one of his daughters on the lyra-viol. Fanny was surprised by the sudden pang in her chest of unshed tears as the notes that seemed an image of Ann were drawn into the air. At the end it was almost wrong to clap but they did and Ann, brought back into herself, brushed away the near-black hair that had fallen forward in a curtain as she played, laughing a little nervously.

As they undressed later after Charles and Fanny had gone she said, 'We never got back to your intelligent sub-humans. What did you mean?'

'Nothing, really. It was just for the sake of a bit of argument. Sometimes I get very pissed off with Fanny going on about her kids and Charlie about his "gidgets". It was an attempt to broaden the conversation.'

'I expect I'll be just as bad.'

'No you won't because you haven't got Fanny's energy. You don't need to talk as much as she does.'

Ann, brushing her hair at the curved mirror of her dressing-table, was silent, not knowing whether to be upset on Fanny's behalf or even on her own. It was when Norman made this kind of remark that her world trembled and he appeared a stranger. Once she had even found herself wondering if he saw her as any different from the animals at the Institute.

He had taken her there one afternoon in daylight to show her round, an occasion different from the faculty social evenings they sometimes attended. She had thought she had wanted to

29

see and hadn't foreseen the effect the place would have on her. As they had moved from room to room and block to block she had found herself panicking as the hysteria rose inside her. She wanted to scream and run away but had fought it with, 'I mustn't, I mustn't,' repeated in her head as mystics entrance themselves with the repetitions of their gods' names.

Not that she had seen anything terrible. Norman, knowing her feelings, had shown her only well housed, warmed and fed creatures who had looked at her with terror or indifference. She had wanted to speak to them, to hold out a finger or tap on the hygienic glass but had drawn back. Such gestures would have offered hope, kindness, and been a lie. But not to make them was to stifle her natural response to living flesh and blood.

Ann remembered a visit to the local zoo as a thirteen-year-old with her father when Professor Briles was being paternally instructive. They had come to the chimps' house, a structure of glass and concrete extended by an outside caged run with small trees and grass. A party of trippers had paused by the bars where one of the residents, a pre-adolescent male, was being particularly charming.

'Ent he lovely?' called out one young girl to her mates. 'I want to get in there with him.' She had crossed the narrow railed-off strip of grass that was meant to psychologically deter and put her hand between the bars. There was no sign of a keeper.

The young male had seized her hand, pressed it to his cheek and then opened the fingers to examine them one by one.

'Thoroughly irresponsible behaviour,' Professor Briles had said, stepping forward. Alarmed, the chimpanzee dropped the girl's hand and stepped back chattering. The girl snatched her hand back through the bars.

'I wasn't doing him no harm.'

'You could have been badly bitten at the very least. I suggest you move away from here.'

The girl had flushed up angrily and was about to reply but a friend had dragged at her arm. 'Come on, Selena. He might report you.'

'What you'd expect,' Briles had said to Ann as he rejoined her. 'Thoroughly irresponsible as usual.'

'Yes,' she had said. But her agreement was given with the private rider that the irresponsibility lay in breaking for a moment the barrier between prisoner and free, in encouraging a relationship however brief that could only bring frustration and greater misery to one of them. It was then that she realized that she could never follow in her father's footsteps as he, having no son, had rather hoped, and turned thankfully towards her music.

The visit to the Institute had brought back that earlier trip. Now as she passed from room to room in a horrified daze, Norman began to seem a kind of tormentor who led her through the infernal circles as Virgil had led Dante but with none of his tendency to shed tears over the damned or their sufferings. She thought of herself as weak, too susceptible, sentimental probably. Other people didn't think as she did. White-cloaked assistants of both sexes, or possibly none behind their masks, moved to and fro finding nothing amiss. It was her own painful vulnerability that was reflected in the small furry bodies. It must be so, for how could she be right and all the rest of them wrong?

In a way the visit to the primate section, Norman's special preserve, was less distressing. They had stopped while Norman talked to Mary the gorilla, explaining the signed dialogue orally to Ann as he did so. 'Mary's jealous of you. She called you a "dirty lady".'

'Why did she do that?'

'Maybe she's having a pregnant fantasy.'

'She's pregnant?'

'Yes. I can't tell her you're my wife because there's nothing in her experience to parallel it.'

'Don't they have wives?'

'In the wild, one dominant male has a kind of harem. But Mary's never known the wild. Here we give them a different mating pattern, one that suits our purposes better.'

'How can you do that?' She meant: how is that possible? But it sounded in her own ears like a reproach, one however which Norman didn't notice.

He was a little irritated by her questions and wondered if she would understand the answer when he gave it. 'Sexual behaviour in the wild is largely a matter of social organization. There seems to be very little that's genetically programmed about it. So if you change the social organization you can usually change the sexual behaviour without much trouble. Animals that would otherwise have an organization rather like an old-

31

fashioned oriental despot's court, with the sultan and his wives and concubines and the young men hangers-on he allows a woman of his choice to, can be put into pairs like any lower clerical couple in a bungalow and mate and produce offspring.'

'Where's Mary's mate?'

'Jo-Jo? We had to take him away. She didn't like him much and bullied him.'

'How did he get her pregnant then?'

'He didn't. We did. She's an AID pregnancy.'

'So it doesn't always work?'

'Mary's in love with someone else.'

'Oh.'

'Her keeper.'

'The famous Mr Knott?'

'That's right,' Norman lied.

'Does it apply to humans?'

'What's that, darling?'

'This theory about the social basis of sex.'

'Oh it must do, mustn't it? Otherwise you wouldn't have had so many varieties of sexual pattern in the course of human history.'

Again Ann felt the ground move under her. She and Norman were the throw-ups of a temporary social pattern. She wanted to ask him where love came in but was frightened of what might be the reasoned answer.

Now as she laid the hairbrush aside she suddenly remembered Mary. 'Has Mary had her baby yet?'

Forester paused before his reply, paying careful attention to the sit of his suit on the coat hanger. 'Which Mary?'

'Wasn't that her name? I'm not sure if she's a chimpanzee or a gorilla.'

'Gorilla. Yes she had it a couple of weeks ago. Mrs Knott is fostering it. Mary didn't make a very good mother. That's how I got so wet, going to have a look at it.'

'Is it a boy or a girl?'

'Male. Doing very nicely with the Knotts.'

'Poor Mary. I suppose she never really wanted it. You said she didn't like her mate much either.'

'Mary prefers humans. She thinks the others are just animals,' Forester laughed. 'Yet she can recognize herself in a mirror and say: "That's Mary".'

'She must think badly of herself then.'

32

'What do you mean, darling?'

'Well, if she can recognize herself in what she sees on others as an animal's body when she prefers humans, it must make her feel, I don't know, reduced somehow and dissatisfied with herself. It must make her despise herself.'

'You wouldn't say that if you really knew her. She's quite a despot.'

Ann was silent. What else, she thought, could Mary do? Only rage or grief were possible from such a perception.

'Besides, that's rather an anthropomorphic view. There's no evidence that she's capable of feeling like that.'

Any more, Ann thought, than there is of what I feel unless I speak about it, and if I didn't know the language or was deaf and dumb, I couldn't except through the same kind of signs that Mary uses. 'Perhaps someone should ask her,' she said aloud.

Later, as she lay awake in the dark beside Norman, feeling her own child as a node of pleasure inside her, and heard the wind and rain beating about the house, her thoughts moved out again across the intervening country to where Mary's baby lay asleep. She must remember to ask his name, she thought, as she felt herself beginning to sink from consciousness.

Thus the infant Gor grew so that by the time Ann's belly was six months round he could sit up and smile and hold things in his hands. And every day as Nancy bathed him she became more frightened that they would come and take him away from her. For there was some terrible mistake. This was a human baby she had been given to foster, she was certain, and the error must surely show up soon. Somewhere there was a mother searching, frantic with loss, while she, Nancy, kept quiet and doted on a child she shouldn't have as if she had snatched it from its babycar outside the automart.

Forester came to see it from time to time and then her gut congealed until he was safely going up the garden path with Gor left behind in the house. Knott kept the baby's record cards and drew the allowance for his nurture, seeing nothing amiss except perhaps for an occasional worry about Nancy's fierce dependence on the infant.

Her new doubts came when his strong arms pulled him up out of the playpen and dropped him in a howling heap she rushed to cosset with hugs and kisses until his tears stopped.

He never crawled but went from sitting to standing while holding on, but that, she reasoned, was alright. Many children, she read in the handbook she had bought herself on baby care, didn't crawl. Her next worry was that he might be a mongol because of something, she couldn't say quite what, about his eyes and the low forehead but his play fitting-together of shapes and building blocks calmed this fear.

Who had his parents been? And what was it all about? How could she keep him for ever? The questions chased through her head as she bent over him and his eyes and hands tugged at her.

It would be satisfying to be able to record that our young hero was gifted with the kind of miraculous growth and strength of other mythical beings, that he strangled serpents in his cradle or was a warrior and beloved of women at seven, but he was in truth a very ordinary child which was perhaps the most extraordinary thing about him. There were no portents, wise men, or unseasonal flowerings except for Nancy.

Often at night beside her husband or during the day, as she cleaned and cooked, she plotted how she would run away with Gor and disappear into the anonymity of a big town. But even as she planned she would come in a rapid circle to the impossibility she had begun from. It wasn't feasible to disappear and remain alive. Only the dead could vanish when they were cancelled from the central databank whose basis was the census return, augmented by tax, employment, benefit, educational and dozens of other records. If she ran away there would be, quite simply, nothing to feed Gor on. She would be ineligible for any kind of public support and her employment rating would be so low on the private employee indexes that she would never get a job.

Her fears made her alternately eager to please her husband, who ensured their survival, and sharp with him in her worry that he might become the agent of Gor's removal. Knott himself kept his usual calm exterior but he watched Nancy and Gor closely. He too was becoming convinced that there was some mistake. Almost, he no longer believed it was the same infant Mary had given birth to. He wondered when he should speak to Forester and, each time he decided the moment had come, a picture of Nancy as she bathed or fed Gor came between him and his resolution.

It was the evening of the day on which Norman had driven Ann to the clinic to begin her lying-in that he went again to

Knott's bungalow to examine Gor. At once he realized, as the child stretched out a string of bright plastic beads it had socketed together and crowed with delight, that something would have to be done about Knott and his wife. They had served their fostering purpose and now they must go.

In the last three weeks Ann had swung between terror and an exhausted longing for the birth to be over. Norman had been good to her, she thought, calm and considerate so that she hadn't dared to become hysterically weepy. He had delivered her at the clinic with a kindly pat and the professionals had closed in on her. Her body was no longer her own to do with as she judged. But then it hadn't been since she had admitted another life into it. Secretly, without ever daring to say so, especially to Norman, she had envied the country people who had their babies at home with only an obstetrician to help. The risks and the deaths were higher of course, she knew that, but the fear and alienation were much lower. It took all her will to say to herself that it was the baby she must think of, not her own distaste for the very word 'clinic'.

The consultant came and looked her over like a pregnant mare and then she was left wired up to the terminal in a white metal bed in a white plastic-lined room, so that she seemed to be the centre of a block of snow that was nevertheless hermetically warm, filled with decontaminated unstirring air. She prayed that something would happen, that her baby would cooperate with her in trying to push its way out before the professionals made up their minds to come at her with their needles and instruments.

When the first pang came she felt a thrill of almost sexual pleasure that was drowned as fiercer contraction followed contraction and she began to think she must surely die. From time to time as the hours passed she was aware of anonymous gowned and masked figures that looked in at her and exhorted her through mummywrapped lips to 'Bear down', and she tried to remember what she had been taught at the pre-natal classes and to fix her eyes and mind on the flickering characters that monitored her body's state from the electrodes attached to different parts of it where she lay, trussed like Gulliver by bonds she might but wouldn't break. She was glad Norman couldn't see her in indignity and pain. At the last, arms with padded shackles sprang out of the side of the bed to grip her legs and hold them apart. The closed-circuit television brought the consultant at the right moment to pull and slap. 'Not bad for small bones,' he remarked.

They showed her the baby briefly before they took it away. It was a girl, they said, and began to stitch the torn flesh, to swab and make straight. At last she could rest.

Knott's first reaction to the letter was that it was meant for someone else because it gave only one 't' to his name. He put it in his pocket to read again later when he was out of the house, away from Nancy's constant watching. When he made his way through the few lines once more he realized there was no mistake. He was being transferred. Either he acquiesced or he was out of a job. The letter assumed he would agree. New accommodation was waiting for him. He was going up a grade. Everything was fine except for Gor. Now he would have to speak, voice his doubts to Forester.

'That baby gorilla, sir.'

'Oh yes. Which one?'

'The one the wife's been looking after, sir, Mary's baby.' Did Forester know that he was being transferred? Knott wondered.

'Yes, that one. Finding it a bit much, is she?'

'No, sir. It's not that.'

'No?'

'No, sir. It's me: I'm being transferred.'

'I'm sorry to hear that. We've worked so well together.'

'Thank you, sir. Yes, I'm sorry too. Someone upstairs decided, I expect.'

'No doubt.'

'There's no possibility we could take Gordon with us? I'd be willing to keep him without an allowance. The wife's got so attached . . .'

'These women!'

'Yes, sir.'

'I don't see how you could. It's Institute property.'

'Yes, sir.'

'I'll have to make some fresh arrangements for it here. How long before you go?'

'Three weeks, sir.'

Forester pulled a face. 'They don't give people much time.'

'There's something else, sir, I feel I ought to mention.'

'Yes?'

'Well, I don't know quite how to put it but if you remember I did say once before that he wasn't quite right.'

36

'Yes, you did.'

'He's, he's so human-like, sir.'

'An albino?'

'No, sir, not the colour. It's his shape and his ways.'

'Imitative behaviour from being brought up in a human household, I expect. I might put him in the apes' kindergarten for a time. It will be interesting to see how quickly he can relearn what should be innate behaviour.' He made a quick note on a pad. Still Knott stood there. If he'd been wearing a hat he'd have twisted it in his hands, Forester thought. 'He'll need a bit of extra attention at first, I expect.'

'You are sure, sir, it was Mary's baby you gave me? I mean there wasn't a possibility of a sort of swap? Sometimes you read in the papers that even human babies get mixed up in hospitals.'

'No,' Forester said firmly. 'It was definitely Mary's baby. I can vouch for that. It's as I believe I said to you before: there's a mutated element in it somewhere. That's what makes it different and interesting.'

'Yes, sir.' He had tried and failed. Nancy would never know how he had tried in his own way. His chest ached with her coming pain. Knott didn't believe in the heart as the seat of emotion. That was for kids and women, but he felt the same surge of clotted fear as if he had believed. Nancy would go mad or leave him and there was nothing he could do.

And he couldn't tell her. He knew with complete conviction that if he told her she would run away with Gor and they would all be destroyed. He would lose his job and they would have to try to live in one of the towns. He would never be employed again because he would be recorded as unreliable, even criminal. The police would find them, however they tried to hide, and at best take Gor away and at worst arrest them both. The Institute was a branch of the Defence Ministry. His offence might not be simply stealing but a crime against the realm, almost a treason. For Gor was destined to be part of a valuable research programme, Knott was equally sure of that. He would have to steal Gor from under Nancy's obsessive care and bring him back.

'I don't know how I'm going to get him away from her, sir.'

Forester put down his pencil. 'As bad as that, is it?'

'Yes, sir.'

'I did warn you in the beginning.'

'That was when we thought he mightn't live, sir.'

Forester sighed. 'Well now, what do you suggest?'

'I'll have to steal him away, sir, and deal with the fuss after.'

'I see. When would be best?'

'I'll have to do it at night, sir, when she's asleep. Knock her out with a sleeping pill or something and bring him back here.'

'It all sounds very dramatic but I suppose you know your wife best. If she's as attached as you say she'll come after him and try to get him back.' Forester was annoyed to find himself falling into Knott's use of the personal pronoun.

'Yes, sir.'

'You'd better let me know when you intend to make the big snatch and I'll drive down and take it from you; keep it away from the Institute until you've gone.'

'I'm very grateful, sir.'

'That's it, then. Let me know on the morning. That should be time enough to make a few arrangements.'

'I'll leave it to the day before we're due to go, sir, the last possible minute if you don't mind.'

It had all worked very well, Forester thought as he drove home. He remembered that he must ring the clinic for a progress report on Ann, and then Fanny, who might really have been the expectant father she had shown such symptoms of advanced couvade when she had rung him at lunchtime. Perhaps such a thing was possible between close sisters. It would make an interesting study. There must be someone on the good guys network who owed him a favour who could give Gor a home for the time being with no questions asked. Forester found himself irritated by having to call the infant by name even to himself but since there was as yet no word for what he was Forester had no alternative. He would have to think of a name for his creation.

He supposed that it was probably best to take, if possible, a term already in use and perhaps something out of anthropology would do the job. He debated between 'anthropoid' and 'hominid' and only inclined to the latter because of the difficulty of saying the indefinite article before 'anthropoid'. And as he considered this the idea suddenly came to him that that was what his wife was: an indefinite article, Ann. The neatness, the appositeness of this thought gave him great pleasure. He rang the clinic's information bank and was given the news of his fatherhood. He could see the tears on Fanny's cheeks as he spoke to her, so clear was the video reception tonight. Sometimes one's correspondent was nothing but a blizzard of microdots. He was free to return to the problem of Gor. There was a private breeder called Jessop for whom he had once got a contract with the Institute. That was just the answer. Jessop had a farm near Aldershot.

Knott laid his plans though he was hampered in everything he tried to do these days by the stone that seemed to have lodged in his gullet, making it difficult for him to breathe and bringing him constant dull pain. All the arrangements necessary to leave their quarters and take up new ones at Midsomer Norton were completed and still he had said nothing to Nancy. Only he knew that they were due to move the following day. 'It'll be tonight, sir, if that's still alright with you.'

'What's that?'

'Gordon, sir. We're leaving tomorrow.'

'Oh yes. I'll make some arrangements. Now what time and where shall I meet you?'

When Knott had left, Forester rang Ann. 'Darling, I'm afraid something rather delicate's on the boil here and I'll have to stay late, maybe even hang around all night. Can you get Fanny to come over?'

'I'll try. Oh Norman, do you have to? I wish I could see you, darling. Why doesn't the Institute have video?'

'Too costly for all these phones. Besides people might spend even more time chatting than they do already.'

'I'm sorry. I'll be good.'

'Darling, I didn't mean you. Now will you be alright? I might creep in later if I can. If not I'll ring you.' As he replaced the receiver he pressed the button that reactivated the video unit. Every telephone had the cutout mechanism but in the new technological etiquette it was thought rude to use it. He had from the first let Ann suppose that the Institute's equipment was old-fashioned enough to be sound only. One day he would have to bring it up to date if she ever seemed likely to visit him at work again.

She was still nervous of the baby and her ability to tend it properly. He wondered if nursing female apes felt the same and made a note of it as a question to be asked of the next one. They seemed as liable to other human natal problems, like morning sickness, but perhaps Ann's anxieties were unique to her, not a common human female experience. He could run a

39

group of humans and apes against each other for points of similarity and difference. It might give useful data on stress reactions among pregnant women with spin-off in psychological warfare and population control. If you threatened a subject group or nation with the loss of its children how would it react? You could call it the 'Herod Factor'.

Nancy's anxiety had led her into evening drinking. Alone with Gor during the day she could stay calm and away from the bottle but the combination of Knott's return and the fall of evening heightened her nervousness. Usually her third quick rye worried and angered Knott but tonight it only relieved yet saddened him. He added the few clear drops to her glass while she had gone for the last obsessive time to peer into Gor's cot.

She was sleeping heavily as he slipped out of bed and went into Gor's room. Quickly he packed a bag with as many essentials as he could think of, slung it over his head and shoulder and picked up Gor who woke and gurgled at him while Knott hardened his heart. After all, whatever it was, and Forester hadn't entirely convinced him, it wasn't his kid. If it was human some other bastard had already abandoned it so why should he feel bad?

Forester was waiting at the end of the road under a ripe August moon that lit the hot darkness. Knott could feel sweat trickling down his body as he laboured under the weight of the infant and his chattels.

'You'd best wedge him on the back seat with the bag, sir.'

'Right, you see to it.'

There was nothing more he could do or say. Knott locked the back door of the car so that if Gor fell off the seat he shouldn't tumble out, and stood back as Forester pulled away. Then he was alone with the back lights redly receding and the hot full moon breathing down on him. He stood a moment to catch his own breath before he walked back to the house where Nancy still lay thickly asleep.

Forester drove quickly but carefully, constantly overseeing the automatic controls. The A30 was deserted as he drove towards Aldershot apart from an occasional couple going the opposite way after a night out in the West End. Jessop's 'farm' was down a cinder track and behind high security fencing which a guard saw him through. It had been put up in the early eighties when breeders' premises had been vandalized by animal liberationists, and was kept in good repair to ward off

40

burglars who specialized in the research animal blackmarket.

'He's all dressed up,' said Jessop.

'He's been hand-reared by a couple as part of an experiment. You'd better use your discretion about how you put him in with the others. They might tear him to bits.'

'I'll be very careful, Norman, very careful. And I appreciate the opportunity to pay you back a bit, just a bit, of what I owe you. You really put me on my feet.'

'Let me know if anything happens. I'll make other arrangements for him as soon as I can but it may not be easy. Meanwhile . . .' He pulled out his wallet and peeled off a hundred in twenties. 'That should keep him going for a bit. I'll be in touch.'

He was relieved to be away from Jessop. The man showed the status of his origins so clearly that Forester found him unnerving and distasteful. He might have been like that. He was glad, though, that it had been so easy. He wouldn't be out all night after all.

Ann woke as he entered the bedroom and took the opportunity to check that the baby was sleeping healthily.

'Wasn't I brave, darling? I didn't ask Fanny to come. I'm so glad you're back.' She put her arms round his neck and he made a conscious effort to smile down into her eyes.

'I've been meaning to ask for a long time but it kept slipping my mind. What happened to Mary's baby?'

'Mary?' he asked carefully.

'You remember: the gorilla I met the day I went to the Institute. You remember, darling. She didn't want it and the Knotts or someone brought it up.'

'The Knotts are leaving tomorrow. Poor Mrs Knott hasn't been at all well. Some kind of mental breakdown. The gorilla baby didn't last very long, I'm afraid. I won't bother with a bath now, I'm too tired.'

Ann lay awake for some time after Norman's breathing note announced that he was asleep. Poor Mary and her baby hadn't had much of a chance. It made her suddenly fearful for her child and she got out of bed gently to look into the carrycradle on its stand. It was time for her two o'clock feed and Ann lifted her out and cupped the corky head to her breast gratefully.

Nancy was late to wake. Knott had been up early removing all evidence of Gor. She went through into what had been his room, unkempt from her heavily uneasy sleep and thick with the residue of the drug in her veins. Her long cry brought Knott into the house from the garden and upstairs.

Her grief wailed speechlessly like a cow bereft of calf. There was no human idiom that could carry it. He had known it would be bad but it was worse than Knott with his unindulged imagination had ever visualized. Because he had taken away all trace that there had ever been a child there she had nothing to fasten her sorrow on.

'Nance, Nance.'

She looked at him without recognition. He heard the sound of the removal van and glanced out of the window. Her eyes followed his and some understanding showed in them for a moment. With a last little cry she fell into the half relief of unconsciousness.

II

THE CHILDHOOD
OF GOR

He had awakened to terror, trembling with the vibration of the car's back seat and his own fright. The half darkness rushed past the windows and the inside was a smothering rug thrown over his head against which he screamed and thrashed and beat his fists. For months he had woken to the smell and feel of Nancy's comfort for all childish crises. Why didn't she come now? He screamed again in rage and fear.

Forester had taken no notice and Gor's thwarted cries had died away. He wasn't used to being ignored by humans and it shocked him into silence. When Forester had placed him with his bag on an armchair he had lain there whimpering while the transaction took place over his immediate future and the notes changed hands. Then when Forester had gone he felt himself hoisted up by the scruff of his clothing and dangled in midair, while Jessop looked him up and down, his smell of hostility rank in Gor's nostrils.

'You're a funny little bugger, make no mistake. Well, he doesn't fool me. He's up to something or he wouldn't be asking favours. We'll just have to see what's in it for Harry and bide our time. But you're certainly like no baby gorilla I ever bred, or saw for that matter. My bet is you're some sort of a cross-breed and he wants you kept out of sight. But why and what for? What's going to be your contribution to the defence of the realm?' Jessop shook the frightened bundle which let out a roar. 'Your lungs are sound anyway. Now let's put you in your bedroom. It won't be quite what you're used to but it's clean and dry which is more than I can say for you,' for terror had caused Gor to mess his paddipants. 'One of the girls can clean you up in the morning.'

Jessop carried him still a-dangle, weeping and choking, out of the room, down a corridor lit with blue neon strip to a far door which he unlocked and on which if Gor had been able to read he could have picked out the words *Primate Quarters*. At once the smell inside caused his skin to prickle. They passed between the big cages where hunched or bundled dark figures half slept, sometimes stirring or letting out a long whiffling breath as Jessop and Gor went by. Only the faintest memory of Mary was brought to him by their smell and that was a disturbing compound of his love and her rejection.

Jessop unlocked an empty cage and went inside. There he dumped Gor on a heap of bedding. 'You'll be safe here till the morning and you can't get up to any monkey tricks. Sleep well, sonny.' He went out, locking the cage behind him. Gor whimpered himself to sleep away from the nightmare of the smells and shapes beyond in the blue twilight.

But when he woke in the morning nothing was changed except that the daylight drowned out the cobalt glow. Gor was stinking and starving and, although he had slept, too exhausted to scream or to take any interest when the far doors were unlocked and an attendant came to thrust food through a small barred trap into each cage, according to its number of occupants, who fell upon it or looked and backed away with indifference according to their temperament. Then the doors clanged to again. Those of the inhabitants who could gather the energy began to groom themselves or each other and some young monkeys in a hut-sized cage started a game of chase among the dead exercise branches, much as prisoners of war play football or do gymnastics. They had torn at the food with their hands, cramming it into their mouths, but Gor, even if the attendant had given him any, was unused to raw vegetable and fruit without cup or spoon and Nancy's proffering hands.

The door clanged again and this time footsteps came to his cage together with a smell and shape that was reminiscent of Nancy. The bars were opened and the figure approached, making little sucking noises and holding out a hand. Gor leapt from his bedheap and flung himself at her to be gathered up in her arms and hide his face against her shoulder.

'Hey, baby, baby,' she crooned. 'You sure stink. Let's get you cleaned up and fed.' She carried him out of the cage and

46

through the connecting door, along a still blue-lit passage and into a room where there was a table and washbasin. It was hard to detach the clinging fingers from her overall and get the little ape on to the table and he began to scream at once. 'Now pack that up, do you hear? Let's get these pants off you. Where on earth did you come from all dressed up like that?'

Emily had been called into Jessop's office that morning and instructed to take a baby gorilla out of the primate quarters. She had been warned that he had been brought up by a private family as a pet and was therefore likely to be a little strange. Knott had thoughtfully pinned a piece of paper to the inside of Gor's pants which read quite simply *Gordon* and Emily soon discovered it as she began to ease them off. But what really surprised her was to realize that the soft belly and legs she was uncovering were naked of hair under the clothes.

'Or almost,' she said to herself. She looked again at Gor's crumpled face. 'If I hadn't been told I wouldn't have known what you were. "Gordon", that has to be your name. Gordon, baby, stop that bawling. I guess you're hungry but I have to get you clean first.'

She pondered carefully. The establishment didn't run to kiddypants but there was an old-fashioned sanpad machine in the little girls' room, or 'powder room', as it was labelled, which she'd often cursed for not providing more up-to-date tampons but that might now give her just the thing. She would have to take Gordon with her and anyway maybe the whole job would be better done in there. She rolled back the soiled pants over the dark pink skin and picked him up.

Jessop's irreplaceable Miss Wilkins who had fussed over him for twenty years was washing her hands as Emily carried Gor in. As she patted her hair into place she reflected that Mr Jessop was far too indulgent with the girl attendants and that the father had certainly been very dark-skinned. She searched back to see if she could remember Emily Bardfield having time off.

'I hope you're not expecting to make a habit of it.'

'What, Miss Wilkins?'

'Bringing your child to work. Mr Jessop is far too good to you girls and you take advantage of him.'

'But this is a gorilla, Miss Wilkins.'

'A likely story. You'll have to do better than that.'

'Well, you certainly fooled her,' Emily said when Miss

Wilkins's rigid back had passed through the doorway and she had shut the door with self-righteous vehemence behind her. She undressed Gor's lower limbs, stood him in the washbasin and washed him down. There was something badly wrong, she knew. She had worked in the primate section for two years now and she had never seen anything like Gor though her experience extended through the whole ape and monkey range. Emily liked working with them. She never questioned why they were there or what they went to when they were taken from her care. She understood them instinctively as if they were her own younger brothers and sisters that her mother said she was so good with. It was Emily who was summoned if a young ape became fractious or sulky.

Now as she dried Gor's buttocks and wiped carefully round the stained penis she tried to think what to do. She couldn't be sure, that was the trouble. There were things that didn't seem quite human but then again perhaps it was a sort of mongol child and such were still human and shouldn't be in a primate cage labelled 'ape'. Emily was sure of that. There was no one she could show Gor to or discuss her problem with and she realized she had to be very careful or she might lose her job. If it was human someone must know and it must be here for a reason that they didn't want found out. Therefore if Emily should open her great trap and spill the lot she could find herself deep in trouble, particularly as it was Jessop himself who had told her to look after it.

When he was clean and dry and reclothed with a couple of sanpads instead of his paddipants she carried him back to the primate quarters and into the kitchen. He bit on the raw banana she gave him, but stretched his hands out to the row of hooked cups that were used for the attendants' tea. Emily poured out some milk in one of them and offered it to Gor who seized it and supped greedily. Then he grabbed a teaspoon, pushed it into his mouth and began sucking on it. Emily crumbled some bread into a cup with milk, mashed it and gave it to Gor who alternately sucked and spooned until it was all gone.

Then she carried him back to his cage. The sound of the connecting door being unlocked made him cling to her and when she finally freed herself from his arms he began to scream and hung on to the bars as she locked the cage door. 'Now, Gordon, be good and I'll be back soon.' But there was no calming his terrors. He wept and howled and Emily could hear

the cries as she retreated down the corridor which had sometimes seemed to her as if she swam in an aquarium from which
there was no way out except by turning up a white belly and
drifting dead to the surface. Now, suddenly, she saw herself as
a gaoler with keys at her belt. The screams died into sobs.

She was summoned by the buzzer in her pocket followed by
the cricket voice telling her to report personally to Jessop.

'Have you seen to that baby gorilla yet?'

'Yes, Mr Jessop.'

'How is it?'

'It was very dirty and hungry. I cleaned it up and fed it.'

'Seemed alright?'

'Very healthy.'

'I told you it's a private customer gone on holiday, wants it
looked after for a bit?'

'Yes, Mr Jessop.'

'So you look after it right. Anything happens to it it's your
responsibility. Understand?'

'Yes, Mr Jessop.'

'Good girl. Anything you notice about it particularly?'

Emily hesitated but caution was bred deep in her. 'Say
nothing and they can't pin nothing on you,' she heard her
mother repeat as if rehearsing the family motto.

'It's all dressed up like you said. They must treat it like a
baby.' Had she gone too far already? But Jessop nodded.

'Maybe the wife hasn't got any kids.'

As the days passed Emily became less sure. Moping in a
corner of his cage on his pile of bedding, his clothes crumpled
and stained, his thumb in his mouth for comfort, Gor now
looked less and less like a human child. Emily worried that he
might grieve himself to death. He had no inclination to play.
Only for a moment when she brought him some bright plastic
bricks did he show enough interest to begin to put one on
another before he suddenly smacked the heap with his hand
and retreated again to his bed. At last she spoke to Jessop.

'He's fretting. Try him in with a couple of young chimps,
see if they'll wake him up a bit. Half an hour in the kindergarten.' After all, wasn't that what Forester himself had suggested?

Emily led him by the hand down the corridor to the kindergarten. It was standard practice to let young apes have time
for play together if they were well adjusted. It made them

49

healthier, brighter and more amenable subjects who would fetch a higher price. She opened the door and led Gor in. Sally and Mick who were building a tent of rugs and plastic frames stopped and turned to look at the two entrants. Emily they both knew well and they came out at once to say hallo.

She had let go of Gor's hand and stepped back from him so that the others would approach him first but as they came near he turned to find her, crying out what sounded to Emily like: 'Na, na, na,' and flung himself at her as he had done on that first day. Sally and Mick grinned with fright at this strange behaviour and their hair began to stand on end. Clearly Gor couldn't be left alone with them. Emily coaxed and cuddled but all three were now nervous and overwrought and she was forced to take Gordon back to his cage where he cried himself into hiccups and then to sleep.

To Gor they had been dark, hairy and huge. They stank of his fear. He was in any case unused to other children, and in an overwrought state that would have made him shy in fright from even smooth, pale human toddlers. Emily decided to say no more about his emotional condition but spent as much time as she could with him until the morning she found the cage empty.

For a moment she thought he had got out, that if she searched she would find him hiding somewhere, probably weeping for her and ready to jump into her arms. Then she saw that the cage was quite bare and clean. There was no evidence that Gordon had ever been inside it. Her first impulse was to run to Jessop's office but she stifled it and took hold of herself. She mustn't do anything silly and put her job at risk. What good would it do her to find out, or try to, where he had gone? There was nothing she could do with the knowledge if she had it. Gordon had been there for a space and now he wasn't. That was life and you learned just to get on with it. But Emily felt sick with loss. She told herself he would be alright and refused to let the unconscious fear that he might already be dead even rise up into the light of consciousness. She made herself a picture of him clean and happy, his face breaking into a laugh like it did when he saw her, and determined to think of him like that.

When the buzzer summoned her to Jessop's office she had herself fully under control. Jessop seemed almost apologetic.

'I didn't have a chance to tell you, Emily. The owner came

back and took that baby gorilla away. I expect you'll miss it after looking after it so well. The owner was very pleased so I thought a little bonus for you would be in order.'

Emily realized at once that she was being paid for her silence and was glad that she'd had the sense not to go running to Jessop in a panic the minute she discovered Gordon was gone. She thanked him effusively and again he considered whether she would be worth asking out some time or whether he couldn't chance the risk. The truth was he liked the girl assistants. They were just his type. Their status level made them both soft and a bit sassy. They weren't too clever for him and they respected his power but their youthfulness gave them a vitality Mrs Jessop had long lost in the pursuit of the perfect executive home. The trouble was that she didn't see that he had a real need of refreshment if he was to keep working and the money rolling in.

Emily Bardfield would look up at him with widening eyes and thereafter would be just the right kind and degree of cheeky, pushing her luck a bit but not too far. He could see her sitting at the dressing-table in the bedroom of the apartment he kept for his little excursions, opening the drawers, spraying herself with perfume, putting on her face. Oh how his gut turned over when they sat there with a lipstick touching the curve of the mouth or a mascara brush tipping the curl of their lashes. They could take the scent away with them or touch him for some filmy underwear, they moved his heart so.

He was aware Emily was still waiting to be dismissed. Jessop hunched and dropped his shoulders. 'It'll be on your slip at the end of the month. Don't spend it all on sweets for those kids; buy yourself something pretty.'

'Oh thank you, Mr Jessop.' Emily bowed out almost backwards. She knew his eyes would be on her as she made for the door. The girls all understood the boss's sudden driftings off and what was on his mind at such times. Most of them dreaded them: it usually ended in trouble. But one or two welcomed the chance and if you lost your job after, well, you were young, smart and strong and anyway it was easier for girls to get new places than for boys.

It was raining as Emily left for home. A dank group was gathered at the taxi tourer stand, wrapped mostly in the transparent raincloaks Hotfast were offering with six cereal labels. Emily stood under her own and looked at the other conical shapes streaming rivulets that gathered in a moat around each pair of feet. There wouldn't be enough tourers. There never were when it was raining and the bargaining would be tough. She wasn't quick enough for the first one and was shouldered aside by people who'd come up after her. The trouble was her heart wasn't really in winning unless she had the smaller children or her mother with her. She could shove for them but for herself she was likely to stand back or even to have gone into a daydream by the time a tourer came in sight and therefore be too slow off the mark. She lacked the necessary conviction that she was as entitled to battle for and occupy a place as anyone else and could indeed always imagine a reason for someone else having it, from swollen ankles to a hospital patient to visit.

The thought of her mother struggling with the children's teas squared her shoulders when the next one came up. A man at the front of their group who looked only just below car status and actually carried an umbrella took on the negotiation with the driver and the price was settled and the stops. Emily looked at him in admiration. It was a very low sum for a wet day.

'Cowboys!' the man said contemptuously.

'Get out,' the driver shouted. 'I don't have to take insults from anyone. Get out of my taxi.'

'I advise you to drive on. You have entered into a contract for a service. We are twelve witnesses and I shall personally sue you for breach if you don't drive off.'

Emily almost felt sorry for the driver, but not quite. No one did. They were generally hated, though regarded as necessary. Most of them could only stand it for a few years because of the atmosphere of dislike and potential violence in which they worked. Then they would sell out to the next cowboy who thought himself tough enough, the tourers becoming more and more battered as they passed from hand to hand. This one had seen long service under many masters. Emily's seat was ripped and flat. Any attempt at stuffing had long gone and the plastic frames were darkly smudged with human grease.

Most of the occupants were getting off at Emily's estate but the man with the umbrella was riding further, almost to where the country began beyond Aldershot. 'Why don't you use your car?' Emily asked him with a sudden understanding.

'I enjoy a good fight.' He winked at Emily, and flourished the umbrella like an old sword in a telly swashbuckler movie. 'It's all that's left.'

52

The group for her estate spilled on to the broken pavement and scurried away, a sudden lift in the clouds letting the sun fall in bright orange fire on their glassy cloaks which threw it back so that they looked like non-humans from some distant planet in *Starwalk*, the longest-running space soap opera. Emily hurried up the front path between her father's neat rows of vegetables and let herself in, wiping her feet and slipping the cone of waterproof over her head. She shook it vigorously out of the front door. Really it had kept her quite dry. It was a good thing they'd been able to send off for so many before the offer closed and now had four between seven of them. Worn with acrylics and two pairs of trews they would even do for winter. They would have to. And for the long wet months of summer they were ideal.

Hotfast had made a fortune. Every household had a cabinet full of it and the whole nation would be eating it up for months while Hotfast's competitors tried desperately to catch up and spent millions on the adagents. All day the air rang with their jingles and offers to a public who had already committed its breakfast feeding as far as anticipation could stretch. The first one to catch the nation at the inevitable moment of irresponsible boredom with the right temptation would make a real killing and the companies were fighting each other hotly for that moment. Every day the news carried accounts of the industrial espionage which was this phase of the war between the food giants as they stole or attempted to steal each other's formulae, market research, advertising programmes and sales reports. Break-ins, phone taps, bribery and even a gun-battle between interlopers and security guards for a time made up for the monotony of the national dish of morning Hotfast.

Mrs Bardfield was in the kitchen. Emily passed through a jumble of legs and arms that was Nina, eight, and Errol, six, in the latest round of their wrestling match. Jessie howled over a grazed knee in one corner with all a three-year-old's lung power. William sat with his fingers in his ears reading at a formica-topped table where they would soon eat. Mr Bardfield, deprived of his garden by the rain, stared from his armchair.

William took his fingers out of his ears. 'Got any money for the telly, sis? It might shut this lot up.'

Emily produced two fifty-cent pieces. At once there was a hush. All eyes fixed on the dead square lens and there was an audible sigh as William pushed home the coins and it began to glow, then flushed with colour. Mr Bardfield leant forward and sighed too. Mrs Bardfield, drawn by the quiet, appeared at the kitchen door. 'Come upstairs, Em, a minute. I've got something to tell you.'

Emily followed her mother clumpily up the uncarpeted stairs. Mrs Bardfield paused at the bathroom to peer into the lavatory bowl. 'That's William flushed it again. He can't bear anyone to see he's been. I've told him again and again we can't afford to flush every time but he still does it.' She led Emily into the main bedroom where their talks always took place if the family was occupying the downstairs and they couldn't sit companionably and undisturbed on either side of the table over mugs of mint tea.

It wasn't just that Emily was the eldest and in some way the most dear to her although the current youngest always nudged at this position. Emily was the wage-earner. Mr Bardfield had been unemployed for years. Under his wife's eye he had first taken up the garden and then found in it a justification for being as he presented her with each first fruit in season and halved their food bill. But Mrs Bardfield with her family income, her dailying and her other labours had carried the real financial burden until Emily was old enough to find a job with Jessop.

Both of them watched William anxiously and gave him the best. It was so much harder for a boy that he would have to do much better in exams than Emily if he was to pass so that he could go on to further education, compete and rise. If you didn't rise you sank and they both knew that temperamentally William was unfitted to a sunken life. Emily was much more resilient. William might well find a short way out of life because the truth was that he couldn't really compete, any more than Emily could shoulder her way to the front for a tourer. His mind was quick and strange, not the material of which good examinees are made. If the world was to get the best out of William it needed to be gentle with him. All the signs as Mrs Bardfield and Emily read them were that it hadn't the time or the inclination.

Sometimes Mrs Bardfield blamed herself for teaching them not to be pushy. Where else but her could it have come from? Emily would be alright because she would be forced to push for her own children and nature would see to it that she did.

But William might be too like his father who had lost his job at twenty-eight just after Emily was born and since then had never looked forward. It hadn't been his fault. A further refinement in robotry had phased him out of the canning factory where he had worked since leaving school. The twelve men who had each handled a machine had drawn lots for who should oversee them all from the new control panel. They had felt this was fairer than trying to choose among their needs, skills and length of service, especially since there had been no skill required for either the jobs they were losing or the post of minder one of them could have. The lottery had seemed a gesture, a comment on the lottery of life and after it they had all gone out and got drunk together, the eleven losers being extra kind in plying the winner with litres of beer till he was sobbing in apology for his luck. Mrs Bardfield still felt a pang whenever she opened a tin that bore the name of her husband's sometime workplace.

She had only herself to blame. She had fallen for and married him because he was gentle and funny and a bit unlike the ordinary run of boys, and because she was moved almost to tears by the way his dark hair curled on the nape of his very white neck. He had wept a lot in her arms at night as the years passed and he couldn't find a job and that was how their next two children between Emily and William had been born. But those two had died in a year of drought when water prices had risen so that many people on the estate had stopped using it except for drinking and an occasional flush. Typhoid had suddenly appeared and flared a path from house to house until all the Bardfields were down with it at once.

'It was just the runs and a bit of fever,' Mrs Bardfield told herself as she dragged from bed to bed. In her own half delirium she became obsessed with the problem of whether to call the doctor. Home visits were free for children and the unemployed. But she herself had a job cleaning, mornings only, for the military in Aldershot. Would they be charged because she was officially in work?

Only when the two youngest had slipped into unconsciousness and the pallor of their skins made her believe they were already dead did she stagger to the only telephone box on the estate to ask for help. It didn't come at once because the partnership of young doctors who serviced the estate as their first practice were both out of their depth and run off their feet by the emergency. In the end a medical team from the barracks was drafted into the area and the epidemic was then quickly brought under control before it could spread from the estate. The local paper had been warned off the story for fear of causing panic and it hardly warranted national coverage except as a minipara of news in brief.

Mrs Bardfield stared out of the bedroom window at the stained concrete houses whose walls wept in the rain. Even now sometimes when she looked out she seemed to see the two dark heads, just like their father's, crouched above the kerb playing some game on the pavement with small bright handout models of spacemen or soldiers.

The fever had weakened Mr Bardfield even further so that by the time he was thirty-five he appeared nearing sixty. He no longer looked for a job but spent his time in the two gardens which had mercifully been apportioned to the houses in the days when such things had been a necessary part of public housing. Mrs Bardfield dreaded the day when the property company, their landlord, might decide to knock down the whole estate and build desirable residences. Then they would have to move to a town where there would be no garden for him, no soil to dribble pleasurably through his fingers or tomato sprout to pinch from between the stem and leaf, letting its sharp nightshady smell tang the air.

Once a month she went into Aldershot to key in the rent and as she did so she prayed, 'Please God don't let them put us out,' and crossed her fingers until she was home again.

It was while she was carrying William that a way of supplementing their income was suggested to her. She could become a maternal host, fostering the foetus of another woman in her body. The checks showed that she was a healthy mother and that in spite of losing two children she was a suitable carrier. As soon as William was weaned she took the offer. Between each of her own children she carried another until after Jessie she had suffered an attack of puerperal fever that had put her out of work.

'We're going to have an addition to the family,' she said now to Emily.

'You know you shouldn't and anyway you don't have to now I'm working.'

'We'll need more money for William's uniform and books and so on next year. They think he'll pass easily. We only just manage as we are, even with your wages. Everything keeps going up.'

'I'm getting a bonus this month.'

'You're a good girl. But that's only once off.'

Emily sighed. None of them liked the cuckoos, as Emily called them. Mrs Bardfield had to be constantly checked and take care not to miscarry and damage the lodger. It made her nervous and short-tempered, as did the drugs she had to take.

'This one's different. It's already been born.'

'Fostering?'

'That's right.'

'How long for?'

'Might be months, might be years. He didn't say.'

'What is it?' Emily knew that in spite of the constant monitoring of pregnant women of status things still sometimes went wrong and a child was born that the parents couldn't face. Then it was common to foster it out or have it adopted by a family that needed the money. Family agencies were the usual go-betweens. A contract was signed setting out the terms, and the agency took a commission and kept an eye on the child.

'He didn't say.'

'I didn't know you'd been to an agency. You might have told me.'

'I didn't go to any agency. I was asked through the clinic.'

Emily felt more cheerful. It was better than a cuckoo though she couldn't explain to herself why. And William would need the money for the next stage of his schooling if he was to get anywhere. 'When's it coming?'

'I've to fetch it tomorrow from the clinic. He's going to pay for a taxi all the way out here.'

The next day was long and monotonous to Emily. From time to time she had a strong sense that there was something important she should be doing only to realize that the need to do it was no longer there, a sensation known to anyone who has lost a loved animal. The habit of feeding and looking after, of seeing and hearing a presence continues until disappointment gradually wears it away.

At least the weather was better. At going-home time she got a place on a tourer straight away at a reasonable price. Her father looked up happily from his beanrows where the first red tongue tips were just beginning to appear and waved to her. The house when she opened the door was quiet. The children must be out to play.

'Sh!' said Mrs Bardfield from the top of the stairs. 'I've just got him off.'

Emily tried to tiptoe on the boards. She followed her mother into the big bedroom. 'He's a dear little thing really,' said Mrs Bardfield, peering down into the cot they had all left their mark on in turn. Just as Emily too hung over it the brown eyes opened. The little figure struggled to sit up, stretching out his arms to her.

'Na, na, na!'

'Gordon!'

'Yes, that's his name,' said Mrs Bardfield. 'A pity you had to wake him.'

Emily realized at once that not even to her mother could she tell their story. She hated to as much as half lie but none of it would have made sense to Mrs Bardfield. It would only have worried her without adding to her understanding. Emily bent over the cot and soothed Gordon. 'Now you just go to sleep and I'll see you later. You're alright here.'

Fortunately exhaustion was on her side. The brown eyes drooped, the arms fell back and she was able to tuck him into sleep. 'What did they say at the clinic?' she asked, to set her mother on a new tack.

Forester had thought the woman was exactly what he was looking for. She was obviously too stupid and too greedy to question Gor's appearance or need of fostering and therefore to become voracious in her demands. Her greed he decided would be kept in bounds by her lack of imagination. A potential blackmailer needed an almost artistic sensibility to visualize how things might be different from what they were and set about changing them. He saw no signs of this in the Bardfield woman. He told her that the money for Gor's keep would be keyed in to her account every month in the usual way and pointed out that she was gaining by not having to pay the usual agency commission. However that didn't mean that she could neglect Gordon just because there was no one to keep an eye on him. Checks would be made from time to time and she would have to bring him for those to wherever she was told.

'What did he say was wrong with the baby?' Emily asked.

'I wouldn't demean myself to ask him. And anyway I could feel he didn't want me asking questions. He was one of them likes to think theirselves way above you. Jumped up I

58

shouldn't wonder. They're always the worst. "Counter jumpers" my dad used to call them though I never quite understood why.'

Emily considered the term. Perhaps it was something to do with a game where your counters could jump over other people's. She saw with great clarity the little plastic circles the size of a eurocent in their bright colours hopping across a chequered board.

'I can't see anything wrong with him and I've had a good look,' Mrs Bardfield went on. 'Maybe he'll turn out to be a bit simple, brain damage or something. They think they know it all but they're not God yet and they still make mistakes. Perhaps that's all he is: someone's little mistake she hadn't got rid of in time. Anyway if he is simple he's got a lovely smile when he's happy, though he was a bit frightened with me at first. I don't know where he's been but he was all clean except for he'd just messed himself with fright.'

Emily bit back an indignant, 'Of course he was clean.'

'I reckon he's got a touch of the tarbrush. Some girl of status been messing with a city non.'

Her mother constantly surprised Emily. Many of the words she used were no longer current. Emily understood them because she had taken them in by a kind of verbal photosynthesis but she didn't use them outside the house. For one thing nobody might have understood them and, insofar as they did, they might have been offended. Many of her friends had what Mrs Bardfield called a touch of the tarbrush.

As with the counters Emily had a strong mental image of this brush dripping asphalt which she knew had once been called tar, but the brush itself was the bright plastic in strong primary colours of her world. Brushes came in different sizes and handle-shapes. You decided in advance what sort would best suit the purpose you had in mind and then you pressed the button on the dispenser which showed the shape and size you wanted, turned the colour knob and punched the release. If the computer was in a good mood what you had asked for fell into the chute. If not it said sulkily, 'Goods temporarily out of stock,' and buzzed like a wasp. More infuriating was when it sweetly delivered the wrong thing and you had to try to get a credit out of the checkout machine which would buzz waspishly in its turn and, if it was really affronted, set off the alarm which activated the whole security system. Usually it

59

was better to take the unwanted object.

Outside her own home Emily used the same basic vocabulary as her contemporaries, a language simplified for the machines and then perpetuated by them but laced by a little transatlantic slang from the radio programmes that poured from every window. This, too, had a touch of the tarbrush, for the language of love, the staple of pop music since singing began, was sprung from the soul and blues songs of an earlier generation.

Mrs Bardfield enjoyed her antique language both as an artistic expression that she could afford and practise about her daily round and as a form of protest. She was also capable as on this occasion of using a word sharply like a blade turned against herself, held against her own throat while she laughed and dared herself to press her flesh hard on it. They all knew people of status called them 'nons' in private but it wasn't a word Emily or her friends used. Only Mrs Bardfield ran her finger along the sharp edge of reality in that way.

She belonged to the same generation as Nancy Knott, to another world that had ended without anyone noticing because their eyes had been fixed on skies from where their death might rain down any old day. They had never expected their children to grow up but those cold-war babies were now parents, wearing about them the last remnants of old rags of speech and attitude that would fall to dust with them.

They had grown up in good times and perhaps that accounted for Mrs Bardfield's suppressed protest. Emily had none of it. Her generation had known no other life and so they accepted things as they were, except in the cities where revolt grew with the weeds in the cracked pavements and on the waste lots of tumbled houses. Emily shuddered when she thought of the cities and the possibility that one day they might be forced there. So far, between them, they had always found the rent. To live on one of the fringe estates of a small town where there was a variety of work was the best they could hope for.

Sometimes like all her friends she dreamed of a way up, to counterbalance the constant threat of that way down to the walled necropolis. For her it would have to be marriage. She would have to catch the eye of a Mr Right. But William and some of the younger children might do it on their own merits.

Emily had always known she would never make it. Her duty had circumscribed her ambition. As the eldest she had to help out, earn as soon as possible, support her mother in keeping the family unit in being. She could never even from the age of eight raise her eyes from this. It would have been disloyal. Her marks had been in keeping with her expectations. No one had ever suggested pushing her. They accepted as she did what level she would find. Yet with a little attention Emily might have surprised them all and herself.

Now for a second she almost resented Gordon and envied him. True there must be something funny about him but in spite of it he was already enjoying, by being fostered in their family, as much as Emily and her siblings had or would have. And one day he would leave them. The better the job her mother did on him to offset his disability, the greater his remove from them would be. He would be found a place where his problem could be disguised by money. One day he might even be in a position to lord it over them or some of them. Yet Emily's anger died. She remembered his fear and his learned trust of her and she was softened. Poor little sodling, it wasn't his fault, she was able to think.

'It's quite a good whack they're paying me. Makes you think. Makes me wonder just what I'm being buttered up for.'

'You wouldn't do anything.'

'I'm not daft. A bird in the hand . . . But they can't stop me thinking me own thoughts. It passes the time.'

Much as she loved and admired her, Emily sometimes found herself holding her breath with fear at her mother. One day she would break out, do or say something rash that would be reported and recorded so that if they ever lost their jobs they would never find a new one, her mother because of her ingrained insubordination, Emily by natural process of family contamination. When the data on Mrs Bardfield was put in it would automatically be transferred to Bardfield, Emily.

Families, after all, were units whose members shared genes, habits, environment, and a parent's delinquency must potentially rub off on a child. An employer needed to know what an applicant's background was before he could decide to take someone on. Still it was better than not having a family, Emily reminded herself. The unattached found it very hard indeed. It was best to have a full complement of parents, with some apparent problem that was common to a lot of people like Mr Bardfield's lifetime of redundancy. That gave you the important appearance of normality.

The thought suddenly came to Emily that Gordon's secret must be on file somewhere if only she knew where and how to unlock it. She would have been astounded to learn that by all the rules of her world he simply didn't exist.

Forester had given this point a lot of thought. Should he create a record for Gordon? Against this he argued that once made such things were hard to destroy completely since the databanks were continually emptied into each other and it was impossible to know just how far a piece of information might have travelled. He decided to leave it until it became truly necessary.

If it ever did. He still didn't know his own intentions for Gordon. Forester liked the knowledge that the hominid was there, his secret, that no one else knew what it was and only a very few that it existed at all. It gave him a sense of power and achievement so strong that it was almost an erotic pleasure. Perhaps he would be content to keep Gordon a secret, meanwhile charting his development so that if the day came to lay open claim to his prodigy he would have the full facts to put before the admiring world. He would give it a month or so to settle down and then have it thoroughly checked. The memory of the Knott woman's reported breakdown crossed his mind. He hoped there wasn't going to be trouble from that quarter but he thought Knott himself would be sensible.

Forester considered briefly whether he should get in touch with Knott but almost at once rejected the idea. It would look concerned, out of character and might raise otherwise dormant suspicions. Already he wondered if some of his obsession with Gordon might be making itself felt. Ann had been very quiet at breakfast and had suddenly said as if he had commented on it:

'Can I tell you about a nightmare I had and then perhaps it will go away?'

Forester forced himself to smile a little. He found other people's dreams boring and would never have contemplated revealing his own.

'Of course, darling. What was it?'

'I dreamt about Mary's baby.'

'Mary?'

'That gorilla you showed me.'

'But you never saw her baby.'

'No. That's what's so unnerving. I couldn't see it even in the dream but I knew it was there. You know the way one does in

62

dreams. Someone threw it down a well.'

'A well?'

'That was the word that I used in the dream.'

'An oil well?'

'No, water. When I was a child I had a book of fairy stories and there were always wells in them: wishing wells, the well at the world's end, the well the prince threw the worm into that grew into a dragon and came up and ravaged the countryside. There were pictures of wells in the book. They were made of a circular stone wall with a bucket on a rope that was wound round a kind of drum with a handle on it. When you turned the handle the bucket came up full of water. In the dream I hoped the baby had fallen into the bucket, just a little way, and I'd be able to pull him up. You did say it was a boy, didn't you?'

'Did I? When?'

'Oh, when I asked you once before. Just after Lucretia was born.'

'I don't remember you asking me although as a matter of fact it was a male.'

'Well, perhaps I only meant to ask and thought I did. You know how that happens.' Ann was floundering now. Somehow she felt she was saying all the wrong things but she couldn't stop or find the right ones because she didn't know what was wrong, only that she sensed a rising anger in Norman. 'You said it had died, Mary's baby.'

'Yes it did.'

'Well, in my dream it was still alive and I was trying to save it. What do you think it means? Why should I dream of it?'

'Probably some hidden anxiety about Lucretia. After all, in a dream a baby is a baby. Your unconscious doesn't want to voice its fear about your own baby so it disguises it as another one so that you can rescue it.'

'But I didn't. I woke up too soon.'

'Then that bears out my point. Why should you have such a strong feeling of fear that it wakes you up about a gorilla infant you never saw which anyway you've been told is dead? It must be a symbol for something much closer to you, your own child.'

Ann put her fingers knuckled to her mouth in a gesture of apprehension that made her seem only a child herself.

'I hope by the way there aren't any more of those books around for Lucretia to find as she grows up, and fill her mind with that kind of old-fashioned fantasy. It obviously didn't do you any good.'

Fleetingly Ann wondered what images Norman dreamed in if he had never learned the language of fairy tale. At the same time she was shaken by what seemed a causeless yet intense anger. She had looked for sympathy to make her bad dream retreat as daylight had failed to make it do. Norman must think it childish of her to have dreamt it in the first place and more so to have told him about it. She felt something inside her recoil as if a small soft-bodied animal had suffered a sharp blow.

It was fright which had made Forester react so angrily. Suddenly he felt transparent as if Ann could see into his head and translate the impulses there into ideas or pluck his thoughts out of the air. Till then he had envisaged them as shut safely inside his skull where only he had access to them. Now he wondered if there were, after all, such things as thought waves that might slop outside the originating brain, if thought might turn out to be a form of energy akin to light, heat or radio and as easily picked up by the right kind of receptor. He had always understood that in the old wives' tales about the existence of telepathy the two minds so linked must be in harmony but he felt nothing of that with Ann and indeed would have believed himself the last person on earth to be susceptible to such a phenomenon if it existed. No, it must be that the interpretation he had given Ann was right and she had been dreaming about her own child, something common enough, he imagined, among new mothers. He let his face relax almost to a smile as he looked at her.

Ann felt a wary relief. For a moment she hadn't known who she was, who Norman was or why he had any right to be sitting there and angry with her. Now she took hold of reality again, not knowing that in that moment something had died in her but only that she wouldn't look for understanding again. It merely made you vulnerable. It had been a last try at something, she wasn't quite sure what, and she had fallen back defeated but perhaps more willing to accept defeat because she could hug the thought of Lucretia to her for comfort. In the following months as she bent over the cot or pushed the pram she sank deeper and deeper into the warm underwater world of maternal absorption, tasting faintly of blood or the sea.

Forester was busy with a new project on motivation: how far could primates be bribed or cowed to perform tasks and what was the best form of bribe? Was it the same throughout the species or did the bribe have to suit the individual? The extrapolation from ape to man was what interested both him and his sponsors. Carrot or stick and what precise shape either should take were of vital importance to the management of society, particularly in solving the problems of the cities. However, his new interest didn't distract him from keeping a sharp eye on Gordon's progress.

Gor was happy. The terrors he had been through began to recede from the forefront of his mind to become an uneasy layer at the bottom that all his life would be liable to stir from time to time letting bubbles of gassy fear float up to break on the surface.

The memory of Nancy and her loss faded too, her place taken finally by Emily. There remained a slight hesitation in him about Mrs Bardfield. Mr Bardfield hardly figured; with the other children he had a variety of relationships depending on their own ages and response to him. But Emily he adored and his face flowered into a smile when he heard her key in the lock in the evening.

He was soon stumbling around without holding on. At thirteen months he surprised Jessie by kissing her. She was undecided whether to roar or laugh until her mother said, 'There's a good little boy. Give him a kiss, Jess.' Thereafter for a while they went everywhere hand in hand. Jessie took him out into the road to join the gang of pre-school toddlers who were its daytime inhabitants and introduced him as 'my little brother sort of'. They sat together on the kerb with a twig each, intercepting an ant stream that was flowing busily from a crack about some unfathomable business and pushed stones and leaves in its way or picked up one luckless insect from his place in the line and dumped him a few feet in alien territory where he would wander in a rapid mechanical confusion looking for his lost purpose and position in the stream.

Jessie became proud of his climbing skill which was far in advance of that of his contemporaries. 'I bet my little brother sort of can climb that fence and yours can't.' Early too she taught him to do acrobatics, to slow roll and hang upside-down from a bar, to go head over heels backwards and forwards. They would push each other and collapse laughing in a heap. Then Jessie would tickle Gor till he whooped with pleasure.

'He's very good-tempered, I'll say that for him,' said Mrs

Bardfield. 'No trouble at all really, and he keeps us all in grub. The only time he gives trouble is when I take him for his check-up.'

'What do they do to him?' Emily asked.

'I never see. He's taken off somewhere and always comes back in a state.'

But on Gordon's third visit Forester questioned Mrs Bardfield herself. 'What about talking?'

'Not really.' She wished sometimes she could 'sir' him. She knew he would like it and that by not doing such a simple thing she might be endangering the whole arrangement. Uneasily she remembered that because this was a private agreement not done through an agency she had no piece of paper she could wave at 'the Doctor' as she called Forester privately. Not that bits of paper were worth much, she consoled herself. How could one of us afford to take one of them to law?

'Can you be more precise?'

'He doesn't say anything really. Except he's got this one sound like "na".'

'As if he might be trying to say "no"?'

'Sort of.'

Forester sighed. It took so long when they were as thick as this woman. You could never get a straight answer from them because of their combination of shiftiness and stupidity.

Mrs Bardfield grew nervous and angry. She knew she was failing. 'Sometimes he seems as if he's trying to say something but he can't make the sounds.'

'We'll have to look into it. I'll make an appointment for him to see a specialist.'

'They do vary, children. My William was a slow talker, whereas our Nina was chatting away at a twelvemonth. Boys often are slow.'

'Yes, yes.' They always had some piece of folklore to offer if you gave them any encouragement. Some of his colleagues found it amusing and he had seen Ann considering the unscientific comments of some geriatric non as if they might hold the key to the universe. He wanted to say to them that they'd never get anywhere while their heads were full of such rubbish and they never bothered to learn the real explanation. His mother had offered him similar gobbets and even as a child he had known he must reject them.

'There's a malformation of the vocal organs,' the specialist told him when Forester had arranged an appointment. 'It's fairly extensive and I've never seen one quite like it before.'

'Do you think it's susceptible to surgery?'

'I just don't know. I can try but it'll be lengthy. Everything needs rebuilding. An interesting job. Who's the child? Not yours, I gather.'

'No, one of the assistants' I take a kind of paternal interest in. I said I'd do what I could.'

'I could make a research project of it and not charge. I might get a bit of kudos I suppose if I publish a paper on it and it's a success.'

It would mean an enhanced career, more patients of status which would mean an enhanced career and more patients, a chair perhaps and invitations to the private yachts of foreign leaders with the inevitable presents, a shining upward spiral. 'I'll have him in my clinic. I expect the parents will sign a release form.'

'He has to have an operation,' Forester told Mrs Bardfield. 'Sign this form and bring him here next Wednesday. I'll take him to the clinic.'

'How long will he be gone?' she dared to ask as she carefully formed her name along the line the Doctor was tapping with a clean forefinger.

'Several weeks perhaps. You'll be paid just the same while he's in the clinic and notified when to come and collect him from here.' Forester saw the relief in her face and misread it.

It was good about the money of course. They needed it desperately, had come to depend on the few extras it gave them. But better was her realization that he meant that Gordon should come back to them. She had dreaded telling Emily about the operation and even more that he was to be taken from them.

To Gor it was nightmare returned. The sight of Forester always made him feel sick and this time as he was led from the room he screamed and tried to turn back to Mrs Bardfield. She had decided quite deliberately to keep herself from becoming too fond of the kid but now all that was washed away by his fear and pleading.

'I was choked, Em, real choked. If you'd seen his little face.'

Emily had seen before and knew exactly. She felt again the hopelessness she had known when she had found his cage empty and, as then, she dredged deep into her resources for emotional survival. He would come back. The Doctor had said so. It would be alright.

Mrs Bardfield had brought back a treat from Aldershot: soypies and fries which was the children's favourite.

'In my young day they were called chips and they were fatter,' she said looking round the table at the expressions of ecstasy. 'We ate them out of paper.'

'Paper?' asked Errol wonderingly.

'Everything was paper then, Mum, wasn't it?' William said, holding up a thin fry on his two-pronged plastic fork.

'There was a song about it, sort of.'

'Oh go on, Mum. Sing us one of your funny songs.'

> 'If all the world was paper
> And all the seas were ink,
> And all the trees were bread and cheese
> What should we have to drink?'

'What's ink?' asked Nina.

'You used it to write with,' said William. 'Didn't you, Mum?'

'Before chippens there was biros and before that there was pen and ink and pencils. Errol, don't gobble.'

'I'm making mine last for ever,' said Jessie virtuously.

'Where's Gordon?' asked Errol.

'He's gone into hospital for a bit.'

Jessie's face puckered. At any moment she might ruin her half of soypie by letting tears drop on to it.

'He's coming back soon,' said Emily hastily, to reassure Jessie and herself.

'Mum, what's pencils?' Nina asked.

'You want to know too much,' Mrs Bardfield said harshly. Nina's curiosity would get her into trouble one day. Girls were best seen and not heard.

Forester realized at once that he had a problem. This was no drowsy infant but an active child who might run off or perhaps worse draw attention to them both by his tantrums. He had wangled the use of the clinic surgery with its waiting-room for his occasional visits but he had no facilities for dealing with a yelling Gor. He rang Jessop although he knew he was putting himself in the man's power.

The dealer was ready to oblige. 'I'll be over in half an hour with something.'

'As soon as you can make it.'

Jessop wasn't really surprised to see it was Gor again. He took out the hypodermic, measured a dose from a small bottle and shot it into Gor's leg while Forester held him.

'That all?'

'Yes, that's all.'

'Any time. You know you can count on me.'

Forester offered no explanation. He had none. Let Jessop think what he liked. But he knew this was mere bravado, that he was posturing before himself to reduce his own anxiety. 'You can carry him out to the car for me. I'll bring it to the service door at the back.' It wasn't just that it would be better for the unknown Jessop to be seen carrying the unconscious form; Forester suddenly felt a physical distaste for the inert figure that made him shrink from picking it up. He had been brought up by parents who didn't touch each other or him except when absolutely necessary and this was now part of his nature, but his feeling for the infant hominid, in drugged sleep with its mouth drooling a little, was the much stronger one of sharp revulsion. Perhaps he should destroy what he had made. It could easily be done. He could tell the Bardfield woman the operation had gone wrong and it had died.

The walk to where his car was parked and the necessary attention to driving it manually to the back door cleared his mind a little. Jessop laid the sleeping body along the back seat.

'Be seeing you.'

Forester nodded but made no reply and set the car in motion. He drove to the gates and locked the computer on to the centre line beam that would take him to Farnham where Graham had his private clinic.

'He's in the car. I had to knock him out: he was making so much fuss. There's nothing wrong with the bawling mechanism.'

'I'll send an attendant out to get him. I'll let you know how it goes.'

'There's no need for anything fancy in the way of care,' Forester said.

'Ah, but I want it to be a success. That's the purpose of the exercise. Just leave it to me.'

'There may be some brain damage too.'

'You mean even if I exert all my skill he may still not be able to talk for other reasons?'

Forester nodded. He disliked the specialist's sardonic turn and was never sure how to answer in case it should be aimed against him, although Graham was more likely to point it at himself.

'What's the IQ?' the specialist asked.

'Normal for his age. I can't remember the exact figure but it's within an acceptable range.'

'Well, we'll have a go, shall we? Nothing to be lost.'

Forester had lied about Gor's IQ. He knew it to a point, for it was one of the things he always tested. There was, though, as he had said, nothing remarkably low or high about it. The hominid had the intelligence of an average non child. As he drove away from Farnham between hedgeless and treeless fields of alfalfa, yellow rape and low soybushes that quilted the countryside with their regular squares he found himself wishing again that it might die under surgery. He felt the whole thing was getting out of hand. The pleasure of having a secret had gone out of it because of the danger from Jessop. The dealer would test the water with some small request and once he had it and knew his power he would become inordinate in his demands, endangering Forester's peace of mind and perhaps his career, even though this might kill off his source of supply. The man was eager to climb and Forester was his chance of a lifetime for a way up.

He would never be accepted of course by people of status as Forester was. He would remain a vulgar dealer with too much money who would try to learn to ride and would never sit right in the saddle. They would let him buy them drinks at the golf or yacht club, wherever his fancy joined him, but they would never invite him to dinner, as Forester was invited because of his wife and his professional status. It gave him some satisfaction to predict how Jessop would make a fool of himself.

He had never met Jessop's wife but he could imagine the type he would have married, by now run to flesh and her hair expensively but vulgarly done in a gleaming fondant. He contrasted Ann's fine-boned simple elegance and for the first time since she had told him she was pregnant felt some rise of desire for her and wondered if it would be strong enough for him to do anything about it or would wilt with the sweetish smell of baby that, however the house was cleaned and the air constantly deodorized, greeted him as he opened the door these days.

Ann had tried. She had got Lucretia fed, changed and safely to bed with the baby-minder switched on. She had brought out from freeze the porterhouse Norman liked best with its faintly gamey flavour, and had prepared real potatoes and a mixed salad. She had lightly cooked frozen asparagus and made herb butter to dip them in. Norman had a residual sweet tooth from the lower clerical cuisine his mother had brought him up on. Ann had concocted a summer pudding from last year's soft fruit which crouched as a pink rabbit on a salver with an accompanying jug of cream that floated swanlike on the palely gleaming surface of the table.

'I think I might look up my pensioners again,' she offered as conversation.

'Oh, why?'

'It would give me something to think about.'

'I thought the baby did that.'

'Well, to talk about then. I had the impression you got rather bored with my baby talk.'

'What would you do with Lucretia?'

'It's only once a week. I could take her with me.'

'You know the risk of infection from the nons because of their low standard of hygiene.'

'They can't help it, Norman. They can't afford the water. Mrs Goulding told me she hasn't had a bath for ten years because it costs too much to fill a bath enough. She has to "stripwash" as she calls it or "wash as far as possible".' Ann laughed. 'She's a wicked old thing. She said she washes down as far as possible, then up as far as possible. "And then I does possible though at my time of life it should be called unlikely." Actually she's as clean as clean. It must be awful not to be able to afford a bath and to be watching the water all the time. They never say because the country people are very proud and reticent about some things but I don't think they always flush the srith.'

She used this year's fashionable term derived from the telly commercial for the product which would make it: 'the sweetest room in the house'. Norman frowned. He had never got used to the way people born to status picked up the current slang, making a private language which he found wouldn't come off his own tongue and that was in its way the counterpart of the older nons' vocabulary.

'Do we have to talk about these things at the dinner table?

71

How you can contemplate exposing your child to such risks I don't know. You know people of status are particularly vulnerable because they have no immunity just because of their greater cleanliness, and yet you want to take Lucretia into it. It's bad enough the risk of your bringing back infection with you.'

'I thought you liked me to have something to do.'

'You have your child. That's enough for most wives. I hoped it would be for you. She certainly seems all-pervasive.' He thrust the last piece of steak into his mouth. It tasted rancid, of his own anger. He would get indigestion.

'I've made you a summer pudding,' Ann tried.

Forester looked sourly at the pink rabbit which seemed to him at that moment to be the colour of thin blood and to have been experimentally flayed in the laboratory. He almost expected to see it breathe. To break the image he thrust the serving spoon into it and severed its head which he mashed before coating it with cream. He would have to do something about Jessop. He wasn't to be beaten down by a nonentity who couldn't rise on his own merit but only by standing on the shoulders of someone who had.

Ann offered no more tokens. With relief she saw that Norman had retreated into his own world. It was safer so. Wherever their surfaces touched they abraded, rubbed sore. The baby-minder began to bleep in her pocket and she was glad to escape upstairs. As she bent over the cot she decided that all the same she would take up her old library run, though leaving Lucretia behind in someone's care or perhaps locked in the car with the closed circuit safety screen on, so that she had only to look at the miniset in her bag to see all was well. That way there couldn't be any risk. She would discuss it with Fanny and if she thought it was alright that was what she would do. She could explain to her sister why she thought such contact with another world was important.

She wouldn't tell Norman, not explicitly. She wouldn't lie about it either. She would just let it come out without emphasis. Ann sensed that he was worried about something. It must be to do with work. Perhaps his current project wasn't going well. Apes were unpredictable, individualistic creatures with differing personalities and strengths of will like the clever but temperamental Mary. Should she ask him what was wrong? Perhaps not. He didn't like her to perceive too much about him, even so far as to know when something was worrying him.

It was funny how she'd been mistaken in herself and had thought it would be enough for her to be at home with her baby. But now that Lucretia was sitting up and crawling she found herself longing for wider contacts. Norman was often late home, edgy and unwilling to talk about his work which, Ann had realized, was the only thing that really interested him deeply. Fanny was too far away and it would have looked weak to be constantly running to her or ringing her up. Shut in their comfortable house together Ann worried that she, and in time Lucretia, might lose touch with the rest of the world. That all-enveloping absorption that she had felt in her baby at first now seemed to have a dangerously obsessive side. Their home might have been floating free as a balloon and as lightweight. Lapped in every comfort, she had no need to go out. Between the telephone, telly and deepfreeze she could conduct her whole life with no more than a couple of expeditions to a town in a year to choose her clothes. Even that she could have done from the dialled catalogues on the screen, except that it gave her as yet no tactile sense of the fabrics, though they were working on it. But she missed the press of other personalities against her own, even if it was only her pensioners she saw and, though she wouldn't have worded it so, the gregarious animal's experience of the mingling of breath and body heat.

The sleeping Gor had been put in a high-sided cot in a little room by himself. It was all very well for Forester to say there was no need for particular care to be taken, Graham reflected, but he knew perfectly well that speed of recovery and indeed success of the operation itself depended on exactly that. It was after all largely what you paid for in a clinic, plus the consultant's skill of course, though many of the community care doctors were perfectly competent and would themselves be able to move into consultancy in time. They were merely young and overworked.

Graham was genuinely devoted to his work. He knew he was good and got great satisfaction both from exercising his skill to mend some of nature's distressing lapses and from the gratitude that flowed over him from patients and relatives. In particular he liked to see children able to smile and articulate as a result of his efforts. His interest in Gor and his self-interest therefore coincided and gave him every incentive to make a good job of remodelling one of the grossest malformations he had seen.

It was a bit of a funny-looking kid altogether but he remembered that when he had examined it before and soothed a little of its fright it had been able to grin at him. Graham liked a sunny child that could show its appreciation. Clearly it didn't care for Forester. Well that was two of them. Although he was prepared to help a colleague, the man had always been inimical to him.

They met sometimes socially as well as professionally, for Graham had been another protégé of Ann's father and had never understood how the beautiful younger Miss Briles had married Forester. If it had been the almost ugly sister Fanny he could have seen it and indeed she might have been good for him and put some blood into the cold fish with her robust energy.

All the tests showed the infant was in good health, although it had the inevitable faint odour that nons carried about with them. Once a month Graham gave an afternoon's unpaid service at a community hospital and you certainly noticed it then, particularly if you had to pass through a waiting-room where they were all packed expectantly side by side on benches. No wonder epidemics ran through them and through the community wards. The unskilled care of relatives and volunteers didn't help either. They never understood how spotless everything had to be to beat brother germ. Graham looked round with pleasure at the immaculate box Gor was lying in.

'I should put him through the wash while he's still asleep,' he said to the attendant who was standing behind and a little to one side of him, 'or we shall have to wear protective clothing when we come in.'

'Yes sir.'

Gor was placed on the conveyor belt, the attendant keyed the console and he slid gently into the plastic dome where warm jets played on him and soft brushes nudged his skin into a rosy cleanliness. At the other end the attendant turned him on his face and he was reversed through the dome again and back while warm air dried him and a fine talcum was dusted over his quiet form. When his back was powdered into a peachy bloom he was beginning to stir and able, still relaxed from the drug and the bathe, to be helped into a small clean bedshirt.

He felt indeed so good that in spite of the strangeness he didn't weep or roar and the attendant began to feel that he might be alright after all, in spite of being an obvious non and it being wrong for a lower clerical like himself to be asked to look after a non child which should by rights be in a community hospital being seen to by its parents.

Still, his not to reason why and there might be more to it than appeared at first. People of status sometimes had whims and this might be one of old Graham's. It didn't do to draw attention to yourself by trying to pull social rank in a case like this or they'd think you were hard-hearted. It was alright for people of status to bend down to take an interest in a non out of benevolence, like old Graham's once-a-month slumming in a community hospital. They could afford it. It was different when you might find yourself back down among them if you were kicked out of a private clinic where 'attendant' counted as lower clerical, into community service where it was only unskilled and strictly non.

When he came back with the kid's chop Gor was able to get up, sit in the high chair and feed himself quite tidily.

'You keep that up, sonny, and you and me'll get on fine.'

His next examination jogged something in Graham's memory that sent him back to his student textbooks, lovingly kept but rarely consulted these days since he knew most of the variations he was confronted with and needed only steadiness and patience to make them conform to normality. But this malformation was almost simian.

He turned over the pages of diagrams showing the comparisons between the vocal organs of the primates. Theories immediately sprang to mind of great social significance. Were the nons reverting? Might one find other simian characteristics reappearing and was this the latest twist of the evolutionary spiral? Or was it the other way round: that these innate deficiencies were what kept them nons? After all, articulacy was all-important in development and it was well known that nons registered a much lower level on the Piakov scale. Several studies had proved it conclusively.

His discovery made the case even more interesting and might even immortalize him. Graham's Syndrome. He could see it in the index to file after file. Excitement released a flow of adrenalin. His heart beat faster, his breathing quickened and his head sang a little, but pleasantly. He opened his desk drawer and took out a pad and a biro and began to make notes. Somehow this needed the old tools to capture its significance and steady his mind. Usually he kept them in his drawer to make a certain impression on visitors catching a glimpse as he pulled it open, for the desk too was old style, but now was the moment to use them.

His hand paused. Did Forester know? But then how could he? He hadn't the knowledge. If he had looked down the child's throat he wouldn't have known what he was seeing and as far as Graham could judge there were no other physical characteristics that were unmistakably simian. There was definitely a touch of colour and he was pretty hirsute but he was no odder than many of the combinations you saw among the nons.

However, now he came to think of it, Forester must be up to something. Altruism just wasn't his line. It must be something to do with his own work for the MOD at the Primate Institute. Which argued that he did know. Graham had thought himself round in a circle.

Was Forester using him in some way? Well, if so, it was even more important to get what he could out of it and keep a proper record. Now he had the child under the roof of his clinic he was committed. He would have to do the very best job he could or that cold bastard might somehow turn it against him, and he would have to get onto record with Graham's Syndrome as quickly as possible before Forester pre-empted him by registering whatever he was up to. He could key up the relevant bank and see whether he had already done so.

There was nothing but earlier work under Forester's entry on the screen when it flashed up in response to his call. Graham was still level then but any day Forester might move. He must get on with what he foresaw would be a series of operations to remodel the vocal mechanism. In the next few weeks that little non child was going to have as much of his attention as if it was his own. The attendant, what-was-his-name, could be promised a bonus if all went well. Then there would have to be intensive speech therapy while Graham kept an electronic eye on Forester's doings.

For Gor the next month was an alternation between waking pain and anaesthetized insensibility. Sometimes, as he surfaced between operations, he was aware of the attendant soothing, adjusting the drip and once dabbing sweat from his brow. Once he half woke to find himself passing through the bather

76

and fell asleep again before it was done. When one day he wakened to ache not pain and was encouraged to swallow a little liquid, he could hardly remember the time before he had entered the clinic, except as another part of a cycle of feverish dreams through which a shape compounded of Nancy and Emily had flitted.

'He's come through nicely,' Graham said when Forester rang. The cool bastard certainly knew how to control his responses, he thought as he looked at the viewer, carefully keeping his own expression light. 'I'll start the speech therapy next week if everything seems to have healed.'

'You realize it may not work.'

'Oh yes. You made all that quite clear. Don't worry. It's been an interesting little exercise but I shan't break my heart if it doesn't come off.'

Not much, Forester wanted to say.

'How's Ann?'

'Very taken up with the baby.'

'You must come to dinner soon. We'll fix it next time we speak about little Bardfield.'

Forester kept his face non-committal. He wished he could have switched the viewer off as he did with Ann but Graham would have seen through that at once. Hearing the hominid referred to as 'little Bardfield' shook him badly. It was acquiring an individuality of its own and becoming less and less his artefact.

Geraldine Evans, the speech therapist, had taken extensive notes as Graham had sketched Gor's physiological difficulties to her while carefully making no mention of Graham's Syndrome or Gor's non background. It looked like an interesting problem. She pushed open the door. Gor was in a tall barred playpen fitting plastic shapes listlessly together. This was a very bored child.

'Hallo, Gordon.'

Gor looked up, stood up and came towards her.

He had a very sweet smile, Geraldine decided. 'Hallo, Gordon.'

'Na, na.'

'What's that? Shall we get you out of there? That's a good little boy. Now you and me are going to get to know each other.' She undid the cage-like pen, took his hand and drew him out. Together they walked along a corridor to Geraldine's speech lab while she chatted to him.

It was the first time anyone had talked consistently to Gor. Nancy had murmured and cooed but he had been too young to respond. Then when the Bardfields had talked it had been above and around him. Mrs Bardfield had expected no response and, not realizing that it might not come easily to him to speak, had made no effort to evoke replies. Her own children had spoken when they were ready. Children did.

Gor was anxious to please, anxious not to be left alone again and if that meant putting his lips to strange objects and twanging at them for the Na Na he was eager to co-operate. She was pointing at herself now.

'Gerry, Gerry. You try, Gordon. Ge-rry, Ge-rry.'

The Na Na stared into his eyes and smiled, pointing at her bosom.

'Gerry, Gerry.'

'Gerry,' he found himself answering.

'That's a very good boy. Now you. Gor-don, Gor-don.' She pointed at him.

'Gor, Gor.'

'Alright,' she laughed, 'if that's what you want to be. Gor, Gor.'

'Gor.'

His throat was very sore the next day but he persevered to please the Na Na Gerry and gradually it got easier and the soreness receded. She was very pleased indeed with him when he said the right thing and the more he said the more quickly she came back again when she had to leave him until she was spending the greater part of the day with Gor.

'You've done extremely well,' Graham told her and for a moment she was almost deceived into thinking he had put a personal warmth into his voice until an inner caution warned: 'Gerry girl, don't make that mistake again. The guy is a confirmed bachelor.'

Graham had listened to them talking together on the intercom for Gerry had feared that Gor would clam up if the consultant was in the room. Forester had been right about the child's IQ. It was perfectly adequate for speech and as far as he could tell from observation there was no brain damage. The problem had been entirely physiological, rather as a child might have difficulty in breathing if it had retained the gill-like structures of the young foetus. His skill had cured it, as he had cured others, and he was entitled to the recognition.

There was no need to name the patient. Indeed it would be unethical to do so. There was no need either to get Forester's approval before inputting his data to the medical bank. Graham had kept careful notes of every state and now had only to cast them into report form. Usually he would have given the pages to his secretary to input for him but he felt a need for secrecy and urgency that made him decide to do it himself as soon as he was ready. Two evenings later he sat himself down at the on-line keyboard and laboriously keyed in his report. The display screen thanked him politely when he pressed the green final button. Now he was ready to let Forester know he could take the child away.

'And he can really talk?'

'Yes, he articulates quite well. There's still a certain insensitivity, a certain lack of control, but there often is in young children. It usually goes with time.'

'You mean he's using actual words?'

'You should hear him chatter to the therapist. Incidentally he seems to have a rather deep psychological aversion to men. That might cause problems. I don't know the precise background of course.' Graham let the unspoken question hang in the air but Forester felt no urge to gratify him. He was turning over the new situation raised by Gor's articulacy and his own failure to anticipate it.

His artefact hadn't died but had shown a natural will to survive stronger than that of many infant primates who had an unfortunate tendency to succumb, at considerable expense, to the deaths of their mothers or separation from them. And now it could talk. It meant that his diagnosis of some mechanical rather than intellectual failure had been right. It also meant that the human was dominant in the hominid's genetic mix. The ability to use language was crucial. The human bias mightn't be so strong in all combinations. It might be possible to produce a whole range of variations between super ape and sub-human. Forester felt himself lifted again, involved in the project, wrapped in his secret.

Graham retired to his private quarters in the clinic when he had input the whole article and spoken to Forester and poured himself a large scotch from a tartan-covered bottle. He had earned the luxury and he savoured it. In his article he had been very subtle in his insinuations about the significance of

Graham's Syndrome, inviting others who might have identified simian characteristics in non patients to communicate with him.

Now as he relaxed with his favourite brand that had a faint suggestion of smoked trout about it, some memory nagged at him.

> I pitied thee,
> Took pains to make thee speak.

He would have to track it down or he wouldn't sleep. It must be Shakespeare. He rang Dial-a-Service Directory and listened to the recorded voice, then he punched the buttons that would give him the complete works and keyed in the quote. It began to roll across his telly screen: Miranda; *The Tempest*.

> I pitied thee,
> Took pains to make thee speak, taught thee each hour
> One thing or other. When thou didst not, savage,
> Know thine own meaning, but wouldst gabble like
> A thing most brutish, I endow'd thy purposes
> With words that made them known.

The words rolled greenly on until suddenly they caught Graham's interest again. It was Caliban answering.

> You taught me language, and my profit on't
> Is, I know how to curse. The red plague rid you
> For learning me your language.

Graham switched the screen off. Surely that was an error and it should have been: 'The red plague *ride* you.' He hoped young Bardfield hadn't learned to curse, not from Geraldine Evans anyway. She fancied him, he knew. But she wasn't at all his style. Ann Briles's maiden simplicity had attracted him most because it was nearest to what in his heart of secret hearts he really hankered for, without ever, of course, doing anything about it: the soft peachdowned limbs of children. Instead he remodelled their pink mouths to make them whole and pretty enough to be kissed as someone else's love object when they were too old to be his.

There were places you could go, he knew: the nurseries as they were called in bull talk. But he never did, though someone who hadn't known Graham's interest but had been merely boasting had assured him that some were very clean and tasteful. His heart had raced but he had kept his comments low key, not wanting to sound either too eager or too puritanical.

From the sessions at the sports club where he played squash to keep in trim he knew he wasn't the only one who hankered after youth and a semblance of innocence. Perhaps, he thought, it was something to do with the technological sophistication and the competitiveness of modern life that made others so keen to share with him what was once thought a distinctly minority vice. In a way he resented their brash intrusion into what had been for him a deeply embedded romantic obsession.

The Family Act, which gave parents greater control over their offspring in an attempt to boost parental responsibility, had made it possible not only for people of status to foster out their children but for non parents to put theirs out in turn, and the prettiest of them could find their way into an employment that brought in good sums to keep the rest of the family. It didn't last long because they grew up rapidly or fell ill and lost their charm. They were said to be getting a better education which usually included gymnastics, dancing and language classes observed through two-way mirrors. Graham's blood churned at the thought and he swallowed deeply on his drink.

Mrs Bardfield was very glad to receive a summons to go and collect Gordon from the clinic. Though she hadn't said so even to Emily she had been growing anxious as the weeks passed that she was being paid for doing nothing, a state of affairs so outside her experience that it made her constantly nervous that it would stop or that she would be forced to refund what she had already spent. Even she sometimes woke sweating with terror at this thought and could get no comfort from the regular breathing of her husband beside her. Now she decided not to tell Emily that Gordon was coming home in case something should go wrong at the last minute. Let it be a nice surprise.

In her worst night-wakeful moments she had been afraid that the child had died and that she would somehow be blamed. Her imagination, which was limited by her need to survive and therefore functioned mostly in a practical way to anticipate and deal with eventualities before they knocked her senseless, hadn't wanted to follow Gor into the hospital where she presumed the operation would take place. Instinctively she knew the Bardfields wouldn't be allowed to visit him and once

81

she wondered if his own relatives would, whether some shadowy but glamorous blonde figure would sit by his bed and look at him through a plastic tent.

Mrs Bardfield didn't care for hospitals. She had had her own children at home in risky comfort. For each of the cuckoos she had been hospitalized twice, once when the fertilized egg was implanted and again for its birth. A part of the community hospital was set aside for this and the consultant moved in his own team to deal with the operation and the birth. The attendants were efficient and impersonal, resenting the time spent caring for the non, surrogate mothers but knowing that at least until the child was safely born their jobs depended on the patient's health. Once delivered, the mothers, now as useless as emptied husks or biodegradable containers, were shunted off as quickly as possible.

'Not that I want to linger there with them cold bitches not wanting to soil their hands with me,' Mrs Bardfield had said to Emily. 'I'd just as soon get home to me own place, even such as it is.'

She waited nervously for the light to go on above the door which was the sign that she should go in. The door at the other side of the room opened and the figure of the Doctor appeared with a smaller figure grasped by one hand. Gordon was hanging back, trying to dig in his toes. As soon as he caught sight of her he wrenched himself free and flung himself at her, almost knocking her over.

'He seems pleased to see you,' Forester said.

'Oh, children are like that. You don't have to take notice of them.' She sensed a danger though she wasn't quite sure what and hastened to placate him. 'There, there, Gordon, you just be a good boy.' The sooner she could get them both out of there the better.

'You will be notified when to bring him for a check-up. He needs as much practice as possible with his speech.'

'He'll get that with my lot.'

'If it isn't enough he'll have to have extra therapy.' The Doctor made a dismissive movement of his head. She was free to go.

'Come along, Gordon.' She took his hand and led him, to the relief of them both, out of the building. Now she came to think of it she had never heard Gordon make any noise much except to laugh. When he fell over or banged himself he didn't howl, not like William, for instance, who'd been a real grizzler.

They got places in a tourer quite quickly and were soon turning the corner of their own Jubilee Street. Jessie was out playing with a group of pre-school toddlers.

'Look Jessie, here's your mum with your little brother.' Jessie stood up from the kerb that was their constant perch like seabirds on a cliff ledge. 'Gordon, Gordon!' she called.

Mrs Bardfield let the willing hand slip from hers and he half stumbled half ran, calling, 'Gor, Gor, Gor!' until the two children were near enough to throw their arms round each other. Mrs Bardfield felt quite choked and exhausted. She would make herself a cup of mint tea unless Harry should offer to do it. She opened the front door.

'Everything go alright?' He came towards her out of the kitchen. 'I'll put the pot on and pick some nice fresh leaves.' As he turned to go out of the door the nape of his neck where one or two hairs were flecked with grey and a little bushy filled her eyes with tears. She must get the scissors out.

The great breakfast food war was won with a song.

> Girl in the red car
> while I'm wondering who you are
> you keep on driving right past me.
> You're not the one I want to see.

It had been pouring from every window as the summer hotted up, the story of non boy meets girl of status when she gives him a lift in her red car: the dream of every workless young non and his baby who saw herself without much effort in the driver's seat of the red car.

'Princess and woodcutter stuff,' said the promotions officer of Flakefirst, *just-add-water.*

'What's that?' asked the sales executive.

'One of the most important psychological categories; deep emotional appeal.'

'Where do you learn all that garbage?'

'All part of the media course in business studies at my college.'

'Does it work?'

'You'll see. We give them a free chip of the song with four packet disks.'

'Five. We need five to really scoop the pool.'

'Who says?'

'The wise box. I gave it the figures and got a prediction.'

'Okay. Five it is. But fast before the song fades and something comes along that hasn't got the same pull. We'll have to buy the song and take it off the air except for our own commercials. I'll get out a whole programme. Pictures of the girl, the car, the boy on our packets and we'll run the story in serial.'

'They can't read.'

'Picture frames and an episode in the commercials. Make a talkie chip of it for extra packets.'

'You're going over the top.'

'No, it's sense. Listen, if you've bought the song you want full potential spin-off. Make a fever of it.'

'If it works you get a bonus.'

'I know.'

'Wonder why you don't hear that song any more?' the commercials began. 'The one that reached deep down and touched your dreams?' Sudden burst of music, just enough to whet the common appetite suffering from withdrawal of its fantasy nourishment. 'That's because Flakefirst have bought it for *you* and it can be yours with only five packet disks from the packets that tell the story of the girl in the red car. In your dispensers now.'

Summer had made them yearn as the temperature rose and people of status fled from its sickly dangers to leafy sea-drenched islands where the local peasants were scoured clean by sun, salt and sand. Almost for a moment Emily was tempted by Jessop's offer of a day at some resort but she knew too well what it would cost.

Ann and Fanny flew with their assorted children to Levkas where they were happy together on the beach though Fanny longed for Charles to follow them out. Norman disliked holidays and was pleased to have the house to himself, to wander from room to room turning projects over in his mind with no need to pretend to even his meagre sociability.

During her annual holiday Emily took a chair out between the beanrows and tanned herself to a rich gold, as if she too had drunk in the Greek blaze that was giving Fanny a deep amber burnish and sending Ann under an umbrella for cover lest she should, with her darker skin, run the risk of offending Norman on her return home. He had once remarked after a holiday that she looked as if she had mixed blood and asked her to wear long sleeves.

Long hot days always brought Mrs Bardfield fear and sadness. There was no saying that lightning might not strike twice in the same place and she watched her brood anxiously while spending extra money on strong disinfectants. Prevention was better than cure which had failed her once, and the whole house was acrid with it.

William suddenly found himself thinking about girls and in particular about the girl in the red car. He steered the family shopping to include Flakefirst as their brekky food and helped himself largely every morning in order to use up the packet quickly, though he found the sweet bluish milk substitute that was produced when you just added the water, and the subsequent mushy flakes rather sickening.

When the holidays came he walked into Aldershot to the estate of officers' married quarters and knocked on doors for jobs until he had enough earned to present his mother with three more packets of Flakefirst.

'Whatever did you buy all that muck for?'

'He's saving the disks for that chip,' Nina chanted.

'There's no call for you to chime in. At least he makes some contribution to the larder.'

'What's a larder, Mum?'

'I've told you before, you want to know too much. Before there was freezers there was fridges and before them larders.'

He collected the song from the dispenser with his heart in his mouth, as he fed the disks in, that it would turn surly and refuse to give him the prize. There had been a queue in front of him of eager Flakefirst fans of all ages and William had worried that the supply would run out just as he put his disks in or that some rough hand would warp it.

'Look at your face,' his mother cried as he joined her at the tourer stand outside the entrance to the vendomatic arcade. She had said at first that she couldn't afford his ride into town and back but had relented with his disappointment. Now she was glad she had, and after all he was less than the negotiated adult fare with his student's pass which was why the tourer drivers tried to avoid groups with too many children in them. It was nice, too, to have help with the bulky shopping.

Home again, William borrowed Emily's chip player without asking. Emily didn't really mind. There was nothing she wanted much to play herself and she was content to sit in the

85

greenish dapple between the rows where the young beans now hung in silvered festoons while the song washed over her from the window of the boys' room and she drifted through a sequence of daydreams in which a tall blond man in an open-top car pursued her into marriage.

From time to time her thoughts wandered to Sandra Canfold who had foolishly accepted the offer of a day out that Emily had prudently refused. Emily wondered when Miss Wilkins would notice.

'What are you going to do?' she had asked Sandra.

Sandra ran a slim hand down her thick black plait as she drew it forward over her shoulder. 'I'm not going under, I tell you that. He's going to pay me.'

'You mean you're going to have it?'

'It's my chance to make a bit. If I just get rid of it I'll just be a non girl who's had a miss. He'll sack me and I'll be finished. I'm going to have it and threaten to take it round to his wife.'

'Suppose he says it isn't his?'

'He can't. I made a tape of the whole thing.'

'What, while you were. . . ?'

Sandra nodded. 'We went to this hotel in Eastbourne where he'd already booked a room. He always knew what he was going to do. Well, so did I. While he was in the bathroom I put the recorder in the bedside cupboard and switched it on.' She giggled, putting a hand over her mouth. 'I made up my mind when I first came here and saw what he was like. You see, I'd never been with a bloke. I'd been saving it up for a rainy day. It's our only asset, Em, you know that. And when it's gone what have we got? There's no sense in chucking it away on some spotty boy.'

Emily had nodded in return, not having the courage to dis-agree and have her notions dismissed with contempt as roman-tic idealism. They were too vulnerable for that.

A lot of what Sandra said made sense, she knew. It was just that Emily couldn't do it, couldn't face the loss of all hope she knew would follow. 'Ah, my girl,' her mother would say, 'you don't want to be the sort of fool I was.' But she did. She ached to be hopelessly, impossibly in love and yet at the same time she longed to be sought after by one of the young princes of her society. A 'counterjumper' as she called them in her mind using her mother's expression, or 'merito', which was her con-temporaries' name for them, would do, Emily conceded. Her ideal, though, was the male equivalent of the girl in the red car. It made her fidgety when she looked at non boys and thought what life with one of them would be. Besides they were so physically unattractive, with their spiky or lank hair and sallow acned skin.

Sometimes Emily spent fifty eurocents on an hour's television, not for the programme but for the commercials that enclosed it. There she saw the kind of boy she aspired to offering a girl a cigarette or swaying on water skis behind a powerboat, his fair hair, fluffy from much shampooing, lifted by the breeze machine. The commercials taught her that she might aspire. They showed her the desirable simulacra of her love objects in her own home paying court to girls no prettier than she was. Such boys were the reward of virtue, taking pains and cleanliness. She rarely saw them in the flesh except under glass through the passing window of a car, for their world didn't really impinge on hers, although they informed her dreams.

Jessop didn't usually go for dark girls. He liked them fair like Emmy Bardfield. It had been a great pity she had said no. Because of it he was in this trouble now with the Canfold bitch. He'd broken his custom about dark girls because she looked so demure and that had excited him. He'd given her a good day out, spent a stack of chips on her and then she'd turned this trick on him. Nearly throttled her he had when he found out. It took all the remembered pleasure out of it to know she'd just been simulating. Well almost.

It was true she'd been a virgin like she said. She hadn't faked that. But the rest. He could spit digits when he thought of it. How much was she going to bleed him? She had looked at him so cool when he tried to threaten her. He'd given her the morning after pill and the little trog had just kept it. Unless he paid up she would stick him with a paternity order that would go on his file or call on his wife with the dear little bundle in her arms. Then to clinch it she had told him her mother was a full Pakky and the baby might be almost black. There was no denying paternity either once they demanded the test. He would have to get a contract drawn up with her for the return of the incriminating chip and a quittance. Then if she gave any more trouble he could sue for breach and she'd lose the lot. She'd know the rules all right. Well Forester would have to pay for this. It was a good job he could lay it off on the side. His wife wanted an extension built and would have wondered why

87

the money wasn't forthcoming. The Canfold bitch would be reasonable and see she couldn't drive him to the point where it was cheaper to confess. That had been his mistake: this one was brighter than the other attendants. He wondered why she hadn't been picked out and pushed to her proper status. Then he wouldn't have been in this fix.

Forester had been waiting for Jessop to make his demand. Even so, he had been able to form no precise plan of action. He needed the stimulus of an actual threat for that. But now the man had to be stopped. Should he counterattack him through his personal life or his business? Whatever he decided there must be no comeback on Forester. There was a pleasure akin to that he got from a project in turning over the possibilities.

He made a few discreet inquiries, much as he would have consulted a bank of research, and he soon discovered that Jessop didn't love his wife and amused himself with girls on the side. He wasn't emotionally vulnerable then. Presumably if everyone else knew about the girls Mrs Jessop did too so there was nothing to be gained from telling her. It would have to be his business. He would have to be destroyed so that he was made incredible and impotent. Forester suspected that Jessop would be underinsured against complete disaster. He was the psychological type to cut that sort of corner.

How should it be done? Not fire. Jessop must be covered for that. Anyway arson was tricky and often left embarrassing evidence of authorship. He must plan very carefully.

Jessop had asked for twenty thousand eurodollars. The man had been quite clever and put it as a request for a loan which they both understood wasn't meant to be repaid. It was only a beginning. Forester understood that too. He might have to pay up this once because there wasn't time to destroy Jessop before the date he had set. But it would be the last. Fortunately Forester was careful with his money and made sure that Ann was too, so that his account would stand the withdrawal of such a sum this time. A plan began to shape itself in his mind.

Ann was pleased to get a suggestion that they should have some people to dinner, including Fanny and Charles. She was always made happy by a chance to see Fanny and she looked too for opportunities to please Norman to offset their growing alienation. She didn't know the other couple he had invited: Tim and Betty Beavors. Ann thought that if she'd been known as Betty and had married someone called Beavors she would have changed to some other form of Elizabeth. It was funny how you could tell from their names exactly what they would be like. For a moment as she automatically spooned apple fool into Lucretia's fledgling mouth Ann wondered whether other countries were the same about names. Somehow she didn't think so, not at least the only people she knew at all well, the French, from her year spent at the Paris Conservatoire. Anyone from any background might be Emil or Renée. She considered the Americans. There were perhaps some recognizably black names but even so she felt there was greater variety and intermingling. Here you could even tell when a name had slipped down the status scale. Tim and Betty would be in Fanny and Norman's vocabulary 'meritos'.

They were. Much as she hated all this docketing of people, Ann had to admit as she served the lettuce soup that it worked. Tim Beavors wore spectacles with lenses like the bottom of a whisky tumbler and a small worried smile. Betty was a little overweight though telling herself she wasn't too much yet because her waist could still be pulled in to give her an hourglass shape, and she was overdressed in tight white silk which gave her the effect of being iced.

She was clearly overawed too and talked incessantly in an attempt to put herself at ease. Ann was afraid that Fanny might be a little cruel to her. Charles was kind in his large sleepy way. Norman was playing some cat and mouse game with Tim Beavors that Ann didn't understand but knew was the whole purpose of the dinner party.

With the stuffed peppers they got on to politics and the Bill to raise the franchise income threshold.

'It has to go up with inflation otherwise the figure becomes meaningless and all sorts of people who are without any responsibility or commitment to society end up by exercising power over it,' Norman was saying.

'Surely it has to keep pace with the tax threshold, doesn't it?' Beavors asked, pushing his glasses back up his nose with an index finger on the bridge piece.

'No representation without taxation,' Charles laughed. 'Who was it coined that?'

'Isn't it a bit of a con trick?' asked Fanny. 'I mean, you could keep on raising the threshold and cutting various levels out until there was only a handful of voters left.'

'You always go to extremes, darling. No government would

ever do that. MPs wouldn't stand for it. This is just a rationalization of the last piece of electoral reform, something that should have been done then: a tax-indexed franchise.'

'Doesn't that mean you always get the same people in?' Fanny persisted.

'You are brave,' Betty Beavors said admiringly. 'I don't pretend to begin to understand, let alone argue about, politics.'

'Does it matter if you do?' asked Norman. 'As long as they're the right people, competent leaders chosen by people with a real stake in the country: the taxpayers.'

'And their wives,' said Fanny.

'Well you have to treat it as a joint income,' Tim Beavors offered, 'otherwise most married women of status would be disenfranchised while lots of little non girls were able to vote.'

'Oh absolutely,' Norman backed him up.

Ann was surprised. She had never thought Norman was particularly strong on female suffrage. 'It's something a man likes to be able to do for his wife, an extra incentive to him to get on,' he added.

Tim Beavors looked with obvious pride at Betty.

'Oh come off it, Norman.'

'Perhaps we'd better change the subject. Fanny's getting irrationally aggressive. What goodies are you cooking up in your department, Tim?' Norman asked.

'I'll bring the pudding in,' Ann said, getting up.

'Do let me help.' Betty sprang up too. 'I do so want to see the kitchen where you make such marvellous things.' Ann, who hated guests in her kitchen, was forced to accept. 'Your sister's very clever. Do you understand all the business about tax linking and joint incomes?'

'Some of it,' Ann admitted. 'Those of us who've got it want to hang on to it, I suppose. When there isn't enough to go round you have to get the best for those you love.'

'It's only human nature,' Betty said cautiously.

'I suppose so. I sometimes wish there was something more.'

When they returned to the table in their small procession of Ann bearing a dish of pears belle Hélène followed by Betty with a jug of cream balanced on the stack of plates, the talk had shifted to Institute shop between Norman and Tim while Fanny and Charles took the opportunity to smile affectionately at each other.

'You mean you've managed to breed a strain resistant to both ampicillin and chloramphenicol?'

'Yes. It's really rather a breakthrough.' Tim pushed nervously against his spectacles.

'What are you going to call it, this prodigy?' asked Fanny who had been half following their conversation.

'Oh, STG because that's the letter we've reached in our sequence of variants.'

'I thought at least it would be dragon's blood.'

'Not very bacteriological,' Tim laughed.

Forester was delighted that his sister-in-law had innocently prised out a piece of information he had wondered how he was going to get. He could change the conversation now or better let someone else do it. Again it was Fanny who helped him out.

'Are you going to play for us, little sis?'

'I'm very out of practice,' Ann said. 'I've hardly touched it since I had Lucretia. There doesn't seem time.'

'And yet you wanted to make time to mess about with the pensioners again.'

'I just feel...' Ann let the words trail and die. She didn't want a public disagreement with Norman nor did she want him to discover yet that she had already resumed her run.

They had all been so glad to see her. 'Someone said you wouldn't never come back but I knew you would,' said Mrs Goulding. 'And you've got the baby in the car. That's right, my dear, you keep her there in this weather. You never know what's going about.'

She made it sound as if there might be a giant or demon prowling the land. Ann remembered some expression about Satan going to and fro on the earth 'seeking whom he might devour' and felt chilled even in the high summer heat.

The Beavors were the first to leave.

'Germs,' said Fanny. 'How can he spend his life breeding germs? And he looked quite a nice young man.'

Forester, who had got what he wanted out of the occasion, said nothing. Sensing his change of mood, the others soon left too.

'Charlie?'

'What's that?'

'Do you think Norman's alright?'

'How do you mean, love?'

'Well, he's very moody and half the time he doesn't seem to be with you at all. Then he suddenly seems to take offence. It must be very trying to live with.'

'Not like me?'

'Not a bit like you.' At another time she might have teased him with: 'Just like you,' but she sensed that he needed reassurance.

His brother-in-law depressed Charles and undermined even his confidence and lazy strength. He was fond of Ann and could see no way to help her, which frustrated his inherent desire to put everything right around him so that he wasn't distracted from enjoying his own life. If Ann could make such a mistake perhaps Fanny had made an equal mistake in marrying him and this, which was only a sudden stab of fear not even a fully formed thought, ate away the foundations of his world and he felt it tremble.

As soon as Jessop was twenty thousand richer and himself that much poorer, Forester went to see Tim Beavors in his part of the huge compound that was the Institute. Whenever Ann visited it she was surprised by its almost park-like appearance and the number of trees compared with the few in the countryside around.

'Just dropped in for a chat,' Forester said. 'It's good to get outside one's own section and widen the view from time to time, don't you think?'

'Oh well, you're the psychological expert. I'm really just a sort of chemist.' Tim Beavors was a shy and rather lonely man and he was flattered and a little excited by Forester's attentions. He had the reputation of not being very sociable among his colleagues and it was reckoned rather an honour to be invited to his elegant home. Tim had casually mentioned his own visit to a group in the clubroom.

'Did his wife play?' he was asked.

'Oh yes, after dinner.'

'They say she's rather stunning.'

'Yes, she is. My wife thought she was very nice and beautifully dressed. She cooked everything herself too, Betty said.'

'I wonder how he does it. There has to be a flaw somewhere. Lousy in bed I expect.'

'They've got a little girl.'

There was a snigger and Beavors realized he had said the wrong thing as he so often did. He wasn't very good at the bull sessions and was generally thought rather limp. Only Betty's plumped curves saved him from worse suspicions.

'Maybe we should do a project together on the motivations of bacteria,' Forester laughed, sinking his hook deeper. 'How's G doing? Or are you on to H by now?'

'No it's still G. If you wouldn't be bored...'

Forester got up. 'Lead on, but I warn you you'll have to come and be bored with my apes in return.'

Beavors flushed with pleasure. 'Oh, I'd love to.'

They passed through a neutralizing current and then put on light plastic helmets and oversuits like old-fashioned divers or early visitors to the moon, with built-in communication equipment. There were warning notices about entering the labs improperly dressed.

'Not to keep things from you but in case the sanitizing procedure missed something and you introduced an alien organism.'

'What about sneezing?'

'Don't do it in the helmet if you can avoid it. It blows your head off. This is the salmonella typhi series. Each one's different, just a bit. We got the idea from studying outbreaks among the nons. Simple and cheap if they get the okay from the Defence boys.'

'There don't seem to be so many outbreaks these days.'

'It's hard to say. They may not get reported. It's hardly earth-shattering news. On the other hand the nons may have learnt to take greater hygienic precautions or have built up some degree of immunity.'

'Rather my department. I'm doing a project on motivation. I hadn't considered fear of sickness as a stick, I suppose because you can't stimulate the conditions with apes.'

'They don't really know what's happening?'

'Oh they understand illness in a way and will bring each other food and sit with another one who's ill or groom them and they will tell you that the other one is sick. But they can't anticipate it. Threat of disease might be an even more powerful goad with humans than threat of punishment or even death. At the moment we're trying various forms of punishment: food or sleep deprivation, non-socialization, infant deprivation and so on. Then we'll try the rewards and try to form some statistically based conclusions on what's most effective. Until now it's been very hit and miss. This should take some of the randomness out of social control.'

For a moment Tim's enthusiasm for Forester wavered. Then his training and his wish surged together to repress any doubts and he was able to be all admiration again. By the time Forester left he knew all he needed and a great deal more that he had made himself be patient with. Beavors and his wife were well suited. She had reminded Forester of a strange bent of his father's. He had loved faintly obscene ice-creams moulded in the shape of a woman, naked, pink and slippery when he ran his red tongue over them as he held them by their plastic feet, all that would be left when he had done with them.

'Dad's girls,' his mother had called them with a laugh as she provided the treat.

Forester, going through his parents' drawers one day when they were out and he was alone in their dingy and tottering semi, had found a plastic bag full of pink feet hidden under a pile of bedclothes. Did his father count them from time to time? Suppose he took a handful – would he be found out? In the end he took two and set fire to them, watching them blacken, twist and shrink to little globules. No one ever mentioned that they were missing.

The thought of what he was about to do excited him. He was plunging deeper into the life of action than his profession usually allowed and yet he felt no fears that he wouldn't be able to bring it off. In anticipation he laid the groundwork with Ann for a night spent at the Institute, with hints let slip of a crisis in his project.

Guiltily Ann felt herself relieved by the thought of his absence for the night. She might go out into the garden after dark and look at the stars between the black palms of leaves or stay up all night and walk in the dawn leaving green footprints in grass opalescent with dew. During the day there was little time for dreaming because of Lucretia's demands but once she was asleep Ann could have long hours of quiet into which she could pour any music she liked if Norman was out. She hoped it wouldn't rain though even as she hoped she began to fashion a dreamcloak out of that possibility too, in which she could drape herself so that the precious hours wouldn't be wasted.

Security at the Institute was mainly outward-looking. The thought of burglary from inside hadn't really crossed the planners' minds. Nevertheless Forester didn't want to be seen or it to be known that he was still inside the compound. Fortunately, though entry was recorded exit wasn't. He was able to lock himself in his room knowing that no one should come in and find him still there, unless like himself they were up to no good. He smiled in the dark at the thought of how disconcerted anyone who had wanted to go through his records would be to see him in their torchlight sitting at his desk as if waiting for them.

No one came, however, while he dozed in his chair. At one o'clock he let himself out of his office and walked softly along the empty corridors to the outer door. He paused and looked through the glass. The primate quarters where an attendant would be on duty were separated from the office. Lights burned there continually and Forester felt a temptation to go and peer through the glass at the sleeping animals. To do so might wreck his whole plan but for a moment the urge was so strong he almost gave in to it and had to shake his head as if to physically drive it away.

Instead he turned into the thicker darkness beside the office and began to make his way towards Beavors's sector. From time to time he had to detour to avoid a lighted window and once he heard distant low voices. The night smell was strong and cool and he made a mental note to think about why humans still experienced what was such a feral sensation as the taste and smell of night and whether it was even stronger among the apes.

His internal pass slid open the doors of the microbiology labs noiselessly for him and closed again when he was inside. He passed through the neutralizing area and dressed himself in the helmet and suit. He wanted there to be as little possibility of detection as he could achieve. To introduce a foreign organism might be the surest way of being found out.

At the row of glass cylinders where salmonella typhi was silently breeding in her several mutations, Forester took out two five-milligramme syringes and placed them on the white bench. With one he withdrew a full quantity of STG and with the other he replaced it with an equal amount of the correct culture solution whose make-up he had learned from Beavors. Then he injected the bacterial fluid into the jar in which he had brought the solution, sealed it carefully, pocketed both syringes and left the lab. It had taken him less than five minutes but he was trembling with the effort.

Now he had to take a gamble. Still wearing the protective suit, he passed through the sensitized zone and on the other

95

side drew out the jar and left it. Then he returned, exposing the syringe he had used to suck up the bacteria in his gloved hand. He undressed and put the suit neatly back in place. His legs wanted to run him away or let him sink in a heap on the floor but he kept moving to his plan and passed through the neutralizing area again, picked up the jar, pressed the button that opened the lab doors from the inside and felt the air cold on his sweating skin. The route back to his own quarters was a nightmare of false alarms to his overwrought nerves and he was sick and exhausted by the time he dropped into his desk chair. He leant forward with his head on his arms and made himself breathe deeply.

And it might all have been pointless if the neutralizing zone could kill through the plastic suit and the glass container. Forester didn't dare go into his own lab to check for that would have meant switching on a light. He must wait until morning. Like a swimmer who has only just made it to the shore he lay collapsed over his desk and fell into a broken sleep.

As soon as it was light enough he went through to his own bench, put a drop of the solution on a slide under the projector and found himself grinning when the animate shapes were thrown on to the screen at the push of a button. Meticulously he destroyed them before flushing the droplet away. Now he only had to wait until he could safely emerge as an early devoted worker.

Ann's night hadn't been at all as she had imagined it would be. She had found herself apathetic, lacklustre. Instead of going out into the dark or the dawn garden she had alternately crouched in a chair by the dead hearth or wandered into another room in search of something, she had forgotten what by the time she reached it, and stood looking about her without recognition. At the same time she was impatient at her own waste of opportunity. Eventually she poured herself a glass of wine and put on a chip of one of the great mezzo sopranos of an earlier period and found herself on the edge of tears.

> My lovely Celia, heavenly fair,
> As lilies sweet, as soft as air,
> No more then torment me but be kind
> And with thy love ease my troubled mind.

She longed for such an emotion to be poured out over her and yet chided herself. Wasn't she very lucky, with a successful husband, a child and every comfort? That was what life was about. Think of Mrs Goulding and the others she met on her pensioners' run and be grateful. Was it too much to ask to be loved as well, for she had become convinced that Norman didn't love her, perhaps never had? She told herself that that kind of romantic love belonged to an earlier age. Perhaps it couldn't bloom in modern air conditioning. Then she saw Fanny and Charles as they had looked at each other while the others were talking and knew that love was possible, not maybe that all-enveloping passion of the song but a loving friendship.

Suddenly she didn't know whether she could live another forty or fifty years without some emotional nourishment. That would be half a century. It was her own fault for weakly accepting the safety Norman offered, denying what talent she had, giving up the struggle for a different life before she had given it a chance. But must she be punished for the rest of her days? 'Perhaps you must,' said the cold voice inside her which she knew was her own when she sounded most like her mother.

She couldn't take her child and go back to that mother and her father. There would be no welcome there. Professor Briles was retired and they had moved to a carepark with medical attendants in residence and every convenience away from the problems of the world to help the inhabitants age gently.

Fanny and Charles would have taken her in temporarily but it was no long-term answer because she couldn't ask them to keep her, even if they had been able to do so. She was trapped. In many ways she had less freedom for all her comfort than an ordinary girl who could get work.

Ann had never looked at her life in these terms before and what she now saw shook her badly. The house seemed claustrophobic and isolated. Perhaps she should go into the garden after all. She opened the front door and breathed deeply but the power to move and liberate had gone out of the stars. They were merely other bodies like the earth, collections of gases or heatballs and there was no longer music from their spheres. She turned indoors. The sensible thing to do was to go to bed.

The next stage of Forester's plan required outside assistance. No one must be able to connect him personally with the nemesis that was about to rid him of Jessop. He made an appointment with an agency for industrial and personal services in Salisbury.

Though historically a city, Salisbury was in essence a country town and that had saved it. It had never had a large non population and those it had were docile country people. Most he saw as he drove through the streets to his meeting were lower clerical, clean and respectable, machine minders like his father, who were too busy tending their houses and gardens in the evenings to dream up trouble.

The office was a discreet eighteenth-century redbrick house near the cathedral. The inside was a mixture of modern comfort and residual elegance to implant an impression of both efficiency and reticence in the customer. Doors slid at a button touch but the ceilings had kept moulded cornice and rose. For a moment Forester was reminded of Ann and of how he had suddenly felt irritated by the blindfold cupid on her viola as she had played for Fanny when Tim Beavors had come to dinner.

'Rick Walters!' The tanned slim figure with white flashes at its temples grasped his hand powerfully and waved him into a chair that sighed as he sank into the depth of its padding. 'You understand how we work? You don't tell us anything we don't need to know. It's a concept we took over from the public security boys: need to know. You ask us to do a specific job, employing us as your agent or servant so that the legal responsibility for our actions is yours. In return we guarantee efficiency and confidentiality. Please read the contract through carefully and then tell me if you wish to go ahead.' He buttoned open a drawer and produced a document on genuine parchment wove paper in faintly gothic printing. Meant to impress the customers, Forester thought, whom Walters will call 'our clients'. Somewhere a hidden recorder would be picking up everything that passed between them to constitute an oral contract as backup.

'I made myself familiar with the position before I came here,' Forester said, taking out his chippen and letting his eye run over the words so that Walters would see his high reading rate. He had thought of using a false name but had reflected that if they were any good at all at their job they would run checks and soon find out. He passed the pen over the document to make a copy of it and then imprinted his signature electronically and indelibly.

'The procedure I want you to carry out for me will be in two parts. The first is a fact-finding job. How you do it is up to you.'

Walters thought, when he had heard what was wanted, that it would be 'a piece of cake', an expression he had decided fitted his chosen image. 'When I know that,' Forester said, 'I'll brief you on the next stage.' He wondered if Walters would hear the quotation marks round 'brief'. This game was absurd and yet exciting at the same time.

'I have the information you asked for,' Walters told him two days later.

'Good. When can you see me?'

This time he took the STG, to the naked eye an almost clear fluid, with him.

For this kind of job you offlaid onto the professionals. You didn't use your own men. A whole new category of burglar had come into existence, specializing in breaking and discovering. If caught they would say they had come to steal on their own behalf, denying any connection with an agency, a connection that was hard to prove. One of them would be ideal for this, Walters thought, not the operative who'd taken one of the girl attendants out for the night, knocked her out with a hypnotic drug, while she thought he was knocking her with something else, emptied her mind and then finished as she had hoped. Walters always used Harris on those jobs because of his accent and the way his clean blond hair fell into his eyes. Each time the girl thought it was for ever and she was saved. Walters didn't care that some of them wept later. Most girls were gulls and deserved what they got when they were plucked. No wonder the non lads he picked up were so contemptuous of them and saw them only as a trap.

They had warned the man to be very careful with his small glass burden. He was to tip it into the feeder tank in the animals' quarters, replace the top tightly and when he reached a convenient spot bury it. He must wear surgical gloves until he was rid of it. He suspected it must contain some lethal poison and he was certainly going to follow instructions and keep the stuff off himself. Well, he wasn't paid to think, except about how to get in, do what he had to and get out completely undetected. He was the best in the business at that and took a pride in his skill. Survival was the thing. He didn't want the glory of a shoot out, just the quiet satisfaction of being so good they couldn't ever stick nothing on him.

With the faintest snap he clipped on the by-pass circuit; now he could open the windows and slip inside. Puss-puss padded between the cages to the far end where a service ladder led conveniently up to the feeder tank on a high shelf. In the bluish dark a shape rustled and he was aware of breathing around him. For a moment he wondered if they were watching and understood. Then he pulled himself together and almost swung up the ladder.

Outside again with the jar in his pocket and the circuit breaker stashed, he set off for open country where he dug a hole and buried the container. A great wave of relief swept him as he turned away from the small grave. He was surprised at himself. 'You need a drink, Puss-puss,' he told himself, 'or you're getting soft in your old age.'

It was eight days before Emily, quicker than most of the attendants to notice changes in her charges' moods, decided that one or two of them were listless and off their food. She reported her worry to Jessop. It coincided with a hot humid spell when mist lay late over the fields as if they were close to the sea, and as the day wore on seemed merely to rise rather than evaporate, and hang in a barrier designed to keep the heat in and the sun out.

'Step up the air conditioning. This weather's enough to give anyone the gripes.'

Then the vomiting and diarrhoea began. 'Must be some bug running through them,' Jessop said. 'Better call in the medic.'

'I'll need some samples of faeces to send for analysis,' the vet told Emily. 'By the time we get the result it'll probably all be over and they'll be bounding about again.'

It was as she tried to spoon a little glucose and water into Sally while she cuddled the moaning chimp on her lap that it came to Emily that she was dying, that indeed they might all be. Shakily she laid Sally down in the corner of the cage she shared with Mick, who seemed to be asleep on his own pile of bedding, and went to the washroom, where she had taken Gor on that first morning, to think. If she was wrong she would be thought alarmist. She had been only a child when her brother and sister had died and she had been sick herself but she was convinced that what the animals had was typhoid fever.

The decision was taken from her by the bleeper in her pocket. She pressed the receiving switch and heard Jessop's voice shrill and tinny.

'Emily, I've just had the vet on the phone. He says it's

bloody typhoid. I'm coming over.'

Jessop was appalled by the stench that struck at him as he opened the door. The violence of the outbreak and its rapid development among all the animals had been too much for the attendants. Apes and monkeys were hunched or prostrate in their own mess with staring fur and glazed eyes. 'Christ,' he said, 'they're all bloody dying. He said to get ampicillin into them and it'd be alright but looking at this lot I don't know. We might save some.'

Afterwards, when she was better herself, Emily was to remember how Jessop had worked alongside the vet and the attendants as they tried first one drug, then, when there seemed no response, another, and swabbed and scoured, and finally dragged away the dark carcasses.

The first journalist rang him while he still had hope. 'We've heard you've got an outbreak of virulent typhoid that doesn't seem to respond to the usual drugs.'

What bastard had told them? he had asked, using a milder expression.

'The usual little bird. Are any humans affected?'

'None,' Jessop said firmly but fear twitched in his gut.

Mick had died in Emily's arms, not peacefully but with spasm after spasm arching his body while Emily stroked his face and cried: 'Baby, there, there, baby.' Then it was Sally she held in her lap.

Jessop watched her anxiously. 'You feeling alright?'

Emily shook her head. 'I'm just tired.'

'Go up to the sick room and lie down for a bit.'

When she didn't reappear he sent Sandra up to see her. 'She's not well. I think she's got it too,' she reported. Now the health authorities would put the whole place into quarantine.

Emily's sickness was compounded by the distress and death she had been forced to see but the antibodies in her blood from that earlier attack made sure that she didn't die. Jessop got in a full-time medical attendant to look after her and Sandra who was the next to go down. They were the two who worked most closely with the animals. The other girls had only become involved when it was already known that it was typhoid, and they had been able to take the necessary precautions from the beginning.

When Jessop heard that Sandra had lost his child he almost laughed. Nothing mattered any more. He was finished. No one would ever deal with him again. Forester had been right in suspecting that he was underinsured. Even if he could have found the customers, and all his old ones had backed away from him as though he was personally contagious, his capital had been in his stock and was represented now by rows of empty cages.

For a time it seemed as if Sandra would follow her baby out of life since no drugs had any effect on the course of the fever, but she was young and strong and managed to survive the crisis although she would be weak for many months to come. Angry and cheated as he had felt, Jessop was relieved to see her pull through. Soon he would have to tell the staff there were no jobs for them and put the premises on the market.

He lay on the bed in the flat he had kept for his girls and looked at his future. It didn't exist. Whichever way he turned, the trap held him and bit into his flesh. There was no escape. They could sell the property but that sum invested wouldn't bring in enough to live on. He couldn't touch Forester again so soon and for so much. Instinct told him that door was closed. If he sold the house it might do it but that his wife would never agree to, or if she did it would break her. Life for them both would be a slough of daily getting by, laced with constant silent if not actually voiced recrimination. It wasn't worth living that kind of life and anyway he couldn't do it to her.

Jessop found himself with almost amused surprise seriously considering his own death as he lay on the bed where he and the girls had had their bit of fun, with a glass of gin in his hand. A lot of it had been good. They hadn't all been like Sandra Canfold. Some of them must have liked him a bit. He looked at the dressing-table where he had watched them afterwards touching up their mouths and saw himself in the mirror, sallow and baggy-eyed from the last few days and sleepless nights. Life wasn't worth living for its own sake; it was only worth living if it was worth living, he concluded as he finished off the gin.

Quality of life, that was what you were taught mattered and that meant to him having what made his life sweet, gave him confidence to play all the games that society required if you were to have the money to buy that sweetness that gave you the confidence to play the games. And so on. Round and round. Some people might have said he was trapped by it but he was no more trapped than they were by their ladder to the top that

102

they hauled themselves up, promotional rung by rung, until by the time they got there they were too clapped out to enjoy the view, exhausted and panting, while he, who'd been content with his roundabout, was still enjoying himself. Or had been.

There had to be a way out. Jessop thrashed against the steel jaws that had shut round him. Animals in traps often chewed off a leg to escape. The human equivalent was the bottle of booze and the bottle of pills. That seemed to be it. His wife had him well insured. She had seen to that side of things while he took care of the business insurance. His death would see her alright. She'd be quite well off and might make a good marriage. He felt rather cheerful about it. There was just the little problem of how best to kill himself.

They would say, of course, that his mind had been disturbed by his losses. And they would be right. He was disturbed and had every reason for killing himself. There would be no question of the insurance company refusing to pay. The trouble was that the more cheerful he felt about the whole scheme the less he wanted to die. The very planning of it gave him a new hold on life.

Why couldn't he just pretend? People were always doing it in movies. He would have to be very clever about it because if anything went wrong things would be worse than ever. He might get done for fraud and Isobel wouldn't get the money. He would have to disappear and the only place he could go would be to a big city. It would be like drowning. He would sink to the bottom out of sight of anyone who'd known him. He might not survive, but he'd have a bloody good try and if all else failed the next time could be for real.

What he needed was a body. Or no, not even that. A head would do or even less: a set of teeth. In the morning he would set about finding them.

It meant a trip to the metropolis, to London. He locked his car on to the Highway Three beam and let it take itself while he thought. He would have to empty the building and make sure he had the place to himself. Well, Emily and Sandra could be sent back to their own homes tomorrow and the medical attendant discharged. He would stay on after the others had left. Old Wilkie would be the hardest to get rid of. She sensed that something was badly wrong and was always at his elbow about to be solicitous. She'd give him her life savings, he reckoned, if he asked.

103

Soon the road was passing through Brentford Heath, part of the outer London green belt that encircled the city to the north of the Thames which formed a natural barrier to the south. Beyond, over the water, lay the non quarters. In the morning those of the inhabitants who had jobs in the city were trained in on company season tickets and at evening they flowed back across the river to their own side. Security checkpoints discouraged them from walking across the bridges unless they could show an employer's certificate or a resident's permit.

Jessop had barely thought about the southern quarters before but now he looked at the names on his travelscope with interest. Wandsworth, Catford, Lambeth. Any time now he might find himself walking about in their strange, exotic-sounding purlieus: London began at Warwick Road after you had crossed the high viaduct over Hammersmith Fields with the river glinting away to the right. He loved the sensation of entering the first of the elegant streets of town houses, Cromwell Road with its white-porticoed façades behind the plane trees, showing sometimes a glimpse of a chandelier or a uniformed servant.

This was a level beyond anything even Isobel had ever aspired to and soon he would lose even the possibility of passing through it for ever. It was probably the last time he would enter the metropolis in his own car and drive along these wide avenues. He headed for the medical quarter of Harley Street where the doctors to people of status and rich foreigners had their houses and where their suppliers had theirs. Here the medical students equipped themselves with everything for their studies, including the traditional skeleton. You could have a choice of two sorts: if you were an aided student you scraped together for a plastic one; if you were a child of wealthy parents you bought the real thing. Nons often raised a few dollars by selling their skeletons or bequeathing them to their families to sell, along with any other marketable parts.

Jessop was shown into the appropriate section of a large warehouse that took up a corner of New Cavendish Street. Idly he wondered what it could have been used for in the old days as he looked down the racks of strung bones carefully labelled and each in its clear plastic shroud, like the raincloaks he had noticed the nons wearing earlier in the summer. Jessop passed up females 9–13 and came to the male racks where he peered at the jaws and selected one with roughly similar teeth and of his own age and height. It was rather more expensive because the nons tended to be shorter in stature, and although Jessop had only been clerical in origin he had been upper rather than lower and had the physique of someone of status. He took his bony double to the checkout and paid in eurodollars so that there would be no trace in his account. Fortunately the machine didn't think him eccentric. It was programmed to accept either, although few people carried cash except visiting foreigners. The wrapping machine delivered him a box when he had paid and he put the skeleton in it and carried it to the car.

Next he looked for the dentistry section of the medical area and bought a drill and filler. Then he turned back the way he had come. He wished he had had the time to take a last look round. Jessop had always loved the city and been glad of the rational solution that had preserved it from the collapse that had overtaken others that hadn't found a way to price the nons out but instead had been given over to them. The metropolis had been saved because that was what it was: the seat of government and finance, the mother city, the matriarch who held the purse.

Fewer and fewer jobs and higher prices had driven away many from the outer boroughs and as the houses had fallen empty they had been bulldozed down to make the new green-belt surrounding the city proper to the north. Jessop could remember when he was a boy that there had still been continuous acres of small houses where now there were fields, woods and heath, with an occasional ugly remnant of a village. The beautiful core of London had returned to almost the configuration it had had at its zenith at the beginning of the nineteenth century.

Jessop carried the box of bones into his office. Everyone, including Miss Wilkins, had gone. He had the place completely to himself. The strings on the skeleton had had to be slackened to allow it to be packed. He tightened them and sat it in an armchair for visitors.

The similarity of the teeth and their good condition had been a bonus. Although dental charts only showed gaps, and fillings if any, it was as well to run as few risks of detection as possible. It was a good thing too that his own teeth were pretty sound: there would be less for him to do. He fitted up the drill, studied his own chart and began, tilting back the skull and wedging open the mandible.

The label had given no details of how the flesh that had once encased these particular bones had died nor of its occupation in life. Had it been married, sired children? Perhaps it had been chaste or the lover of another identikit of flesh and bone. Now it would lie as his surrogate more socially exalted than it ever had in life. He thought of its funeral, such of it as was left, and wondered if Isobel would weep over it. He wished faintly that he could have found its family and paid them some kind of bonus for its extra service to him.

His thinking had changed with the purchase of the skeleton. At first he had thought he would set fire to his proxy in his office, leaving a suicide note, but that had begun to seem full of hazards and opportunities for the whole thing to go badly wrong. He had now switched to the idea of an accident. There could be no question of the insurance not paying up then and there was likely to be less minute inquiry into his remains.

When he was finished he slackened and boxed up Fred, as he had found himself calling the skeleton, and put him back in the car with the holdall that now contained all he could take out of his life. Then he rang Isobel and said he was on his way to a dealer near Melksham he had done business with before, and wouldn't be back till the next day. He was sorry about the small select dinner party he was missing but he was sure she could manage without him. It sounded like an epitaph on their marriage. There was nobody else he had to say goodbye to.

For the last time he walked between the empty cages which still smelled faintly of their recent occupants. The image of Emily Bardfield's face as she had cradled the dying Sally was suddenly as strong as if he had seen it rerun in video. He hoped she would get another job when she was fully recovered and everything would turn out alright for her in the end. It was time to get on with it. He joined Fred in the car and set off towards Basingstoke.

At Andover he turned off the main highway going west. Surely he was very close to where that swine Forester lived. It was a pity he hadn't had time to get more out of him. At least the Canfold bitch would be set up in life and without his little bastard round her neck. He would have been happy to have done the same for Emily. Jessop drew up at a motel. He was going to have a last blowout, a good though short night's sleep and an early start in the morning. Fred could sleep in the car.

The alarm call on the breakfaster woke him at four-thirty. He ate all he could and pocketed what was left. He was going to have to think of things like that from now on. Then, his bill debited to his account, he set off into the whitening dawn and, as soon as he found the spot he wanted, pulled off the road into the fringe of Savernake Forest.

Fred was dressed in his clothes, not that Jessop intended there should be anything left of them, and seated in the driver's seat. Jessop took out the extra gallons of petrol and his holdall. Then he released the brake, set the automatic and stood clear while the car gathered speed and plunged through the undergrowth until it smashed into a tree. He ran forward and soused the wreck, and in particular Fred, with petrol, threw in a lighted cigarette and ran back.

The effect was all he could have wished. The clothed figure slumped over the controls vanished in a surge of flame that shot twenty feet into the air. Jessop stood watching as both skeleton and its fibreglass coffin were consumed along with the surrounding brushwood. A tree caught and another. So much the better if the wood around the wreck burned so fiercely that no one could get near it for some time. But the smoke would attract police and forest rangers and besides there was the risk of his being caught in the advancing flames. That would be too ironic. Jessop picked up his holdall and walked away, turning his back on the rising sun.

As soon as Emily felt almost strong enough she joined the scrum for a tourer and took herself in to work. She found the building locked and silent with a For Sale board the only brightly coloured object at the end of her long walk down the track. For a moment she felt faint. This was some nightmare and she would surely wake. Indeed she had dreamt it before, hadn't she? She got out at the top of the track and as she walked along she became aware that there were weeds growing where she put her feet. That was the beginning of the dream.

Now she turned to look back at the way she had hurried along, not noticing because she was almost running and that made her breathless after her long days of weakness, and saw that the weeds, grown tall, leant their heads in from the side of the path showing that no vehicles had brushed past them recently. Their seeds would drop on to the track and sprout as in her dream. She looked up at windows become filmed with dust, and blank; at the alarm system and the high door in the wall shut against her and already wearing a curiously neglected air as if she had been away for months not weeks. It was no dream although in her barely recovered state it seemed one. She would go round to Sandra's and see if she knew what had happened. The Canfolds lived on a small estate for ex-soldiers and her father's army pension, at the edge of Aldershot Military Town, quite near.

She would walk, Emily decided, for now every cent would count until she could find another job. She didn't allow herself to think in terms of 'if'. It was a long walk but there was no hurry and she dawdled a little dreamily. Now was the moment for the young man in the open top to squeal to a halt beside her, but the nearest she came to that was when a truck of young soldiers called and whistled at her as they bowled dustily past. As so often, the sight of them gave Emily a sharp pang of anxiety for William. How could he ever fit into their world? He must work hard and get on. Soldiering was a chance for many boys just a few years older than William but the competition for places was tough and those who succeeded were very different in temperament and physique from her brother.

How right her mother had been to seize the chance given them by Gordon – or Gor, as they had come to call him because that was what he preferred to call himself. Since his return he and Jessie had become as inseparable as twins and he was talking more and more. He seemed to have forgotten his stay in the hospital and laughed and hooted with delight at life most of the day as he stomped along behind Jessie or wrestled with another of their gang of toddlers. Whatever happened the Doctor mustn't take him away yet, not until she had found another job at least. Her thoughts diverted her along the two miles to Sandra's but she was weary by the time she got there.

Mrs Canfold wore her thick black hair in a plait like her daughter but one threaded with strands of clear silver. Sandra had lied when she had told Jessop her mother was a full Pakky but her Indian blood was dominant and as well as her dark hair, had coloured her skin and refined her features so that sometimes Emily thought she was the most beautiful woman she had ever seen, even on movies or the telly, and then felt guilty towards her own mother. Diva Canfold herself would gladly have swapped her looks for Mrs Bardfield's doughy skin and energy.

Jo Canfold was out when Emily reached their maisonette, drinking with pensioner cronies at the Duke of York. By the time he was stood down at forty he had reached sergeant and his pension was princely by the standards of the Bardfield family. In this house they drank real tea, a habit Jo had got into in the sergeants' mess.

Sandra was still in bed. Mrs Canfold showed Emily into the bedroom which she shared with a younger sister and left silently. The shock to Sandra's body had been much greater than to Emily's, partly because she had lacked Emily's painfully earned resistance and partly because of her miscarriage. The face that looked at Emily from the pillow was sallow and thin and her hair showed dull as a sick animal's coat. It brought back all the misery of those days to Emily and once again she saw Mick's face as the tremors had passed through him. She drew up a chair to the bed.

'How you doing, kid?'

'Oh Em, I am glad to see you. It's so boring lying here and you know what my mum's like.'

Emily nodded. For all her beauty and her husband's pension, Mrs Canfold found life an unending tragedy from which she had long ago retreated inside herself.

'I've been down to Jessop's and it's all shut up with a For Sale notice outside. I thought you might know what's happened.'

'Haven't you heard? It was on the news. Jessop was killed in a car crash. He set half the forest on fire. They thought it might have been suicide because he was going bust anyway after all the animals died but no one could prove it.'

'But why didn't anyone tell us?'

'They don't have to if someone dies, my dad says. It cancels all contracts in some way. Mrs Jessop came out of it best. She'll sell all the buildings and land, and she's got his life insurance. What'll you do, Em?'

'I don't know. I haven't had time to think. What about you?'

'Oh, I'm alright. I've got that little nest egg in the bank, and none in me.'

'Did you really get it?'

Sandra nodded and grinned. Her face was looking less sallow as she talked and smiled and her eyes had taken on a gleam deep in their previously matt black pupils. 'I might set up in business. You could come in with me, Em. We'd share a place. Only people of status because we'd have something to back us and so we wouldn't just have to take any old sludge,' she said using the usual female term for unemployed non men.

'Where would we go?' Emily was only half listening as she turned over all Sandra had told her. Jessop was dead. She was sorry about that and remembered how he'd worked during the fever, not baulking at the muck or stink. He hadn't been a bad geezer, just in that one way and maybe even that was understandable if he didn't get much affection at home. Gossip had always said Mrs Jessop was more interested in her home beautiful than in how the money was made or the man who made it.

'We could find somewhere in Aldershot and go for the young officers.'

'My mum'd kill me.' At last Emily had fully registered Sandra's suggestion.

'She needn't know. You could just say you'd got a job and we were sharing.'

'I'd have to send money home.' Emily felt that somehow she was using all the wrong arguments.

'Of course you would. So would I. You don't think my dad'd let me get away without.'

'Did you tell him about the money?'

'You're too right I didn't. He'd have had half of it off me at least and slugged it away in a few months. Probably drunk himself to death in the process and then where would it leave Mum? Come on, Em, what do you say? We'd do ever so well: you so fair and me so dark and neither of us looking slag.'

'I'll think about it,' Emily said. She didn't want to offend Sandra by turning the idea down straight away or by seeming to be offended herself. She recognized that people might look at these things very differently and that it was all a matter of temperament. Her own romanticism, however, recoiled at Sandra's suggestion and she was unwilling to give up that dream that still held out a shrinking hope in the corner of the box, whatever ills and furies buzzed about her head.

Forester had been very pleased by the simplicity of his success. He had no doubt that Jessop had either committed suicide or been killed while attempting to run away. Whichever it was, Jessop was off his back for good and he had brought it about by distanced manipulation. His death was a bonus Forester hadn't expected but it gave him no qualms. He had been a little worried when the news had broken that two girl attendants had been involved in the mysterious epidemic at Jessop's. Fortunately their recovery had prevented too many questions and any further curiosity had been consumed in Jessop's funeral pyre. Clearly the man had been incompetent to have allowed the disease to spread unnoticed to humans and had panicked and killed himself.

The agency had been paid and would keep silent; so would whoever they had employed to do the job. They were all professionals. It was a pity Forester couldn't use his knowledge as a warning to anyone else who might attempt to interfere in his life, like Graham, for instance, with his ridiculous syndrome theory which had brought him membership of the Royal Academy of Sciences and would probably get him a chair if not a birthday honour. How Forester longed to be able to reveal the anthropoid and show the man up for the conceited jackass that he was.

It seemed as if Emily would have to leave home. Jobs, even for girls, were harder to come by at the moment in their area. Mrs Bardfield stood looking out over the tops of the houses opposite, towards where the first field of low soybushes began, and felt as if she was quietly bleeding to death inside. How could she let her go or manage without her? She had talked of perhaps sharing some job with Sandra in Aldershot and that wouldn't be too far, but today she had taken the coach down to Salisbury where she had heard of a job going in her old line. Travel was expensive. She might have to find a place in a hostel to live near her work.

'Mum, Mum!' It was Jessie's voice calling to her up the stairs. 'Mum, Gordon's gone into the fields!'

Mrs Bardfield never remembered how she got down the stairs. She was aware of herself running, and of how slowly her legs went up and down even so, while the ground seemed to stand still under her as if it were all uphill, instead of flat between the next row of houses, across the road and between the next till she came to the narrow green verge before the crops began, and the warning notice that all the children were taught to heed before they could form the letters that made it.

She could see Gordon and another small boy moving among the bushes that stretched to her horizon, their blue plastic dungarees catching the sun and almost shiny against the grey

111

leaves. There were gaps in the security beam, fades that sometimes let an animal slip into the field where it might browse but never find the spot again where it had entered or if it did the patch would have moved like a map of the shifting desert that could never hold itself still for long.

The beam was a high frequency pulse that stunned and killed if the animal was small enough or damaged irrevocably if it was big enough to survive. A philanthropic lawyer had once tried to get compensation for the parents of a child who had been caught in it but the courts had ruled that there was no liability because the injury had been sustained while the felony of trespass was being committed. There was, as Mrs Bardfield said, 'Nothing for hard luck.'

Birds might have flown above the invisible wall but these were such rarities since the death of insect life that their depredations were ignored. It was the tooth of rabbit, mouse and rat that the beam barred from the fields where they would have munched and gorged.

Mrs Bardfield caught back the impulse to cry out to the two children. She might startle them and cause them to run straight into it. Trapped herself, she searched up and down for inspiration and help. There must be some way to get them out. The two figures seemed small as mice among the neat rows of scrub running as far as her eye could see in chains that bound the unhedged soil from blowing away. Every two years the harvester trundled into the field, tore up the bushes, stripped and chomped them. Later the sower would come and put in next year's crop. The estate children all gathered to watch the giant machines at work until they were out of sight. Alfalfa and rape did turn about with the soybushes so that their lives were calendered by the changing colour of the fields. Always Mrs Bardfield saw events afterwards in the grey, purple or yellow of that year's crop.

Now in her mind's eye she saw the windows of the cabs with the small black figure of the driver high up in the air. Sometimes they would wave down to the watching children. Mrs Bardfield saw a hand against the sky. The drivers were above the beam then when the machine passed through it into the field. Or was it switched off for them? No, because as the harvester tore and crunched, any small animal that had managed to pass through one of the fades and had lived happily ever after in that Garden of Eden was startled into flight towards

112

the edge of the field where it dropped dead. The nearest child would prod at it with a brush until the furred, warm corpse was manoeuvred on to the verge and carried home. The unwritten rule was that, as in a game of chance, the prize was to the lucky. No one jostled or tried to claim unjustly that he had been nearest and the spoil should go to him. Mrs Bardfield remembered William's pride when one year at harvest he had brought something home for the pot.

The only answer was to raise the children above the beam. She must find a ladder tall enough.

'Jessie, you stay here and if they look as if they're going to come back tell them to stay where they are and I'll be after them if they don't.'

Again she ran cumbrously but back the way she had come.

'What's up?' Mr Bardfield unbent from the row of seedlings he had been thinning, his fingers neat and gentle among the tender leaves.

'Gordon and another kid are in the field.'

His face crumpled. He had no advice to offer. Long ago he had lost the power to decide and to act. She hadn't expected anything else. 'What are you going to do?'

'Find a long enough ladder. You knock and ask down that side of the road. I'll do this.'

No single ladder was tall enough. Four were brought out and carried up to the field where Jessie waited. Gor and his accomplice were standing together facing her now with frightened faces that might easily collapse into tears like melting wax. Mrs Bardfield directed the tying together of the ladders into a large 'V' which was pushed half-way into the field by the group of adults that had now gathered.

Her theory was to be cruelly tested. If she was wrong or the ladders not high enough, the children would be irrevocably injured. The other boy's mother was being cared for by a neighbour as she waited in her kitchen unable to stand watching the attempt at rescue.

'Gordon,' said Mrs Bardfield firmly, 'you climb up first because you're best at it and show Leroy how to do it.'

Obediently Gor seized the second rung and began to pull himself up. As he neared the apex he would be over the beam or within it.

'Leroy, you follow Gordon.'

But Leroy put his fists to his eyes and let out a howl of

terror. Gor stopped in his ascent and began to climb down again. At the bottom he took one of Leroy's muddy fists and gripped it round the rung. Then he took the other and pushed him up till he was standing on the first strut.

'Come on, Leroy. It's easy.'

Slowly the two children climbed, with Gor often having to unclench and move his friend's hands or force his knees up till his feet rested on the next rung. Mrs Bardfield watched them approach the test point in a chilled calm. She had realized at the outset that whichever child reached it first might drop in a stunned heap. She had chosen Gor because she couldn't bear the other woman's pain. Fond as she had become of him she knew there was nothing like your own and that a bereaved mother must suffer more than she would, though the loss to her own family if Gor was taken away had almost made her hesitate. Now, though, it was Leroy's head that inclined further and further towards the beam. The choice had been taken from her. Her fists were doubled so that her fingernails bit into her palms. Jessie heard her mother sigh as Leroy's head was silhouetted at the top.

It took all Gor's skill and persuasion to get him over so that he could begin the climb down. As soon as he reached the ground he began to wail and run towards his own house. Gor touched down after him. Mrs Bardfield clipped him sharply on the ear in her relief and then threw her arms round him and he too began to howl.

The tale of his helping Leroy was all over the estate. Emily was stopped by a neighbour on the way home and told, a little of his fame rubbing off on her by propinquity. 'It makes you wonder who his parents were. There must be good blood there. That's more than ordinary guts for a little one.'

The other children came bursting in from school to question Mrs Bardfield and be told and retold. Jessie too basked in the fame of her little brother sort of. 'He'll get a swelled head,' said Mrs Bardfield. 'If they hadn't been where they shouldn't in the first place it wouldn't have happened. I'm for a quiet life.'

For a time it looked as if she might be right. Gor had become a little prince among his people. The mystery of his origins helped to beglamour the neighbours and gave endless opportunities for invention and speculation in lives that were short on romance. His toddler peers competed for his friendship and brought him small tokens to buy it. Had his nature not been essentially cheerful and modest, and Mrs Bardfield a firm corrective, he might have become very spoilt.

Emily had got her job. Forester had been interested in the turn of chance that had brought an answer from the anthropoid's foster sibling to the Institute's radio announcement of a vacancy for an attendant. The girl might well have got the place anyway because of her experience, even though it was tainted with Jessop's reputation, but it amused him to weave his web tighter.

The man had questioned her closely about the happenings at Jessop's. Obviously everyone knew about it. Emily had considered not mentioning her previous workplace but that would have meant leaving out the qualification that would give her the edge on other applicants. When the questions came and elicited from her that she had been one of the typhoid cases she felt her chance slipping away. She had been surprised then to hear him saying: 'You will of course need a security vet for here but if that's satisfactory I think you will be suitable.'

She was a pretty girl for a non. Forester didn't usually find them attractive. He knew that men, and women too, of status sometimes got an extra fillip out of crossing the levels but he was too close to them in his upbringing to find them exciting. They always had that faint smell of unbathed humanity. Given some better clothes and more hot water, though, this girl could have passed. For her mother's daughter her features were surprisingly refined. 'I see you live near Aldershot.'

'Yes, sir. I'll have to get a place in a hostel in Salisbury.'

Forester nodded. Her problems didn't concern him. She would be an auxiliary, not a permanent, as Knott had been, and would have to find her own accommodation.

'Are you sure you want to go that far?' her mother asked.

'No I don't, not really. But there's nothing round here. The money's better than at Jessop's so I'll be able to pay for my keep and come home most weekends.'

Mrs Bardfield was cheered a little. 'You wouldn't rather go with Sandra?'

'It wasn't much of a job,' Emily said carefully. 'And if this one doesn't work out I can always go back to it. It'll still be there.'

Mrs Bardfield asked no more. She sensed that Emily was keeping something from her that perhaps she wouldn't want to know. Emily found a place in one of the hostels run by a charitable trust for away-workers. She had never had to leave home before and at first she lay at night in the dormitory cubicle listening to the sounds from other sleepers or wakers, her throat tight with unshed tears.

Gradually she became accustomed to the new routine of morning alarm call, communal breakfast and an evening in the sitting-room where they took it in turns to feed the telly. On Friday night she caught the highway coach and her heart lifted as she was dropped off at the Aldershot junction and was on the last leg home. Sometimes she would go to visit Sandra who had set herself up and was now as glossily groomed as a cat come home after a long straying. Sandra had her regulars among the young officers and told stories of keeping them apart with much laughter that Emily sometimes found a little tinny. Julian must be out of the apartment before Joscelyn came and there must be no sign of his ash in the alabaster ashtray, telltale droppings that would be pounced on.

'You can come in with me any time, Em. Go on. Living in a cruddy old hostel! Why don't you?'

'I'll think about it,' Emily always said. Her weeks were passing as if she waited in a limbo of the emotions, slipping away almost unnoticed until she had been at the Institute and in the hostel for over two years and still it seemed she had arrived only yesterday.

William was taking the exam that would determine whether he left to flop into a pool of unemployed teenagers or went on to college. The teachers were confident; William nervous and grave.

Mrs Bardfield waited too. Things couldn't go on so quiet: they never did for long. It was therefore no surprise that she heard Gor say at the kitchen door: 'Dad's fallen over.'

He was stretched out on the earth with a little dribble coming out of his mouth. His eyes fluttered at her, begging. She lowered herself to the ground beside him. 'Run indoors, Gor, and get a mug of water,' she said to give the child something to do. Then she took Henry's head in her lap. 'That's alright, my lover, you're always mine.' His eyes stilled and closed. Later she found the damp patch on her shirt, one of his cast-offs, where she had held him against her.

'It would have made more sense to bury him in his garden,' she said to Emily as they came back from the crematorium where a very little breeze had scattered the token particles

116

through the Gardens of Rest. Things always went in threes, bad ones that was. With good things it was all life could do to manage one at a time. Well, she was ready and waiting.

The summons to pack up Gor's things and take them with her to his next check-up she saw at once was the second.

'What does it mean, Mum?'

'It means they're taking him away.'

Yet even before she could do it, the third was on them. The time had come for the anthropoid to be moved on to the next stage of the experiment, Forester had decided. The Bardfields were redundant. The girl could go. She had never been made permanent and her presence irritated him. Her approach to the animals she attended was too anthropomorphic, as if they were human children. It made them calmer and easier for her to handle but the added emotional responses distorted the experimental results.

They would find the next rent but not the one after, Mrs Bardfield knew as she led Gordon into the clinic and felt his apprehension transmitted through their joined hands. There would be no respite. If they didn't leave at once the bailiffs would be sent to throw them out. They would have to make for a city where rumour said there were empty squats. Her mind was already sorting their few things into what they would take and what they would try to sell. Emily had begged her mother to let Gor go with them but even though it was their first disagreement and it hurt her own already raw emotions she was firm. It was best for him. He was going where he would be well looked after; much better than they could do for him, she comforted herself. He would be spared their downfall.

He tried to cling to her of course as she had known he would but she pushed him away. He dug in his heels and beat at Forester with his free hand.

'Will you please hold him while I give him a sedative.' And she did, feeling both that it was her ultimate betrayal of him and that it was for his own good.

'You must try to think of him happy somewhere, Em. We haven't got time for tears.'

He felt himself sinking under the drug and tried to fight it as it was carried by his treacherous blood to the brain that was still resisting. When he woke he was in a small room in a clean white-quilted bed. There was a little table and chair, an unreachable window and clean new clothes hanging from a rail above a set of drawers. He turned over on his face and snuffled into the pillow until he fell asleep again. His schooldays had begun.

III

INTERLUDE
THE SCHOOLING
OF GOR

He would soon learn that crying did no good. It was Matron's maxim to begin as you meant to go on so there was no point in mollycoddling a new boy. They all cried at first but it quickly wore off. Crying exhausts itself and the weeper, and the natural impulse for survival of a young creature asserts itself in the end. Montgomery College, named after a heroic general of the Last World War, was intended for officers' orphans and run on lines very different from the methods of its namesake whose bereted portrait hung in the mess.

Not all the children were orphans or service offspring. Some were the sons of overseas diplomats and officials who preferred not to expose them to the hazards of foreign schooling. A few were non military orphans who were admitted on low or no fees and gave the school its charitable status. That was how Gordon Bardfield got in through the representations of his guardian, a distinguished biologist working for the Ministry of Defence.

Brooding over Gor's thickening file, Forester had decided to push the anthropoid to its limits. He could with no difficulty have taken it back into the Institute for intensive training and experimentation and for a time this had been his intention. But looking ahead to the moment of revelation he suddenly saw how much greater the impact would be if he could place before the world a young man of status, and then whisk the cloth away and show the ape, rather than a clever monkey punching the right buttons with a human forefinger. So far it had managed to pass against a non background, indistinguishable from its foster siblings as black on black. It was time for the second stage of the experiment.

Would the hominid be more ape than man in its motivation? Would it develop the necessary human ambition to do well or would the desire for play and comfort which he had to contend with in his apes be dominant? What might he learn about how to provoke the urge to succeed as a method of social engineering? Sometimes the nons seemed to be closer to his apes in that respect, to show almost a kind of psychological Graham's Syndrome. He pushed the thought away angrily. The consultant's specious triumph would rankle until he could find a way to reverse it.

Now it gave him pleasure to think that he had planted his creation in Montgomery College. It was true that he was there only on probation. All the aided boys were. There was no point in persevering with them if they weren't able to take advantage of the benefits the school could give. On the other hand the head liked them to come to him young, so that he could have the forming of them. Then if a child didn't respond it was clear that it hadn't the aptitude.

The school buzzer woke him again in the morning. The drug had largely cleared from his body but he felt heavy and lethargic, and his face was puffy with his tears and sodden sleep. Matron had been told the reasons for his unconscious state when Forester had carried him into the castellated building whose brick had mellowed to the blackish hue of dried blood. The long journey after an emotional parting from his foster family was explanation enough for a seven-year-old's exhaustion.

Instinctively he realized that the sound required action on his part. Gor sat up and swung his legs over the side of the bed. Usually he ran in to Jessie when he got up and she helped him wash and dress. He looked down at the new sleeping suit he was wearing and tugged the zip open. Then he realized that if he took it off he would be rudely naked with the day clothes intended for him out of reach. He dragged the chair over to the rail, climbed on to it and took down the aided boys' uniform of blue dungarees and teeshirt. There were blue pants and socks on the hanger in a plastic bag which he opened out of curiosity. At the foot of the bed were blue and white sneakers.

The door opened. A boy stood there who, Gor realized, was about Errol's age, though taller.

122

'What's your name?'

'Gor.'

'Gor?'

'Gordon.'

'We use family names here. What's your family?'

Gor thought hard. The question had never arisen before.

The boy sighed. 'They get younger and younger, and whimpier and whimpier every year. Come on. What's your family?'

Gor could see he was losing patience and that as with Errol in a similar mood the sharp dig or slap might be his next move. The only name he had heard fortunately coincided with his registration. 'Bardfield.'

'At last. Well, I'm your captain, Bardfield, and you do what I say. If I give you an order you jump to it. Okay?'

Gor nodded. He was used to being ordered about by older children.

'Aye, sir. You call me sir. Okay?' Gor nodded. The boy sighed again and rolled up his eyes. 'Aye, sir.'

'Aye, sir,' Gor said obediently.

'Progress at last. Come along, little Bardfield. Pick up your clothes and trot along to the showers.'

Gor followed his captain along a corridor to a door that if he could have read would have given him the unknown word 'Showers'. The captain pushed open the door and his ears were assaulted by the shouts of several small boys screaming and shoving each other under the jets of water at the far end. 'Put your clothes in a locker and get in.' Fortunately his captain accompanied this order with gestures that showed Gor what the locker was.

He put his new clothes in it and stood hesitating. 'Dear Bernie,' his captain sighed again. 'This one's even worse than most. Do you intend, little Bardfield, to get into the shower in your sleepers? No? Then take them off, little idiot, and put them in the locker.'

Slowly Gor did so and stood embarrassed and wishing to hide himself. 'It's a pretty disgusting tadpole, this one. Get down to the other end and wash yourself, ugly bug.'

Gor crossed the few paces to the jetting water as if it was a mile of Jubilee Road. The group of small boys watched him come silently. 'He's called Bardfield and he's a new sprog in C platoon.'

'You're very dark, Bardfield. Are you a blackie?'

123

'He's very hairy. He's a monkey.'

'He's a black monkey.'

They gathered around, pointing and shouting.

'He's got a bigger widdler than you, Curtis.'

'Curtis has only got a piece of twine, haven't you, Curtis?'

'Yours is like a horse, Bridgey.'

Two of the boys pushed each other until they slipped on the wet tiled floor and fell floundering and wrestling together. Someone pushed Gor. He felt his feet slide, grabbed at anything for support and brought another boy down with him. They scrabbled a moment. Gor realized the boy was trying to hold him down under the jets. He laughed and wrapped his arms round the squirming smooth skin that had the bonelessness of childhood still. They struggled only a second or two before Gor had the boy's head under the jets while he laughed and hooted.

'Serves you right, Empers. The monkey's beat you.'

'Come on, tadpoles. Under the driers,' the captain shouted. Gor scampered with the rest to the hot air cubicles. 'Everyone out and dressed in two minutes and I'm timing you.

They fled to the lockers and dragged clothes over damp bodies. The others wore khaki shirts and shorts with knee-high white socks and brown shoes. Politely they didn't comment on Gor's blues. The boy he had pushed under the shower helped him with the laces of his sneakers. 'It's best not to untie them when you take them off. Then you can get into them more quickly when the captain says get dressed.'

'In twos, squad. To breakfast.'

They formed up; the boy Empers beside Gor. 'Heads up, tadpoles. Don't slouch.' Gor suddenly found he was hungry. The bowls of breakfast food, the cups of strong tea and thick slices of bread and jam vanished into the chomping jaws.

Gor had never tasted other than mint tea but he found his new drink immediately acceptable. Jam, too, was a find he was happy to have made.

'Take the monkey to get a cap issue, Empers,' the captain said when they had eaten, 'and then to the store for books and stuff. You know what he needs.'

'Aye, sir. You have to have your cap with you always,' he explained to Gor, pulling his own brown peaked one from his shorts pocket. 'You have to wear it if you leave barracks, even if you only go out on the square or the camp.'

Gor nodded as if he understood. His cap was blue and forage style. His ears stuck up on either side of its boatshape and it emphasized his rather long face and prominent brow ridges. They left Quarters, as Empers told him that part of the building was called, and crossed the square to the classroom block where a row of dispensers like the automarket gave out books, writing blocks and chippens.

A voice over a loudspeaker system made the boys jump.

'Bardfield on parade to Commanding Officer B Company.'

'That's you, Monkey. I'll show you where to go and wait for you. We've got ten minutes before classes.'

'At ease, Bardfield. That means you take your cap off. Now can you read that?'

Gor stared at the page. He knew that reading was something older children did. Jessie had gone to school last year and had come home with letters on a page which William had helped her to decipher, sitting with her at the kitchen table while Errol and Nina laughed at her difficulties. 'You didn't find it so easy, either of you,' said William. 'Come on, Jess. Once again.'

'Can't read at all?'

'No, sir.'

'I don't know why they let you aided boys in without some kind of test. Alright: Remedial I for English and Math. Join Section 3 of C Platoon for everything else. We'll see how you get on.'

'Good,' said Empers. 'I'm in threes. I'll come and find you in Remedial I.'

It was fortunate that Monkey Bardfield had found or been found by Empers. Such are the vagaries of school fate that it would have needed only the slightest variation for them never to have met though under the same roof, and there isn't the smallest reason to suppose that anyone else would have done just as well or even been willing to guide Gor through the intricacies of social and scholastic life at Montgomery. Empers had already been there a term when Gor joined late. He hadn't found a friend in the eft pool and had been feeling lonely as the rest shared secret passwords and helped each other with fatigues. The impulse to push Gor and then grapple with him had been quite spontaneous and even he hadn't known that it was a bid for affection. He had simply reached out. But when Gor responded with laughter and a strength that was part hug, Empers's second impulse was to hold on to him.

The great advantage of his new friend was that he knew nothing. Without push, which was foreign to his nature, Empers could boost his own poor confidence simply by teaching his friend all he had already absorbed. In return Gor's full warmth was turned on him and his strength used in Empers's defence in all those tussles that arise where young animals are kept together in a peer group.

It was soon discovered that Gor came out top in any such combat but his general cheerfulness and his refusal ever to hurt an opponent prevented any resentment that a sprog should be lord of the camp for his age group. When older boys bullied he fought back but bore defeat and that earned him the amused respect of the upper levels of the childish hierarchy.

He soon learned to read and write and sum but without distinction. The subjects where he shone were all physical activities and art. He swam with the ease of a water rat or as if the water was suddenly so salt he was unsinkable. He ran, climbed and vaulted as though made of rubber. Already captains of teams were waiting to pounce as soon as he was judged old enough for competitive sport outside his platoon. He seemed simply to take a ball from the air as if it was stationary.

Art wasn't a subject that figured large at Montgomery. It was taught by a young woman quite recently come herself from learning. Its inclusion in the curriculum at all was a concession to pressure from the wife of the bishop who was one of the college governors. It looked good in the brochure, too, when perused overseas. Mothers particularly were reassured by the picture of their young with paintbrush, charcoal or chalk in hand. It was the very traditionalism of the materials and tools that seemed a corrective to the rigours of maths, electronics and business management. However there was no need to spend much on the salary of the person who provided what was essentially icing on a fruit cake stuffed with the real plums that would enable them to take a good place in the world.

Perhaps it was because Gor found compensation in Miss Forbes for the lost female element in his life that he was even more eager to please than usual. In her turn Alleta Forbes was amused by his funny grinning face.

'Well, what have we here?'

'It's Monkey, ma'am.'

'Monkey?'

'We called him that the first day he came.' One or two of

them sniggered. She wouldn't enquire too closely or the situation might get out of hand.

'He's really Bardfield, ma'am,' said Empers.

Personally she disliked calling such tots by their family names but she bowed to it. Discipline was difficult enough for her as it was without the familiarity of first names.

'Well, Bardfield, what do you like to do? Paint, draw, cut out?'

He didn't know for he had never done any of them but he liked colours. He looked at the paints and pointed. 'That.'

'That, please, ma'am,' she corrected. He blushed, a deep dark red almost the colour of Montgomery's brick. He is very like a monkey, she thought, but rather sweet. Why were children so cruel? 'Alright, you shall paint.'

'I'll show him, ma'am.'

'Thank you, Empers.' She was glad the child seemed to have found a friend at last. Alleta arranged a selection of coloured fruits on a table. 'Whoever does the best picture can choose a fruit for himself.'

Empers showed Gor how to mix the paints and soon he was working happily. Forester would have been interested in his application but would probably have misunderstood his motives, which were a compound of wanting to please, wanting the fruit and a pleasure in the activity itself, which generated together enough energy to keep him bent over the paper for a long time with his tongue sticking out a little against his long upper lip, quite silent while the others gossiped and baited each other. By the end of the period he had painted the fruit shapes in clear strong colours to produce recognizable primitivist images. The prize was his and the praise. Because it was Monkey Bardfield no one dared call the winner girlie.

Alleta Forbes was delighted. Suddenly in one class it was respectable to paint and the standard of work improved accordingly. Section 3, C Platoon, began a mural based on the exploits of the college namesake. Alleta sketched and the boys filled in, suggesting modifications to her cartoons, things they wanted included or that the figures might do. She had quickly realized that if she hoped for the project to be acceptable to the college ethos military deeds were the subject to depict. Soldiers in the quaint uniforms of the period bivouacked under the desert stars or read letters from home, propped against sandblasted trucks she had copied from the evocative photographs in a history book.

The boys wanted to show the cumbersome moving castles of tanks in combat. In her researches Alleta read how men were roasted alive trapped in the metal dungeons of them or struggled out, living torches that tried to quench themselves in the sand. She wavered between the theory that it was good to show the children the full horrors of old-fashioned war with its lingering deaths and mutilations and the fear that such images would only breed morbidity or a hankering for violence disguised as heroism.

'Strange,' said the Commanding Officer of B Company when he first inspected the paper panels pinned along the corridor, where the boys came to work in their own time, as well as in the official art lesson, such was their ardour now, 'how all ancient warfare repeated itself. Those might be the Spartans before Thermopylae.'

The CO was due to retire soon and Montgomery would lose one of its outstanding characters, a scholar from another age who knew Greek and Latin, though these were no longer curricular subjects but could be acquired for love or extra points as optionals. Every year one or two boys, drawn by his uniqueness, were to be found with him in some corner, heads bent over the thumbed and worn old texts. His *raison d'être* in the college was military history and strategic studies. Many boys went on from Montgomery to Sandhurst, the united services university.

Forester was amused and fascinated by the first end-of-term dispatch on Gor's progress. He had predicted the physical aptitude. The 'below average but making up lost ground' in general subjects was in reality more than he might have expected. Gor's scholastic ground was not so much 'lost' as a vacant lot. It was the glowing report for art that intrigued him until he deciphered the forename. Then he decided that, just as Emily Bardfield had done, this woman had lost her heart to the anthropoid and her judgement was suspect. On the other hand apes liked to draw although the results were usually uninterpretable. They recognized objects in drawings and photographs without difficulty and could name colours. It was an interesting question whether creativeness was a more primitive activity, rooted in the animal psyche, than the ability to reason. Both were there in his apes in rudimentary form. Gor's general character was described as cheerful, willing and indus-

128

trious. Here the human was predominant, Forester decided.

Bardfield's guardian had made no provision for the holidays. When he realized his mistake Forester tried to contact Gor's foster family but the clinic had lost touch with them, they were no longer at their old address and calls to the central computer brought forth no new one. For the first time the ease with which people might vanish from society altogether struck Forester. He found it very disquieting. To be wiped from the record or rather to remain there in stasis was a kind of death. He dialled his own number and was comforted by the up-to-date precision of his entry.

Arrangements were made for little Bardfield to stay on at Montgomery for the long leave. Empers was upset that his friend would be left behind alone and Gor did his best to cheer him by pretending that he didn't mind so that when his mother came for him Empers was able to get into her car without guilt. Gor waved until it turned the corner and then went back to Quarters heavy-hearted. Restlessly he wandered from room to room. He stood for some time looking at the mural but it appeared flat and grey and he couldn't imagine how he had worked at it with pleasure for long hours. Matron, a cook and a village girl who came in to help prepare the meals and clean Matron's room were left. Matron had shut herself away for a rest from boys and was quite unapproachable. The village girl was taciturn through fear or stupidity. Only Cook made any effort to speak to the child, inviting him into the kitchen for cups of tea and tales of boys long gone and appetites she had ministered to.

On the third day, roaming through the camp, he found a gardener. It had been overcast when he had left the building, crossed the square and reached a shrubbery like a miniature jungle, glossy-leaved with evergreens that shut out the sky. Beyond was a stretch of lawn and the kitchen garden. Suddenly the leaves over his head began to patter under splodges of rain broad and heavy as a shower of eurocent pieces. Gor felt the hair on his head stiffen under his cap. Above him thunder smashed through the air as if the clouds had solidified and their peaks were colliding. He wanted to yell with terror. Across the grass the rain fell in continuous strands like a bead curtain that pounded against the hardened summer earth. The rain was a being, a presence that would destroy him. Yet he must pass through it whichever way he went. Suddenly through a shift in the slanting warp he saw a blurred figure behind glass. For a moment he didn't know whether it was rescue or the rainmaker but he found himself running on trembling legs towards it.

'Come in, kid, you're nigh drownded.'

The greenhouse was warm and dank and smelled of mildew and loam. Rain drew continuous scribbles on the glass that distorted and screened the garden outside. The man seemed very old. His skin was a coppery tan coursed by wrinkles like the rivulets on the windows. His hands were carved from long·seasoned wood, stained with earth. Yet the fingers were supple enough to hold a small oblong of paper into which he was tucking some brown fibrous shreds. He rolled the paper into a cylinder while Gor watched, and moistened one edge with a finger dipped into a small plastic bottle. For a moment he held the cylinder and then he put one end in his mouth, flicked flame from his hand and applied it to the other end. A sweetish rich smell filled the greenhouse with the smoke, recalling for Gor the days when Harry Bardfield had lit a bonfire in the corner of the autumn garden. The old man inhaled deeply. To Gor it was all magic for he had never seen anyone smoke before.

'What's the matter, kid? What are you shaking for? Are you cold? It's not cold in here.'

'It's the rain. It was so loud. It frightened me.'

'Don't let the rain frighten you. That won't hurt you. It makes things grow, the rain. It don't do no harm.'

'Will it make me grow?'

The old man laughed. 'Maybe if you stood out in it long enough it might.'

'How long?'

'Oh you'd have to stand out all day like the plants so the rain and sun could draw you up.'

'I want to grow tall.'

'So you will, little feller, in time. You have to be patient. Everything comes to him who waits. That's why I'm still waiting.'

'What are you waiting for?'

'Well, that I don't know but I'll know it when it comes.'

'Will you tell me?'

'If we're still around each other I will.'

'What do you do?'

'I'm the gardener.'

'Like Dad.'

'Is your dad a gardener and you're at the school?'

'He fell down in the garden and died.'

'Perhaps he found what he was waiting for.'

Gor shook his head. 'No, he didn't.

'How do you know?'

'Mum said he didn't. She said he never had anything except making things grow.'

'Well, that's not so bad, not so bad for an epitaph.'

'What's an epitaph?'

'That's what they say about you when you're dead, sums you all up, like. Look, the rain's stopped. You can go back now.'

'Are you always in here?'

'Most often or hereabouts.'

'Can I come and see you again? There's nobody left except me. Empers's mummy came and took him away in a car.'

'You can come any time. But you'd best not tell anyone. We'll keep it secret.'

'Alright.'

'Go on now, off you go. My head gets tired with too much talking.'

Gor had a purpose again. He could go and see the gardener although he wasn't always there and sometimes he was loath to talk much, saying he was tired. At other times he said things that the child hardly understood and that came to have the colour of magic sayings which would unlock mysteries or could be used as charms against mishap. On the second day he asked the child's name.

'Gor,' he said, using it for the first time since he had come to Montgomery. 'But they call me Monkey here.'

'And are you?'

'What?'

'A monkey.'

'They said I looked like one.'

'Boys is cruel to each other. When I was a lad I was known as Hooter, because of the big nose, you see.'

Gor looked at it. 'It doesn't look very big to me. The CO's is much bigger.'

'There you are. So maybe you don't look like a monkey, not that much anyway. Like my nose.'

'I see.'

'But you may be one. Are you?'

131

'I don't know.'

'A monkey's a boy who's always up to wicked tricks.'

'No, no I'm not.'

'Then you're not a monkey at all.'

In the second week the painters came to erase the scuff marks of a year of boywear from walls, floors and ceilings. There were two of them and they let Gor help them with the automates that sprayed on fresh, clean-smelling coats to every surface. The painters spent a lot of time in the kitchen and there was much chatter with the cook in which even the taciturn village girl joined, and which Gor listened to, though, as with the old man in the greenhouse, a great deal of what was said went clear over him. There was no air of mystery to their discourse however: it was simply grown-up talk he didn't understand.

'You'll be too busy to come and see me when the holidays are over,' the old man told him as the beginning of term drew near. 'But if you need me I'll be around, remember.'

'Can't I even tell Empers about you?'

'Best not. It's our secret. Young gents aren't supposed to chat to old gardeners.'

'What's a "gent"?'

'They call them people of status now but they used to be gents, gentry, gentlefolk, only they weren't always gentle all of them and now they're mostly not at all. Folk are more wolfish now but even wolves didn't tear each other's throats out.'

Empers was delighted to see him. 'I didn't mind so much coming back this time until one day I was afraid you might have gone away.'

'I'm not in Remedial any more. We can sit next to each other all the time. What did you do on leave? Where did you go?' Forester thought about the next holiday. It would look odd if his guardian left Bardfield at the school alone always and nothing must look odd enough to be worth someone inquiring further than he wished. It was a great pity that he had allowed the Bardfield woman to slip so completely out of his grasp.

The solution came to him quite suddenly. He had arrived home early to find Ann still out on her school run. Lucretia had begun kindergarten in October. She could already read, write and sum on a junior calculator because Ann had spent patient hours teaching her with the help of the telly which kept a wilful child's attention longer than even the most inventive mother would have found possible alone.

Forester heard the crunch of tyres on the gravelled drive and glanced through the window to see mother and daughter getting out of the car, one dark and one fair head. He would have to do it very carefully but he thought that Ann's own nature would be his best weapon. The main problem was that he sensed that his creation didn't like him and might disclose some of his past history. That was a risk he must take.

Ann found the story very upsetting as Norman told it: a brilliant colleague who had been killed with his wife on a skiing holiday leaving a small son. Neither of the parents had had any relatives and the child had been admitted to Montgomery as an aided orphan. Norman had been one of the executors and therefore the college had written to him to ask what was to be done with the child in the leaves.

'Leaves?'

'It's a college with a rather military flavour. That's what they call holidays or vacations. We left him at the college for the summer but it's a problem. We'll have to try to board him out somewhere.'

'How old is he, did you say?'

'About a year older than Lucretia, I think.'

'Why don't we have him here?'

'Oh, I don't think so. Who knows what he's like? He's had a tough time; he may be rather disturbed.'

'We could have him for a week and see.'

'Suppose he bullies Lucretia?'

'I think she's more likely to bully him and if he did manage to put her in her place a bit it would be nothing but good for her. I'd like to try it. I worry sometimes that we, I, do so little for other people. I'm safe and comfortable here while thousands of people have absolutely wretched lives by our standards. At least we can try giving a little boy a home for a few days.'

Forester shrugged his shoulders as if acquiescing against his judgement and at the same time placing the responsibility for the experiment on her.

'It's very good of you and your husband to have him for a week,' the matron was saying as she led her into the hall where two small figures were sitting with bags. They both stood up. Which one was Gordon Bardfield? They were wearing quite different uniforms but Ann still had no means of telling which

133

was which.

'Bardfield, this is Mrs Forester who's very kindly taking you into her home for part of the holiday.'

The child in blue saluted. 'How do you do, ma'am.'

'Hello.' Ann fumbled for something to say. She felt a faint disappointment. The little boy in brown had been her hope. This wasn't a pretty child and it was looking very gloomy. She hoped it wasn't going to be morose. Perhaps Norman had been right and the whole idea was a mistake. At least it was only a week.

Two terms at Montgomery had changed Gor. He had grown from an infant into a boy in the pressure tank of the school. 'This is my best friend, Empers. His mother's late.'

'Then we'll wait until she comes, shall we? It's dismal waiting alone.'

'Thank you very much, ma'am,' the blue child said and smiled, first at his friend and then at her. Ann felt a wave of relief. The smile transformed the rather ugly little face so that you forgot the individual features that were so like those of The Oicks in the popular cartoon series that they might have been deliberately put together in caricature: low peaked forehead, broad mouth and long upper lip.

'Would you like to see our mural, ma'am?' he asked her now.

'Is it far?'

'No, ma'am.'

'Suppose your mother comes while we're away from here?' she asked Empers.

'She'll see my bag, ma'am, and know I won't be long.'

Really they were very composed, these small creatures. She allowed herself to be led into another room, filled with long battered tables, hard chairs and a smell of ancient fat and cleaning powder.

'This is where we mess.' The term seemed very appropriate. 'And that's our mural, C platoon's.'

It was much better than she had expected for children's work and, although it seemed to be concerned with war and soldiers, it was very still and non-violent. 'It's very good. What is it about?'

'It's the story of the general the college is named after, ma'am. He fought in the desert, with tanks. That's why there's all the sand. That's two tanks firing at each other.'

'And which bits did you two do?'

134

'I did that soldier reading a letter but Monkey did lots of it, didn't you, Monk, because he's the best at art. He did the sky there and the palm trees and that truck that's all burned up and those two soldiers washing their clothes.'

Ann took it in without listening. The boys would call him Monkey of course. She wondered if he was mobbed up for his painting as well as for his funny face. They went back to find Empers's mother had arrived.

'I hope we haven't kept you hanging about. The boys insisted I should see their mural.'

'They would. They're so proud of it. Are you ready, James? Have you got everything? Turning to Ann she asked, 'Is Gordon going home with you?'

'Yes, he's coming to stay for a week.'

'I'm so glad. We hated leaving him last time all alone, didn't we, James?'

Gor would never forget his first sight of Ann. He had sensed her nervousness and that apprehension had unconsciously pushed him to invite her to see the mural. Part of him had hoped for some glory out of it. He would have turned cartwheels, something he did with great ease, to catch her eye. He too had been nervous. Suppose the lady who was coming to collect him didn't like what she saw. Would she refuse to take him? Would he be left with his bag in the hall while she hastily explained to Matron that she couldn't have him after all and drove away? He felt the lightening of her mood and knew that everything was going to be alright.

Some of their anxiety returned as they got into the car but both worked hard and by the time they reached Salisbury they were at ease again. 'We have to collect my daughter from her school on the way home. She's a year younger than you, I think.' He waited in the car while she went into the building that was a smaller version of Montgomery and came out leading a little fair-haired girl by the hand who bounced along as if she was a stoolball on a rubber thong.

'This is Gordon, Lucretia. Say hallo.'

'Hallo. Mummy, I was top in English and dancing.'

'That's good. What were you bottom in?'

'Nothing. I wasn't bottom at all in anything. What were you top in?' she suddenly asked Gor.

'Art and PT.'

'What's PT?'

'Physical training.' And as he saw she didn't understand he added, 'Games and things.'

'We call it gym at our school. Mummy, can I have my tea on a tray, please, Mummy.' She lengthened out the vowels in pleading.

'Yes, as it's the last day of school and Gordon's here.'

She made up two trays as soon as they were indoors and had taken their coats off and Gordon had been shown his room.

'Bring your tray and you can watch telly with me,' Lucretia said grandly and Gordon, who was used to being told what to do by girls, obeyed her even though she was the younger. Ann sighed with relief. That seemed as if it was going to be alright. She did hope that he wouldn't be too trampled on.

Gor first heard Forester's voice above the speakers on the screen so that for a moment it seemed one of them, interwoven, and then the different timbre told him that it wasn't mechanical but came from a real presence of flesh and blood within the house. He felt as if he would choke with fear. He wanted to get up and run through the French windows into the dark winter garden and on and on but he sat quite still gripping the arms of the chair.

'It's Daddy,' Lucretia said and jumped up. 'I'm going to tell him I was top in English and dancing.' Gor sat still, his eyes on the telly screen where figures performed meaningless actions and spoke in gibberish. What should he do? The Doctor, as Mum had called him, would come into the room and he would have to move and speak. Lucretia had called him 'Daddy'. Had he brought Gor here to torment him further in some way? He heard footsteps outside on the hall floor.

'Daddy, this is Gordon.'

He forced himself to stand up and salute. Training supported him. 'How do you do, sir?'

'Hallo, young man,' said the Doctor, looking deep into Gor's eyes so that his will was channelled into Gor's being and was carried to every part of him while his eyes went on pouring out their power. 'You sit down again and go on watching. I'll talk to you later.' Automatically Gor obeyed but 'later' didn't come. Soon it was time for bed.

Perhaps the man would come into the room while he was asleep. Perhaps he was quite wrong and it wasn't the Doctor, only somebody very, very like him. Gor believed he would never sleep but all at once it was morning and the man was

136

gone. He would come back at night but in the meantime Ann and Lucretia made the day busy and enjoyable. In the evening he was able to say, 'Hallo, sir,' and almost look into his eyes. By the third day his heart no longer thudded and threatened to stifle him. He must have been wrong and this was a different man or else there was something he hadn't understood.

'I'll keep him here another week,' Ann said to Norman on the fourth evening.

'It's up to you. You have all the extra work.'

'He's no trouble at all and he actually keeps Lucretia out of my hair so I can get more done. I'll ring the school.'

It was Christmas. He was given presents and shared in all the trappings of the season. He had never been so happy. Gradually Mr Forester seemed less and less like the Doctor.

One thing puzzled Ann. She caught him once looking out into the garden rather forlornly. It had snowed and they had built a snowman, the three of them together. Wearing an old hat of Ann's and a scarf, it stood still in the middle of the lawn looking towards the house. 'Is something the matter, Gordon?'

He turned to her, the smile coming back into his face like the shift of cloudshadow across downland. 'I was just thinking about some people I know and wishing they could all have presents.'

She knew so little about his background yet she feared to ask, partly because in her ignorance she might scrape against something raw and partly because she respected the rights of children not to be emotionally imposed on by adults just because they were young or small.

'Perhaps they have.'

'I don't think so.'

Ann felt she should ask more, that there was a wound here that might be soothed by speech. She cast around for the right question. 'Were there a lot of them?' It wasn't quite right but it was all she could think of that was oblique enough not to cause the child to shy away.

'There was Emily and William, and Errol and Nina, and Jessie. Then there was Mum and Dad but he died.' Gor ticked them off on his fingers.

'And where are they now?'

'I don't know. They sent me away.' He could no longer remember clearly the transition from the house in Jubilee Road to Montgomery.

In a sudden impulse Ann put her arms round him. 'You will come back to us for the next leave, won't you?'

He stood back a little and looked up at her. 'Please.' He didn't mind now going back before the other boys. There was the gardener to find and tell all about it.

'I've got a word of advice for you though you mayn't take it: don't come to depend on it; don't get cheeky.'

He might have saved his breath. Gor had no more ability to stop himself coming to depend than a morning glory can hold from opening its blue ruff to the sun. But his luck held. Forester watched his *in vivo* experiment and waited for the moment to terminate this phase. Ann grew increasingly attached to the boy and soon looked forward to his presence for part of the holidays as to that almost of another adult with whom she could have grave discussions about many things. She discovered too that although his own voice was completely untunable he loved to hear her play or to listen to a chip with her.

Gordon never became upset either by Lucretia's tantrums but would often distract her with a game when she threatened to make herself and everyone else miserable. One summer day when he was twelve he lay on the lawn, his face in the thick grass, snuffing up its warm green scent and heard the voices of Ann and Lucretia coming from a distance across the garden. He felt as if he could melt into the ground with happiness. Beyond were the inevitable fields of purple, yellow and grey but within the bounds of the weathered brick wall, espaliered with rose and peach, green softly dominated in leaf and blade.

Ann had made trellised arbours and set an old-fashioned sundial whose moving finger of shadow still fascinated Gor for the stealth with which time crept away. He had come upon Ann once the summer before holding up a hand against the sun to blot it out.

'If I do that, I can stop time,' she said.

'You don't really,' he said with an eleven-year-old's logic. 'You just don't see it going, that's all.'

> 'Ah yet doth beauty like a dial hand
> Steal from his figure and no pace perceived.'

'What's that?'
'It's a poem about growing old, like me.'
'You're not old at all.'

'Yes I am. I feel old inside and I look at my outside and see it ageing and I think sometimes that I still haven't lived.'

Gor had no answer. It was a remark almost as opaque to him as some of the old gardener's. He understood that she wasn't happy, something he had given no thought to before, and the garden was momentarily shadowed as Ann had shaded the sundial.

Because she shared his interest in painting she showed him books of pictures to stimulate him in his own work. 'Look, Gordon,' she said one evening, laying a thick volume in front of him, 'that's Time as people used to see him.'

An old man in strange clothes who looked like a gardener in fancy dress was carrying a long curved implement across the page.

'What's he got in his hands?'

'It's a scythe for cutting everything down. That's what they used before there were harvesters.'

Her words brought back Jubilee Road with a rush and for a moment he was confused by an image he couldn't quite recall of climbing and a voice saying, 'Before there was chippens, there was biros,' like a poem.

'It means that Time cuts us all down.'

'He looks like the gardener at Montgomery.'

'Maybe he is. You ought to paint him.'

'Can I paint you?' he asked him when he got back.

'Why would you want to do that?'

'I've never tried a portrait. That's what it's called.'

'I know.'

Gordon blushed. 'I mean Ann told me.'

'You can try painting me if you want as long as I don't have to sit without a smoke.'

It was his first attempt at likeness and perhaps it wouldn't have succeeded if the gardener had been less remarkable in his appearance or if Gor hadn't known his features through and through. The old man looked at it with smoke dribbling from a corner of his mouth.

'Does that look like me to you?'

'Yes, I think it does.'

'I haven't seen myself for years. I never look in the glass. If you say so you're probably right, kid. I'm very old. Old Father Time, that's what I am.' Gor didn't mention the picture Ann had shown him.

'It's very good, Gordon. Is it someone you know?' Alleta Forbes asked. She was leaving at the end of term to get married to an army officer. She hoped it would be alright and they would eventually find something to talk about when the first sexual excitement had diminished. Of all the boys she would miss Gordon most because he had shown the only real talent.

Should he tell her about the gardener? The habit of secrecy wasn't easily broken. He compromised. 'There's a gardener I sometimes see, mainly in the holidays, working when there's no one else about.'

'There's an exhibition in Gloucester soon. I'm sending a couple of my pictures in. I'd like to put that one of yours in too. It may not be selected of course but I think we should try. Would you like to, and not be too disappointed if it doesn't come off?'

The Gardener was chosen and even won a small prize in the portrait class. Gor wrote eagerly to Ann telling her all about it. She passed on the news at breakfast to Norman who seemed amused by Gordon's success.

He had asked her who he should paint next. 'Why not do a self-portrait?' she wrote back and regretted it as soon as she had expressed her chip. She had bought Gordon one of Charles's pocket readers for inprint. His gidget had made him a lot of money over the last few years and enabled him and Fanny to move to a bigger house with stabling for more horses. Her riding school was doing well too. The readers made correspondence easier but as Ann had feared the tactile pleasure of writing on paper had gone from it. She was glad there were still books though they too became rarer every year.

Gor looked at himself in the mirror. He had never really looked at his face before. Glasses had been for combing one's hair or making sure one was generally tidy enough to avoid trouble. He supposed he was ugly and that he should try to get it all down in the cause of truth. 'It's only a bit like you,' Empers said when he saw the result. 'It's too rough somehow. Try one of me.'

That was better. There was a wistfulness still about Empers and Gor caught it. Next he painted Alleta Forbes's portrait as a kind of leaving present. It was the first woman he had tried to portray. 'I wish you could see it,' he wrote to Ann, 'but she's taking it with her.' She felt a pang of an emotion she couldn't quite identify as she read his words.

If he had been happy at twelve, at thirteen he had entered the valley of pubescent gloom that everyone must pass through, though the legends don't tell us how such heroes as Cuchullain and Lancelot fared there and perhaps the stories of their youthful prowess are meant to gloss over this time. Here Gor passed the full two years while those closest to him noticed that they saw less of his smile than they were used to.

Ann in particular found its absence hard to take. If Gordon was to become as cold and strange to her as Norman her life would seem intolerably bleak. His life was the Institute and his work there. She hardly existed for him except as a necessary adjunct to his career and status. They kept a shell of public correctness intact but it housed nothing.

The time was drawing near when Forester would have to make some decision about the hominid's future. The very success of his experiment had caught him off balance. It was hard to see his creation, Mary's baby, in Montgomery's re-creation, a young man with all the attributes of a person of status. How would he be able to convince the world when he made his revelation? Gor's schooling had given him greater conviction in his role than Forester would ever have and sometimes when he heard Gor's voice across the garden he felt a tremor of anger and envy pass through him.

Gor himself, though Forester scarcely seemed to be the Doctor any more, knew that he was uneasy in his company and avoided it. He understood that it was good of his guardian to give him a home and he dreaded the moment when he would be no longer a schoolboy and would have to leave it. Soon there must come discussion about what he was going to do. Indeed he was a little surprised that it hadn't begun already. The fifth upper year which was Gordon's fifteenth began the countdown for public examinations. He was a captain of platoon now, in charge of a group of sprogs. Perhaps he would be a captain of industry or a designer. Secretly he would have liked to be a painter but he didn't know if that would be possible. He would need money and as far as he knew his shadowy father had left him none.

Once he had asked Ann about those long-dead parents but she had been able to tell him no more than that his father had been 'a colleague' of Forester's which presumably meant he had worked at the Institute. He must ask Norman, she had said, but Gor had shied from such questions.

Forester wondered about the questions too and about the hominid's degree of self-consciousness. The apes recognized themselves in mirrors and photographs and had a strong sense of identity. 'Me' was a concept that came easily and early to them. Soon he would be able to enter his creation's mind and lay it all bare. No one had ever been able to question an animal before with all the subtlety of a common language. He must choose the right moment to begin the stage of emptying out, retrieving the data that the hominid's brain had been storing up for him. But when and how? It was Lucretia who made up his mind for him.

It was her fourteenth birthday and she was giving a garden party with a barbecue on the terrace. The air was heavy with the scent of madonna lilies and sizzling meat. Several of her school friends and their brothers were there as well as her cousins, Gor, and Empers who sometimes came to stay with him when they were on leave. Ann soon sensed that something was wrong but found it hard to decide what. No one seemed to be left out. There was a great deal of noise and laughter, a usual sign that a party was going well. Why then did she feel so uneasy?

Lucretia was a bit over exited, her voice tending to break into almost idiotic laughter at nothing. She was flirting outrageously too. Ann sighed. She always had, even as a four-year-old. As far as she knew it didn't come either from Norman or herself, this tendency. Perhaps it was from Mrs Briles. Now poor Empers was being forced to dance to her tune. Gor as usual looked on smiling tolerantly.

She could almost have envied them their youth, fresh looks and animal vitality, above all their opportunity to find love. They could even afford to squander the time on fleeting but highly charged encounters. Except that that wasn't what she wanted, which she suspected didn't exist except in the imaginings of artists who were irresponsible enough to embody them in tantalizing shapes that gave an illusion of reality.

'Come on now, Cressy,' she heard Gor saying. 'Leave Empers alone.'

'Why? Do you want him yourself? Gordon's jealous,' she chanted like a child and when he refused to rise but went on smiling. 'Oh you're such a goody goody stick, Gordon. I'll show you before today's over.' She had never subjugated him as Ann had feared at first she might but she had never given up

142

trying either.

Fanny came to collect her brood. Ann offered her a glass of punch. 'Heavens, whatever did you put in this? It's lethal.'

'Nothing much.'

'Then someone's laced it for you.' At once Ann understood the party's strange effervescence. She drank a glass of the punch, something she hadn't had time to do before, and found it just as Fanny had said. She had to admit it was a great improvement on her own tame concoction. Ann scooped herself out another.

The teenagers were thinning out. Empers helped her carry the debris into the house. He stacked plates and glasses in the dishwasher while Ann waved off the last car load of guests. She brought the punchbowl into the house and she and Empers had a glass each, sitting at the table turning over the visitors in companionable gossip. Ann found herself being uncharacteristically sharp and clever, and giggling as though she and Empers were the same age.

Lucretia had got a great deal of punch into Gor with a simple game of forfeits in which the penalty for the wrong answer was to drink a glass straight down while standing on one leg. He wasn't the only one she had penalized in this way but he was her main target. As the rest began to leave she kept at him, just pausing to drag him off to wave goodbye. All at once there was only one group left. She looked quickly round and saw Empers follow her mother into the house with a stack of plates.

'Now you have to come with me.' She seized Gor's hand and drew him towards a corner of the garden beyond a yew hedge where there was a summer house they had played in when they were children together and Gor first came to stay. 'Now this is our house,' she said breathing quickly, 'and you have to kiss me.'

Cressy's face was turned up to him, her lips slightly pouting, her eyes round and intense. Without thinking he bent and kissed her. She put her arms round him and kissed him back until his whole body was swept through as if someone had put a flame to the punch in his bloodstream. He pushed her back against the wall of the summerhouse and kissed her again and again. 'I've got you, goody, goody Gordon, you're all mine.' Cressy laughed up at him and he kissed her again while she dug her nails in his back through his shirt. That was how Ann found them, suddenly aware of their absence and following

143

their voices through the garden.

She leant against the yew hedge not knowing whether she was going to faint or be sick. She mustn't let them see her. Ann retreated towards the terrace. She must call them. But her voice seemed stuck in her throat. She went back into the kitchen. 'I think they're hiding somewhere. It's the punch, I expect. Would you go and call them, James? Tell them I'm making coffee.'

'Okay.' He stepped out into the garden that was still daylight although only half a disc of sun fireballed on the horizon, sending long flames to light up the purple and yellow fields in a last burn of colour. Ann held her hands to her hot cheeks. She mustn't show what she had seen when they came in. She moved to the sink and splashed handfuls of cold water over her face and mopped it dry. She could hear Empers shrilling in the garden. 'Monkey! Monkey! Coffee time.'

His voice reached through Gor's consciousness and tore him away from Cressy. He felt beside himself.

'Go on, Monkey. Your boy friend's calling.'

He took a step towards her and stopped. 'I said I'd get you and I did.' She laughed at him. He had to go into the house and face Ann and Empers. Surely it was written all over him. He needed to be alone to recover but he couldn't. Would he be able to stop shaking, to speak? He came round the yew hedge onto the lawn.

'There you are,' said Empers. 'Where were you?'

'I fell asleep by the summerhouse.'

Empers laughed. 'It was the punch. That tall boy, Joanna something's brother, put a bottle of pure alcohol in it for a lark. I decided not to have any but to watch. Ann and I've been drinking it up in the kitchen. Here's Cressy. You'll both have fat heads tomorrow.'

Gor was grateful for Empers's chatter. They crossed the terrace and went into the kitchen. He knew at once, from the set of Ann's back, turned towards them as she reached into the freezer, that she suspected something and his face burned. He went upstairs to the bathroom and made a performance of peeing, washing and cleaning his teeth. When he went down again they had all retreated to the drawing-room with their coffee and music was playing. Gor looked quickly at Cressy. She appeared completely composed and it came to him to wonder who else she had done such things with.

144

Boys played with themselves and other boys all their spare time at Montgomery but although Gor satisfied himself most nights he and Empers didn't touch each other. He had never kissed anyone before and he had no power to control the sensations that Cressy had set flowing through him. It was a relief when it was bedtime and he could escape by himself.

Empers left in the morning. Ann dreaded his going for it left her alone with Gordon and Cressy and what she had seen. As Empers had predicted, Gor was badly hung over when he woke as well as feeling guilty and, though he didn't know it, physically frustrated. It made him almost morose. Cressy on the other hand had weathered the punch much better and was made more cheerful still by Gordon's obvious depression.

Ann found her mind refused to leave alone the scene she had almost walked into. She wanted to talk to someone about it. She tried Fanny but she was out all day supervising strings of small children on horseback. In the afternoon she drove both children into Salisbury: Cressy to stay with a friend, Gordon to replenish his paintbox. He would catch a coach back. On an impulse Ann decided to drop in at the Institute and discuss it with Norman.

The security guard on the barrier telephoned through for verification before he would let her in. She drove to Norman's part of the compound, parked her car and made her way to his office.

'What a nice surprise,' he said.

'It seemed ages since I'd been here. I thought I'd drop in. You don't mind? I'm not being a nuisance and stopping your work?'

'Of course not.'

'As a matter of fact I wanted to talk to you about something. I'm worried about Lucretia and Gordon.'

'What about them?' he asked carefully, straightening a pile of cards on his desk.

'I came across them kissing after that party yesterday.' She knew at once she had made a mistake as Forester's hand scattered the pile of cards. He was surprised by his own fierce reaction. His hand shook with anger.

'I'll soon put a stop to that.'

'What will you do?'

'I'll put him back where he belongs, behind bars.'

'Oh no. You can't do that. After all it's only natural at their age and I'm sure she led him on. I suppose I'm upset because I thought they were like brother and sister.'

'It isn't natural, not for him. You don't understand.'

'He's a big boy. Strong and well developed . . .'

'He, it, isn't a boy at all.' He hadn't been sure he would say it but the words were out.

'I don't understand.'

'Gordon Bardfield so-called doesn't exist. He's just a thing, an experiment of mine.'

'But . . .?'

'He isn't human, just humanoid: the test tube product of a gorilla ovum and human sperm. He's Mary's baby.'

For the second time in less than a day Ann was unsure whether she would faint or be sick. She had to go out, away from Norman and this place.

'I'll make the necessary arrangements. I'll send some knockout drops or a couple of strong attendants. As you say, he's big and well developed for fifteen.' Ann stood up. 'Where are you going?'

'I have to get back. Fanny's coming over,' she lied, hoping her legs would sustain her to the door and her car.

'Where is he now? "It" I should say.'

'In Salisbury, shopping.'

'It'll take me a day to arrange things. You'll have to keep very calm so it isn't alerted to anything. Can you do that?'

'I think so. I must go. Will you be home early?'

'No, rather late. It'll all take time. You're not afraid of being alone, are you? They don't attack anyone they respect.'

'They?'

'Apes.'

'No, I'm not afraid.'

She forced herself to walk to the car, open the door and drive away as if she had heard none of it. She drove five miles down the road and pulled off the beam on to a country lane, found a flat verge, parked and switched off the engine before she let herself lean her head against the wheel and shake with sobs. She had made a terrible mistake in telling Norman because it had brought out a latent hostility to Gordon so powerful it had obviously unhinged him. She could see how the boy's appearance would lead to such a fantasy being formed and how Norman's work would reinforce it and provide it with a seemingly rational framework. She wept for all of them.

146

What she didn't know was how far Norman could impose his fantasy on reality. As she understood it, Gordon as a minor was completely in his power. Norman intended to have him locked away, 'behind bars' he had said. Presumably he could and would have him committed to some institution, certified by a colleague as deranged or defective and with no parents to care for him. Gordon would resist, thereby confirming the view that he was a violent lunatic. She couldn't bear him to be locked up, perhaps for the rest of his life. But what could she do? She had never before this had to commit a forbidden act against the authorities of her world. All her life she had had simply to conform, to do what she was told or what was expected of her. Open rebellion was against her nature, almost beyond her comprehension. Yet now there seemed no moral alternative. She had brought this on Gordon by telling Norman what she had seen. It was her responsibility. She started the car and drove back to Salisbury.

He was still waiting in the coach station she saw with relief. 'Gordon, Gordon!'

He had been sitting on a bench, head bent, hands held between his knees like a dropped puppet. Now, at her voice calling his name he looked up and smiled. 'Get in, I've come back for you.'

She drove faster even than usual, and without speaking. All Gor's guilt was reawakened. 'I want to talk to you,' she said when they drew up before the house. She knew.

'I want to say . . .' he began and faltered. Was he sorry?

'There's no time for that. Come upstairs.'

He followed her into what had become over the years his room. 'Get down your bag.' He was being sent away. It was just, but something snapped painfully inside him. 'I made the mistake of telling Norman.' She didn't have to explain what. 'He's very, very angry.' She opened a drawer and began to transfer his clothes to the bag. 'It's important that you're gone before he comes home this evening.'

'I'll ring the school to let them know I'm coming.'

Ann put out a hand. 'No, Gordon. You can't go back to Montgomery. That's where he'll expect you to go; that's where he'll look for you.' He stared at her, bewildered. 'I said he's very, very angry. He's going to have you locked up if he finds you. It's not just an ordinary anger. I think he might even kill you.'

147

All Gor's buried terror of the Doctor was laid open by her words. Sometimes he had dreamt of Forester holding a syringe and wakened sweating. Now the dream came to him waking and he felt weak with fear. Not for a moment did he doubt that Ann was right and that Forester might have it in his power to kill him.

'You'll have to go where he can't find you and you mustn't tell me where. I have to be able to say I don't know, and mean it. I've got some money for you. You'll have to walk to the highway and get a coach. I shan't be able to give you a lift to anywhere. You see that, don't you? If you can think of a way one day to let me know you're alright without its being traced . . .' She felt her breath catch. Outside the sun was going down the last reaches to the skyline. Norman had said he would be late but had he meant it? Suppose he met Gordon walking to the road? 'You must go now.' She gave him a bundle of eurodollars. Then she took a gold bangle from her wrist. 'Take this too. You can sell it if you have to. Now, have you got everything?' she asked as she always did when she packed him off at the end of the holiday.

He put his arms round her and kissed her cheek. Then he picked up his bag and followed her downstairs. 'I won't come out because then I haven't seen you go.'

At the end of the drive he turned and looked back. He couldn't see if she was watching from a window because the glare behind had thrown the front of the house into deep shadow with blank dark eyes as if it was uninhabited. As he looked the setting sun caught the ridgepole and threw long swords of dazzling light above it that flashed and blinded him so that he had to blink as he turned his back on the house and the lost garden.

IV

THE APPRENTICESHIP
OF GOR

He had never been on his own in the world before and he hardly knew how or where to begin. Had he been able to go to Montgomery he could have asked the gardener, for he sensed that the old man was a survivor and could have told him a lot, but the college was closed to him. When he reached the highway he had to decide whether to take a coach east or west, which was the first big lone decision of his life. He chose west because that was where Empers lived and more than anything he needed someone to talk to, even someone who knew less, if that were possible, about everything than he did. He got off at the Yeovil junction and found a payphone. It was comforting to hear Empers's voice.

'Where are you?'

'Yeovil.'

'Whatever for?'

'It's too long to tell you on the phone. I've been kicked out of everywhere.'

'Dear Monkey. What for?'

'Don't keep asking that. I've got to see you. Then I'll tell you all about it. But you mustn't let anyone know you've seen me. That's why I can't come to your house. Can you meet me here somewhere?'

'Okay. I'll think of something. I'll see you at the coach station at eleven o'clock. Where will you sleep?'

'I haven't decided,' Gor said, quite as if the problem had already crossed his mind.

He felt very lonely after Empers's voice had ceased. Calling him and arranging a meeting had given him a purpose. Now there was nothing. There was a waiting-room where he could sit for a while but he sensed that a fifteen-year-old boy shouldn't linger too long. From time to time a policar cruised into the station yard and a scanner swept through it. After it had passed over him Gor felt it had sucked out his soul and that he was less himself than he had been. He imagined himself being emptied out somewhere and compressed onto a chip for future reference, and looking round at the few faces above the anyhow-slumped figures on the station benches he saw that those who were still capable of feeling felt the same. Some had the appearance of having been scanned so often they seemed to be empty shucks.

Gor bought himself a soypie and a cola from the dispensers, partly because he felt empty and partly to give himself an excuse for being there. His clothes set him apart from the other would-be travellers. They were clearly nons going somewhere at the cheap night rate, with a few possessions in uniform cheap brown plastic holdalls. He remembered that they were being given away with something once when he had switched on the radio.

In the morning the extractors would be turned on while the building was sealed for half an hour and the accumulated dust and litter sucked away but now the day's leavings lay desolately about, soypie wrappers and cola tumblers, fragments of plastic that had held carefully put-up sandwiches and, inexplicably, one broken female shoe. Gor finished the stale pie, bought a locker key and deposited his bag and stepped out into the yard. He crossed it and turned into the dimly lit streets of the town.

It was the southwestern centre of the agribusiness and the most important buildings were the red brick offices of the consortia who competed with each other for a slice of it. Gor paused for want of anything better to do to read the enticements to investment as they flashed on and off in one of the windows. 'Own your own little piece of England,' he read. The illustration was like no countryside he had ever seen except in a history book. Cows grazed in a green meadow and a man leaned over a gate between hedges, smoking like the gardener but from a round container on a stem while he looked at the cows. 'Even the smallest sum could get you a share of the good earth.' Then there was a statement from the chairman of the board, full of confident predictions about the future of the company. At the bottom was the scrawled signature of Empers's uncle, Sir Saunders Empson.

Further along was a market for agritechnics. Behind these windows giant cultivators of all kinds waited in their yellow or red gloss as yet unstained by the soil. Gor had seen them at work in the fields distantly but being at close quarters like this with only a clear skin of glass between stirred some memory he couldn't quite recapture. The company was advertising a new breakthrough: the 'Farmer' series which no longer needed an overseeing human. There was even a small one called the Farmer's Boy for trimming grass verges by itself.

All the companies ran lotteries. Your numbered share was at the same time a ticket in the monthly tombola. Twelve shares gave you a chance to cover the board and win a prize. Last month's winning numbers flashed on the window display screens together with the prizes to be won and a graphic of the progress of the board to date this year. Down the high street the windows winked at each other for there were few passers-by to see them.

The automart arcade was open all the time, with its telly security on line to police HQ to prevent theft or vandalism. There were no shoppers for the dispensers to solicit but they went on chirrupping and flashing their products just the same. Gor would have gone inside just for a place to be and something to look at but the warning notices explaining the security system deterred him. A lone figure which suddenly appeared in the picture of a deserted automart could bring a hornet crowd of buzzing policars.

Sounds of music drew him further down the road. An amusement arcade rang with popsong and the clang and bleeping of the machines. There were people here too. A few of them had come there to play; the others as somewhere to gather where there were lights and music. They divided into the two sorts by age. A woman of about Ann's years pulled repeatedly at a lever on an upright display that channelled a shower of bright balls into cups below. She seemed hardly to wait before she fed in another coin and jerked again to release a new shower. A man as old as the CO of B Company played a slow thoughtful game of spacechess with himself, a simplified electronic version of the traditional one with symbols of the Emperor and the Empress and the galactic hierarchy down to the lowliest rookies in black or white jump suits with rayguns at the ready.

Two boys detached themselves from the mixed group of loungers to cross the invisible line and engage in a fierce starwar, each cheered on by a party of boys and girls suddenly animated as if the button had been pressed that brought them all into play. Most of them were in Gor's age group yet even here he stood out because of his solitariness and his clothes. He caught them looking sideways at him and then at each other. He was all at once afraid in spite of his better-fed strength. There were too many of them and he was carrying more money in the bundle given him by Ann than most of them would ever have seen. He looked around casually, and then slowly turned and left as though what he had been seeking wasn't there, which was true in a way. He would have been glad of the companionship and the expertise of these townees. He was surprised to find himself wishing that one of he girls had looked as if she might speak to him. Lucretia had opened a sluice that wouldn't close again easily.

When he got back to the coach station even fewer people were left. Ann had shown him pictures of Roman soldiers collapsed asleep about a tomb but although he was reminded of them now they hadn't the desolation of these figures who seemed to belong to some world where the acutest suffering was quite simply to wait eternally. Still, as long as they were here he supposed he could be too. He would huddle up on a bench with his back to the door and windows so as to be as inconspicuous as possible. The night dragged its length as if it were inching wounded coils towards a dying ground. From time to time a coach drew up and a shape would gather itself to its feet, pick up a bag and go out to become another of the slumped, upright bundles inside it, or a grey face that stared apathetically down from a window. Twice a policar made the rounds.

'Is it okay to stay here all night?' Gor asked one man who had shown a momentary interest in their second visit.

'You're not supposed to go to sleep, stretch out, you know, but as long as you're more or less sitting up the pollys don't bother. They'd only have the trouble of taking you in and you might mess up a nice clean cell. They could stick a vagrancy on you or even an LWI, but they wouldn't get much out of it unless they were lucky and you showed up as having form. They'll be more interested in the kids on the streets. They're not broken yet like the rest of us.'

Most of this was in a foreign tongue to Gor though he was grateful to the man for talking to him and wished he would go on but he relapsed into the stupor of the rest. Morning began to wash out the darkness from the windows. More people with brown plastic holdalls arrived to disguise Gor's presence there. He got himself a cup of warm coffine from the dispenser and then found a lavatory where he could wash his face and hands in a pitted grimy basin but not dry them. Gor combed his hair and looked in what was left of a broken mirror that showed half his face in distortion. Already it began to look as grey and listless as those around him. He felt the image that stared back at him eating its way in. It was a worm in an apple that would dwell deep inside, gnawing its way to the surface until it met itself again. Then he would look in the mirror and see nothing. He shook his head to chase the thought away.

Empers was punctual at eleven. 'This is a dismal place,' he said as they walked along the streets to be out of earshot. 'That's why I never come here.'

Gor told him hesitantly, and trying not to blush, about kissing Cressy.

'I knew something had been going on. You did only kiss her though, didn't you. And she must have started it; she always does. I don't understand why he's so angry but if Ann says he is she must be right. Didn't your parents leave you anything?'

'I don't think so and in any case it would be in his control because he's their executor and my guardian.'

'What will you do?'

'Ann gave me some money but I don't know how long it will last.'

'I think it's cheap in the cities. That's where people go, don't they, when there's nowhere else? I know my uncle's always banging on after dinner about all the layabouts in the cities. Look, I haven't got much but you have it. Let me know where you are and I'll see if I can get any more. Which one will you go to?'

'Which what?'

'City.'

'I haven't thought about it.'

'Bristol's the nearest. Go to Bristol and then I'll be able to get in touch with you.'

Gor, who was usually the leader of their group of two, was

155

surprised and comforted by Empers's practical matter-of-factness. Empers insisted on staying until the coach for Bristol came in. Gor felt the loneliness sweep over him as Empers's spindly figure dwindled from sight but knew it would have been even worse had it been the other way round. The coach carried him northwards through Glastonbury before swinging west to join the national route along the coast. Once he thought he glimpsed the sea, a grey blur that might have been only a cloud low on the horizon. He knew when they were approaching the city because of the almost imperceptible frisson that ran through his fellow travellers. They were coming home.

The way in lay through the tangle of shanty town, the suburb of plastic shacks that fringed the city proper beyond the river. It wasn't known who had been the pioneer to spot the possibilities in temporary structures as a way round their housing problem. At first people had made their own but soon firms had moved in to supply a booming market. The first necessity was speed of demolition and, of course, re-erection, but the ease of taking down was more important than that of putting up because it had to be possible to unclip and pack a home into mobile containers so that when the permit for a temporary structure ran out it could be moved at once. Often two groups would synchronize their permit buying and simply exchange sites. The land the shacks stood on was outside the city limits but not entirely beyond its jurisdiction.

The shacks were of all colours and gave the effect of a box of toys emptied out by a child who had lost interest and gone away. The coach roared down the stretch of highway that ran through this outer calyx of the city as if it too was glad to be nearing the end of its journey. Beyond shanty town were streets of empty houses with shuttered windows repeating the coloured plastic patchwork of the shacks. It was all so alien after Ann's garden and even Montgomery that Gor shrank inside at the tawdry desolation.

The coach spewed them out at the station and the others hurried away. He almost sank down on one of the benches to weep, his loneliness was so great. Almost he longed to see the Doctor with his syringe coming across the yard. He would be a familiar face and bring oblivion whatever might happen after. He hardly dared let any picture of Ann rise up in his mind yet they wouldn't be kept down. He saw her holding a little earth in her hand, and crumbling it while she explained its composition, with the sunlight and flicker of leaf shadow across her face or that face with the smile of the blindfold cupid below it, echoing her own half smile as she played oblivious of them all.

She had told him to go and although it had been to save him there was an element of rejection in it that in his dazed and lonely state had the sharp edge of banishment. Then came the thought that she would want him to survive, to find somewhere that would be sanctuary in this city, to let her know somehow that he had done so. Gor looked round at the faces of his fellow beings to see who might give him some guidance. Presumably they all had somewhere to lay their heads at night. They must be able to help.

Most people were travellers and it was hard to judge who might give him some answers. A man in company livery with the word 'Supervisor' on his cap and shoulder flashes came into the yard. Surely he must live in the city and would know something.

'Excuse me. Can you tell me where I can stay?'

'Most people don't want to.' The supervisor pushed his cap back a little and looked at Gor who was already as tall as he was. 'Run away from school, have you? I don't suppose you'll want to say. Well, I expect it'll soon all get sorted out and you'll be on your way back. There's a hostel where you might get a bed though they'll probably want to see a certificate from your employer. The Grand and suchlike only take people arriving by car, bona fide travellers, you see, because they're classed as inns.' He laughed. 'Keeps out pedestrian riff-raff. Well, you can't be a bona fide traveller if you're walking, can you?' His voice had a burr to it rather like the gardener's that Gor found reassuring because of its familiarity. 'Best bet is to try the hostel but if they won't take you you needn't be out in the open air. There's plenty of empty houses. Mind you, I'm not advising, only stating facts. Watch out for patrols, both the pollys and the Ugs. Anyone found in an empty property can be done for trespass, vagrancy, LWI and about three more I can't rightly recall. That's if you're clean.'

Once again Gor was baffled by the opacity of the language but he was grateful all the same for the supervisor's interest. The man pointed out the way to the hostel and Gor set off with his bag. He walked smartly to encourage himself and soon reached the street the supervisor had named. A group of men and women had gathered on the hostel steps. They seemed to be waiting for something. Gor went up the steps to read a notice beside the door.

It was obvious to him at once that he had no chance of getting in. Applicants who were seen at 6 o'clock had to produce a certificate of employment. It was emphasized that this would be checked on the spot. There was no point in forging one. Gor wondered why they had to be produced at all since the information was available at the touch of a few buttons. Any attempt at fraud was a punishable offence and would be treated as such. He supposed those in the waiting group knew all this. Gor carried his bag down the steps again.

Once more he was without a direction to turn in, but to stand still would attract attention. Those waiting on the steps had already looked at the tall young man in his clothes of quality with unwelcome interest. Since one way was as unknown to him as another he turned towards the west and the sun and began walking, not quickly but as though he had a purpose. Now for the first time he was able to notice the difference between the size of the buildings in this area and the number of people about. There were tall office blocks yet the streets were almost deserted. He passed the university, emptied he supposed by the long vacation. Even so it had a rundown air. Weeds grew in the courtyards, the railings were rusting where the paint had peeled, litter had gathered against the doors as if waiting to be let in. They had discussed the 'concrete colleges' at Montgomery, the sweatshops where aided students mostly pursued their vocational studies after the best had been siphoned off by the Londoxbridge Trinity. There had even been a college debate on whether their function entitled them to the tag 'university' since they didn't cater for the whole man but with their mixture of short and evening courses merely crammed for enhanced employment. The motion to strip them of the title had been carried with the traditional pounding of feet and thumping of tables in the officers' mess which Gor had graduated to that year.

A little further on to the left he paused to read a cracked and dried out board whose indistinct lettering told him that the stained concrete structure, with its three-pronged tower like snapped off teeth, was the Roman Catholic Cathedral. Gor followed the road upwards. There were many empty houses here but they were tall town houses often with a notice on them

158

stating that the building was unsafe and that people entering did so at their own risk. His route up was stopped by a steep gorge but he continued climbing along the side of it until he was halted again by a barrier across the road and a new warning sign announcing that the suspension bridge ahead was unsafe and, further, that anyone using the bridge for improper purposes rendered themselves liable to prosecution or, in default of themselves, under the Families Act, their next of kin. Gor found it impossible even to guess what improper use a bridge could be put to.

He walked round the barrier and went a little way along the road to where the massive iron cables rose from their housing to the top of a tower. A perpetual wind sighed along the gorge and the structure seemed to sway with it though that might have been only a trick of the light and the airy drop from the slung roadway to the water far below. It caused his legs to tremble as if he might fall even though he was nowhere near the side.

'Yer!' The shout made him jump. A boy had come out of the blockhouse where the cables began. 'What be you doing?'

Gor walked back towards him. 'I was looking at the bridge.'

'Just looking?'

'Yes.'

'You're sure?'

'Definitely.'

'I'm on watch today. I missed you come by. I must have fallen asleep. When I woke up and looked out of the window there you were. You looked a natural to me, bag and all.'

'A natural what?'

'Jumper. They do often come with a bag and leave it. That's if the watch don't spot them. It's harder at night, of course. I don't know why they bring a bag unless they come straight here from the coach station, daresn't go home. Yes, that'll be it.' He seemed relieved by his explanation.

'I came from the coach station.' The boy who had relaxed a little became tense again. 'I'm looking for somewhere to sleep. All the houses I passed seem to have danger signs on them.'

'That's mainly to frighten people off. But you have to pick carefully. You won't want chunks dropping on you in the night. I expect you do know what to look out for.'

'No, I don't. I've never done it before.'

'Oh.' The boy looked worried. 'I'd go along with you but as

159

soon as I turned my back sure as sure someone'd come along.'

'What do you do if someone does?'

'Press the button and summon assistance.' He fished a small intercom transmitter from his pocket. 'Look, you go down that way back towards the centre. You'll find something along there. You do know not to be seen going in, don't you? Pick a smallish house. They're safer.'

Gor thanked him and set off again. The brief contact with the boy had cheered him up a bit and made him able to plan and decide. He would find a house, get in, leave his bag and go down to the centre to buy food and some less conspicuous clothing at an automart. Here was a terrace of two-storey houses mostly shut up. He walked along one side, crossed the road and came back on the other, picking his choice residence. He decided on the middle of three that were empty and that had a wide passage running along the end one. Gor walked past until he reached it and, with a quick look round, ducked down the passage bent double.

At the bottom there was a back lane with gates into the gardens. The gates hung drunkenly and convolvulus, whose pale pink cups sweetened the air, had climbed up them in a thick hedge. Gor threw his bag over the middle gate and vaulted over after it, hearing the rotten wood crack as he rested a hand on the top. He was almost in. He ran through the garden doubled up, and flattened himself against a wall to listen. There was no sound except the slight sighing of the wind that seemed to have followed him up from the bridge. A window big enough to climb through showed a crack open at the bottom. He heaved against it with both hands until it shot up with a bang. Not waiting to see the effect of this, he scrambled inside with his bag and pulled the window down after him.

The house smelled of damp and sad disuse. Gor went from room to room investigating. From the remains of a fire in a grate and a scattering of plastic wrappers and containers he wasn't the first to have camped here. The shutters were of red plastic and the light filtering through them was given the jewelling of stained glass and lay in ruby puddles on the plastic-tiled floors. Gor decided he would sleep a little and go on his shopping expedition when it was dark. The house had a small waterless bathroom and a kitchen. It seemed somehow familiar and comforting to him and he put some of the clothes

160

from his bag under his head for a pillow and fell asleep in the reddish twilight of an upstairs room which was cleaner than the rest.

When he woke it was true dark. He hid most of his money and the gold bangle wrapped in a few clothes in the empty cistern. Then he went down the garden and freed the gate from its convolvulus bonds so that he could get in and out without leaning his weight on it. A smell of cooked food came to him on the summer air, reminding him that his last meal had been in Yeovil. He set out towards the city centre. Remembering the supervisor's warning he kept a lookout for anything resembling a patrol although he wasn't sure that he would recognize one when he saw it. 'Pollys' he understood from its use among the boys at Montgomery but 'Ugs' was new to him.

There were so few people about that any walker was conspicuous. Gor tried to make up for this by keeping in doorways and against walls, making little rushes and then waiting and listening. He finally reached a street which was an automart arcade and paused at the entrance. After the dark ways he had come it seemed an Aladdin's cave full of many-coloured treasures under magically blazing light, but once he crossed the threshold the eyes of the security system would be on him, transmitting his image who knew where. He must be quick and purposeful, and give as little reason as possible for anyone to be suspicious of him. He picked out the dispensers he needed, took a deep breath and went inside. Quickly he pressed the right buttons, gathered up his purchases and went to the checkout where he laid them on the conveyor for totalling up, fed in his money when the till told him how much, gathered his goods again and went out into the night. It had all taken about five minutes.

His heart was thudding and he pressed himself into an alcove in the façade of a tall block to get his breath back. Suddenly at the end of the street he saw a policar drift past, its scanner turning like the seeking head of some reptile. Gor shrank as far into his niche as he could and watched. The policar reached the entrance to the arcade and paused while the scanner searched. It might, of course, have been a coincidence but he didn't think so. Slowly it moved away from the entrance. Every instinct in him wanted to run but reason held him still and at last it disappeared round the corner from which it had come.

It was essential for him to change his appearance now that it had been monitored. Gor went round the back of a large boarded-up structure on which he could faintly make out the single mysterious word ODEON in raised letters. Shucking off his jacket and trousers he folded them neatly and as small as he could and after clambering into the cheap dungarees he had bought, he stowed his old things in a new brown plastic holdall. Then he combed his hair towards the right and over the tips of his ears instead of behind them. He had no mirror to tell him what difference this made but he hoped it was enough. He hoped too that the pollys wouldn't think to enquire too closely of the till what he had bought. If they were looking for him it was crucial that they shouldn't identify his change of clothing which they could easily have done from the stock code the till had processed. With everything safely packed in his new anonymous bag he stepped out into the street again and made his way back to his new home.

Gor managed to survive the next few days without incident. As long as he was careful he could go out in daylight and walk about like an inconspicuous native. He made no attempt to get in touch with Ann or Empers. A lethargy had crept over him and as the days passed he hardly knew any more who he was or why he woke in the morning to eat and wash as much as he could in stolen water and then to wander the streets until exhaustion and apathy sent him back, to sleep and wake still tired.

There were one or two other people living in his street. At least there were a few unboarded houses but he saw nothing of their inmates. For all he knew behind the plastic shutters there were others living like himself but short of investigating every one there was no way of finding out and in any case he might not be welcome. He knew how he would now react to an intruder: with suspicion and a voice grown hoarse with disuse.

He had slept in the afternoon and woke restless in the long summer twilight. He would chance a walk but in a new direction away from the centre. It hardly mattered where. As he walked in the warm evening the dull ache in his body became a writhing pain that almost made him howl with loss and grief and he lost all sense of time and direction, blindly putting one foot before the other as he tried to beat it down. What was the point in living if it was simply to endure pain? He saw no direction, purpose or possibility in his life. On that walk he reached

162

the point where the caged and heartbroken creature turns its face to the wall.

It was blind pain that led him past the notice and on until he was brought up against the barrier and the waiting guards.

'What's the matter, mate? Can't you read?'

Gor lifted his head. The road in front was blocked by a long gate made from a pole mounted on a swivel at one end and a post at the other. From it hung a sign which read: UGWHQ. There was no turning away. The guards moved towards him.

'I'm sorry. I wasn't looking where I was going.' It sounded weak even in his own ears. The guard laughed.

'Pull the other one, it's got bells on it. I think we'd better take you along and find out what you're up to. Come on.'

Gor hesitated. 'Quiet now or we'll have to get rough.' They placed themselves on either side of him and walked him along the road. After the first few metres of empty houses Gor became aware of the presence of people. At some doors chairs had been brought out and men and women sat there lazily fanning themselves and talking easily. Children played in the dusk. Further along a group of people were busy in what seemed a communal kitchen and eating area. Even as they approached a signal was struck on two pieces of metal and a voice called: 'Come and get it!'

People began to walk up from the houses and seat themselves at an assortment of tables, on each of which he saw was set a posy of flowers and leaves in some kind of container. He heard laughter for the first time since he had come to the city, not raucous but falling on his parched ears like the sound of running water.

The guards walked him on to building at the far end which was larger than the others with ornate mouldings above a long window frontage pierced by a heavy door. Another man leant against the door, arms folded. 'This joker wandered into camp.'

The door was opened and Gor and his guards stepped inside. They sat him down in a chair, with one to watch him while the other went in search of someone else. Then he was taken into another room where a man sat behind a small round table. 'Sit down.' He waved Gor into a chair opposite him. For a moment he sat silent, contemplating Gor. 'Why did you come here?'

'I was walking.'

'You decided to ignore the notice that told you this area is no-go?'

'I didn't see it.'

The man looked at him in silence again as if weighing up his next question. Then he drew a chippen block towards him and took out the pen. 'What is your name?'

'Gordon Bardfield.'

The man put down the pen and looked at him. 'We can check, you know. We have our own access to all known national computer files, except for the state security index of course. But we can check the general register. How old are you?'

'Nearly sixteen.'

The man got up from the table and went through into another room. As the door opened to admit him Gor heard the chatter of a computer room and glimpsed an array of equipment. He had realized that he had fallen among the Ugs that he had been warned against but he still didn't know what they were. He sat calmly waiting for the man to reappear with his identity confirmed. If they could do all he said it would only be a matter of a couple of minutes before he was back. The door opened and the man came in. He stood on the other side of the table and looked down at Gor. 'No such person as Gordon Bardfield, aged fifteen plus, exists.'

Gor half rose in his chair and then sank back. He put his face in his hands. The man sat down again and drew the block towards him. 'Now let's begin again. Give me your real name.'

For a moment Gor thought of giving Empers's name. That would be there he was sure and they were the same age. Then his head went up. 'Gordon Bardfield.'

His interrogator put down the pen and spoke over Gor's head. 'Would you tell the commander I'm sorry to interrupt his supper but I'd be grateful if he could come back here. We have a problem.' The guard left. There was silence in the room. The man leaned back in his chair and swung a little. Then he wrote on his chippen block. The door behind Gor opened.

'Something the matter?'

'This boy was brought in after he wandered, so he says, into the camp. He also says his name is Gordon Bardfield but there's nothing on record. I thought you ought to have a look at him.'

The figure of the commander appeared at the edge of Gor's

sightline. He seemed to be about thirty, spare and hardly filling the uniform dungarees that bore no evidence of his rank. He too stood looking down at Gor. 'What's your name?'

'My name is Gordon Bardfield.'

The commander turned to the guard. 'Would you please fetch my sister.'

Again there was silence while they waited. Then the door opened once more. The commander looked towards it. 'Em, this boy says his name is Gordon Bardfield.'

There was a sound of footsteps. Gor didn't look up. A woman's voice said, 'Will, do you remember? You do or you wouldn't have asked me.'

'Look carefully, Em, and tell me what you think. It's a long time and it could all be a trap.'

'I know.' There was a pause. Then she began again. 'Gor, do you remember me?'

He looked up quickly. 'I don't know. I almost do but I can't quite . . .'

'Put your hair back, Gordon.' She reached out a hand and brushed it back for him. 'It is him, Will. I'm sure of it. No one else's hair grows like that in the front. It's Gordon, Will, it's Gordon.'

Gor looked from brother to sister without understanding but with that odd sense of half familiarity, a snatch of barely heard tune. 'We'll take him out to Mum and see what she says.'

'I think we can sort this one out, Martin,' the commander said to the man behind the little table.

'We'll get back to the barrier then,' said one of the guards and they left the room.

Gor walked between Emily and William back the way they had come to the eating area that now seemed like a big open-air restaurant with all the tables filled with diners.

'Mum,' William said pausing at a table with two empty places. 'Do you remember the boy you fostered once?'

'Gordon,' she said firmly. Mrs Bardfield was a little stouter but to those who saw her every day she hardly seemed any older. She looked at Gor. 'It could be,' she said. 'Give that kid another nine years or thereabouts. How old are you?'

'Fifteen.'

'And what's your name?'

'Gordon Bardfield.'

'And where've you been all this long time, Gordon?'

'I've been to school and in the holidays I stayed with Ann and Mr Forester, the Doctor.' His answers came childishly.

'The Doctor?'

'Yes.'

'That's what I used to call him, remember, Em?'

'What are you doing in the city?' William asked.

'Oh, sit the boy down and give him something to eat,' said Mrs Bardfield.

A chair was brought for him. The other people at the table, an elderly man and woman, moved round to make room. 'Go and get him some implements, Em,' Mrs Bardfield said.

He didn't feel like eating but he knew he must try. Emily brought him a knife, spoon and fork and a dish of vegetable and soy hotpot with noodles. It tasted so good that Gordon was able to eat most of it after all. People were fetching pots of tea from a long table and bottles of wine and spirits were brought out. There was also a large keg of beer on a stand which some drew from. A small band filed, to the sound of catcalls and clapping, into the space in the middle of the assorted tables and began to tune up. Soon the first brave spirits who can't keep their feet still once the music starts were dancing, then more and more people of all ages took to the tarmac floor. Gordon wondered what Ann would think of it all.

'It's not surprising you don't show up on the computer,' William said later when they were seated in the house where the Bardfields lived. 'That can't be your real name.'

Emily looked at Gor.'I've never told anyone this before but I knew Gordon before ever he came to us.'

'Go on,' said Mrs Bardfield. Emily told her and William how she had looked after him at Jessop's.

'Jessop. There's someone of that name who's in charge of admin at the hospital.'

Gor hardly heard. It was all coming from a long way away. Someone had given him a glass or two of wine and what with everything, Mrs Bardfield saw, he could hardly keep his eyes open. 'No more tonight. It's time we all got some sleep.'

Gor tried to stand up. 'You stay with us tonight, Gordon.' Emily said. 'Then we'll sort a few things out in the morning.' He fell asleep hearing the reassuring murmur of William's and Emily's voices as they talked on into the night.

When he woke in the morning he was puzzled by the absence of a reddish tinge to the light until he remembered where he was. He lay for a bit thinking things out. He must get in touch with Ann and tell her what had happened, and Empers too. 'Can you find your way back again?' Emily asked when he told her that he ought to go and get his few belongings from his old house.

'Oh yes.' His smile faded.'If that's alright, I mean, for me to come back?'

'Anyone can come here if they want.'

'Why don't they then?'

'Some people aren't ready or they're afraid of something. They prefer to be on their own.'

Gor couldn't imagine how anyone could choose the loneliness he had endured instead of the companionship and cheerfulness of the camp.

He reached the house without difficulty and left it without regret. The convolvulus would soon seal up the rotting gate again. In time it might take over the whole house, reaching tendrils round the shutters and in at the windows and cracks, creeping its pink, easily bruised trumpets over the roof until the house was drowned in them and crumpled under their weight.

'He says he had to run away because the man Mum calls the Doctor was threatening to lock him up. Apparently the wife Ann warned him and gave him some money,' Emily told William.

'I wonder how we can find out who he really is.'

'This man you mentioned last night called Jessop, it couldn't be the same one, could it?'

When Jessop had first arrived in the city he had followed the same course as Gor, shutting himself up in an empty house, and avoiding all human contact. He had been able to monitor the progress of his deception by checking on his wife's bank account. Knowing their joint number and privacy code he was able quite simply to ask the computer for a statement and the figure would appear on the screen. He knew therefore that the insurance company had accepted his death and paid up and that she had sold the property.

He had enough money to live on for some time in his present style for he had the sum he had been ostensibly carrying to the dealer he had been on his way to visit. That wouldn't last for ever, though, and the future would have to be looked to. He had no intention of skulking in a rotten house alone for the rest of his life though he rather enjoyed the masquerade for the first few weeks. There was a great sense of freedom in walking about in the uniform dungarees, pretending to have a purpose but with no responsibilities.

Even his natural buoyancy began to sink however as he observed the life around him and wondered how best to lay out his special talents. There were the employed who led lives shut away in unboarded houses for fear of contamination from the unemployed. Of these many were on benefit while the rest were like himself, exiles and runaways. For Jessop to take a job was out of the question because of the rigorous searches any potential employer would make. He cursed himself for not providing a new identity before committing the old one to the flames.

As a dead man he wasn't, of course, entitled to benefit. For a stark moment he saw himself embarking on a life of robbery in order to eat once his money ran out. The trouble was he had no talent for it. He was neither violent nor cruel by nature and though necessity is said to be a great teacher he felt he would be both incompetent and dispirited by it.

Jessop turned his mind to study the structures within the city that might give him a living, both financial and stimulatory. He needed to be doing something; his metabolism demanded it, otherwise he would end dead of despair and apathy to be gnawed on by rats. He sometimes looked from his windows at other shuttered houses and wondered how many of them were now inhabited by the dead and the rats who came to dine on them until they were like unopened tombs each one housing only bones. He knew about this because the first house he had tried to move into had been like that. When he had found its silent dweller Jessop had waved a hand in a kind of salute and backed out.

He didn't blame the rats. They were all in it together and if he found a means to gnaw his way into this system wouldn't he be ratlike too? Sometimes these days he thought about his apes and regretted how little he had known them or about them, and the fates to which he had thoughtlessly sent them. He remembered Emily Bardfield's face as she had watched them die and knew she had been right to care as she did. He found himself enticing birds on to the windowsill with fragments of his food just to watch their squabbles and their courtships and the whirled wings of the stout fledglings demanding food from anxious pared-down parents.

Jessop felt most affinity with the sparrows who seemed so like himself that at any moment one of them would speak to him. Where was the real difference except in the complexity of what we humans did with the same basic structure? In one way they seemed to have solved a key problem much better: they knew how to interface the communal and the individual. They lived pinion by pinion. They squabbled noisily but the approach of a common enemy turned them into a shrieking homogeneous cloud to drive it away. Yet amidst this community was the life of each nest apart from the rest of sparrow society, a world of love and procreation. They mobbed but didn't destroy, and they allowed a necessary privacy. Jessop thought regretfully of his apartment and a girl's face in the mirror touching a pencil to her lips. He had to get out and bend life to his needs again. If employment was out of the question how was it to be done?

It took him a little time to realize that there were other potential employers in the city. There seemed to be two groups of Ugs, as they were called by those who didn't belong to them. One was based on the plastic shanty town. The other operated from a no-go area on the north of the city. There was a third group which he became aware of in his nightly wanderings that was sometimes confused with the others, especially in radio and, he presumed, telly reports of events: the criminal network that ran the drinking clubs, amusement arcades and girl and boy prostitutes who set out their wares in them at night in the city centre. He supposed there might be a job for him there but he shied away from it as he had from solitary crime.

From shanty town shock waves of rioting flowed over the bridge and pulsed through the city from time to time. It was after such a wave when the streets were littered with flotsam of broken plastic, stones and rubber bullets and still faintly acrid with riot gas that Jessop decided to follow the retreating tide to its source and see what it might yield him. The difficulty was in getting back again. There was a real danger that once having crossed to the other side of the Avon he might find himself marooned there.

It was easy enough to get over, he had observed. You went with the trickle of returning workers in the evening, looking exhausted and faintly hangdog in your dungarees. The pollys stood back at the toll almost as well protected as spacewalkers in their security suits, their features slightly distorted by the curve of the plastic visor of their helmets as a toothbrush handle seems to bend in a glass of water. As Jessop walked past them with the nerves in his thighs and calves all ajump he saw a man going into the city on the other side of the bridge having his employee certificate or some other identification examined. Well, he would worry about that later.

On the other side he turned into the section of shanty town that lay to his right. Further along, the twin towers and slung web of the suspension bridge threaded the gorge with its elegant cat's cradle. He supposed one day the ancient structure, that seemed the toy of the great engineer who had built it, would drop down into the water leaving the towers looking across at each other like divided lovers until they too fell to their knees and toppled down the gorge. It was a kind of iron lyric against the evening sky that made his throat catch. He was getting morbid being so much on his own and would have to do something about it pretty quick.

The jumble of plastic shacks reminded him of cartoon films he had seen as a child. They should house gnomes or the legendary Martians that everyone now knew didn't exist but were still part of the collective mental furnishing.

Supper was being cooked outside most doors in a pot balanced over a calor gas burner. There could be little room inside the shacks except for sleeping and they must be cold in winter and hot in summer as an unregulated greenhouse. At intervals along the track there were standpipes and lavatories put up by the regional council in an effort to keep down disease. The whole rootless growth was inexplicable to Jessop where there were so many empty houses. When rain came the tracks between the haphazard rows must become miniature bogs and on this warm evening there was an unmistakable smell of putrescence.

A girl outstared him from beside a cooking pot with a look that was an invitation, but much as his mouth watered he was too unsure of the rules in shanty town to chance his luck. At last at the end of a row he came to a point where several tracks met and there was a longer domed structure with the appearance of being some kind of centre. Jessop gathered his courage and went in.

There was a mart with the usual basic dispensers and what

170

he was pleased to see was a bar where you could buy drinks in one corner of a large amusement arcade whose dozens of machines were busily at work providing entertainment. There were even a few stools to sit on. Jessop got himself a gassy beer and perched on one of them to sip at his bottle and watch.

He was joined eventually by a little old woman who settled like a bedraggled rook on the next stool. Jessop nodded to her. He would be glad to talk to someone.

'Evening.' She smoothed the folds of a black skirt over her mottled legs. It looked as if it had been made from old curtains and had vertical stripes of fading where it had turned to a deep brown. It was unusual to see anyone in anything other than dungarees. 'Look at them,' she said, jerking her head at the fruit machine players. 'Daft. You can't tell if they're playing the machines or the machines are playing them for their money.'

Jessop laughed to encourage her. 'Here night after night, some of them,' she went on. 'Spend a fortune and all for a few free goes. That's why I said, "Who's player and who's played?" I swear some of them things looks as if they're ready to bust with laughing after a bit.'

'I see what you mean,' Jessop said. Several of the pieces were so constructed that they appeared to have an almost human face with knob eyes and gapped mouth that after a few beers might well begin to laugh and leer.

'At least my pension goes into my belly not into a machine's.'

'Are most people here on a pension?'

'Unemployment, retirement, disability or widow's.'

'No one works?'

'What at? There's one or two goes across to a job for a time. But it don't last and they're soon back. You see them go, all sure they're going to get out of here and you see them return. It's only ever temporary. They never get taken on.'

'Why's that?'

'You don't end up here, so it goes, unless your record's bad and once you're here that makes it worse.'

'Is your record bad?'

She laughed. 'Might have been if I'd been a bit younger and more up to the mark.'

Jessop was delighted with her. She was the most sprightly thing, apart from the rats, that he had come across since reaching the city.

171

'I'm luckier than most. I don't starve and I don't really want any more. As long as I get out for a drink and to watch the fools looking for a fortune in a shower of cents I'm not too bad. I used to dream of getting away like everyone else but give it time and common sense and you realize you're here and it's where you'll stay.'

'What was the row about yesterday?'

She laughed. 'They have them from time to time. Seem to need to. Frustration, I suppose. Somebody gets up and says the benefit's too low and then they all get excited and rush over the bridge and rampage about until they bring out enough pollys and wagons to knock a few down and they settle back again. Then everything goes quiet for a bit. It's like lancing a boil. Only this one never goes away, just simmers until it blows and then starts all over again.'

'What does Ugs mean?'

'They're not UGs, this lot. They're just a rabble though it suits the pollys and everyone else to say they are. You scratch any one of these and you'll find he's all out for himself and his own inside whatever the fine words and fire eating.'

'But Ugs or UGs, what are they?'

'It stands for "urban guerrillas". That's what they were first called and it's stuck. The real UGs live over there.' She waved a hand in the direction of the river. 'I'd go and join them if I could and get away from this lot.'

'Why don't you?'

'I don't suppose they'd want me. Living here's made me not much use, like the rest of them. Selfish really, just thinking about coming here for my beer and to laugh to myself at the fools. And anyway how would I get there? You either need an employer's paper or a resident's permit, otherwise they can do you for vagrancy. No, once you cross over there's no going back.'

That problem was beginning to worry Jessop increasingly. His boredom he realized had made him hasty. 'There must be some way across.'

'It's for the nimble and lucky, with a head for heights.' She nodded towards the suspension bridge. 'A few try it. No one knows if they get over or just drop down and are carried out to sea.'

'Why can't you just walk across?'

'Because the middle's gone all except for the cables.'

'It looks alright from here.'

'You try it and good luck.'

'I think I'll have to. Here, let's have another. Drink to my success.'

Yet another beer later Jessop set out for the suspension bridge, climbing up towards what the old woman had told him was called Nightingale Valley but none sang now though it was getting towards dusk and their voices might have floated down the gorge or across to the other side. Jessop longed to be a bird or even its clear song pushed out on the night like a fragile leaf boat on a stream of air.

He was almost reconciled to failure and death. He couldn't sweat or fret any more. He reached the end of the bridge. The tower stood sentry, a lighthouse against the almost drained sky but eyeless with no guiding beams. Perhaps by the time he reached the middle it would be too dark to see the gap and he would plunge wailing through. He walked on.

The road was broken and strewn with fragments that caused him to stumble out of nervousness. The wind soughed and moaned about him and he thought he felt the whole structure sway with it. The black ropes of the cables cut across his vision arching down towards the centre. Fear came back even stronger as the night air and his walking dissipated the effect of the few drinks. All was black now or his sight had blurred. He must be near the middle but he couldn't see anything. He stumbled again and the sweat broke out all over to trickle coldly down his body and soak into his teeshirt. Any moment he might fall or the wind pluck him off the road and slam him down. He hardly dared look up for a second.

The left-hand cable rose in a black arch against the sky. It was rising. That meant he had passed the middle. She had said the middle was gone, he was sure. Perhaps she'd meant the middle of the road not the middle of the bridge and the gap was still to come. He was almost staggering now; his legs ached with weakness. Still he kept on. It seemed as if he had been crossing the bridge all his life in the dark and the wind. Then he saw the far tower ahead and almost started to run. It would be too malign if he fell through now just as he had begun to hope. Jessop held himself back and walked the the last few yards. At the foot of the tower he leant against the wall and half sobbed as he drew breath. His chest was as tight as if he had run all the way.

173

It was all a lie; the bridge wasn't broken. Perhaps the story had been spread to stop people crossing. Perhaps they had told each other and the rumour had acquired a kind of truth. For them it was broken and even if he walked back down again and told them the reality he sensed that they wouldn't believe him or be grateful for the information if they tried to believe. Jessop stood up and began to walk down the other side. It was only a matter of time of course and maybe the structure was already unsafe for any but a lone walker. Perhaps he had just been lucky and any day it might crack with someone on it. But he had done it and he couldn't believe that others couldn't or hadn't as well, though they had never returned to let the rest know. Probably they too had thought they wouldn't be believed.

Later he was to wonder whether the old woman had known exactly what she was doing all the time and was smiling quietly to herself over her beer, knowing he was safely across. In the morning he would try the other group to see if there was a place for him there.

They weren't as well organized when Jessop presented himself at the barrier of the small no-go area as they would become later. Nor had they been joined by Mrs Bardfield and her family. They were grateful for new recruits. Even so, Jessop felt he had been very thoroughly turned over. He had decided to tell the truth, more or rather less.

'And why do you want to join us?'

Jessop breathed deep. 'Because my money will run out and I can't sit around doing nothing.'

His interrogator smiled for the first time. 'That sounds honest. How do we know that you aren't a polly plant?'

'Check my records. You'll see I'm dead.'

'I already have. What does that prove?'

'You could kill me. I'm completely in your power.'

'We don't kill people. We try to make them live. Your case will be discussed. Meanwhile walk about the camp, talk to people, see whether you think you would fit in.'

Jessop began his walkabout. He grinned at a girl mending a fence. 'Hallo, baby.'

'Hallo,' she grinned back.

'What you doing tonight?'

'Washing my hair.' She laughed at him. Jessop felt more cheerful than at any time since he had set fire to his bony

174

replica. The boss had been a bit of a sobersides but then maybe pioneers always were. The important thing was that the life around him seemed purposeful and yet relaxed. Houses were being put in order but no one shouted. Everyone he saw was doing something easily as though it was worth doing and they had all the time in the world to get it as right as their own temperaments and talents would allow.

'What did you think of it?' his interrogator asked.

'You're asking me?'

'We need administrators, people who can organize. You ran your own business and built it up. You could be useful.'

'Then try me.'

'Alright, we will. You'll live in and get your keep and a small wage.'

'Where?'

'We're starting our own hospital in a disused college. That'll be your first job.'

He had been there ever since while the no-go area expanded and more and more refugees from loneliness and disorder came in. Jessop was quite surprised to find himself not only rather good at the job as he gradually took over the whole administration but enjoying the constant hard work that was only secondarily for his own benefit. Even in his own firm he had wanted to be easy with the people who worked for him, against all Miss Wilkins's inclinations and advice. In the hospital he found he could carry this out and even encourage others who found it hard at first to accept responsibility without formal hierarchy. He was eager to make it work and not find himself an outcast again.

From time to time he would meet a girl who, like himself, wanted the relaxation of an evening's pleasure. After the first such encounter he had examined his own reactions very carefully. He had always believed that the inequality between himself and his girls had been a necessary element for him but either he had been mistaken or he was changing. He found he enjoyed watching them as much as he had but he no longer needed them to be in his debt or power. The girl at her own glass combing her hair turned his gut over as much as the ones who had stolen or begged the perfumes he kept for them.

William found him at work in his office. 'Stephen Jessop?'

'That's right.' For the first time in years he felt afraid. His mind flicked through the past few weeks to see what might be

175

wrong. There was always something. No organization ever ran perfectly because if it had it would have had to be inhuman.

'I believe you knew my sister?'

Jessop's heart touched bottom but still felt as if it was going down. 'What was her name?'

'Sorry. Bardfield. Emily Bardfield.'

So that was it. It had never occurred to him when he had seen the name in the list of commanders that there could be any connection, though of course he had thought of her at once. How, though, did she think of him? Did this rather serious-faced brother intend to right some old wrong by getting him removed? They wouldn't send him away. Anyone was entitled to stay there now if they wanted but he would have lost his place, his sense of belonging to something.

'We'd both like to talk to you about somebody if you could spare the time. I know how busy you are.'

'Delighted.' The relief flooded through him, displacing the despair so palpably he wondered there wasn't a great dark stinking puddle of it under the table.

They arranged to meet away from the Bardfields' own quarters and without Gordon. William realized that the boy had been through a damaging experience. Too easily tears pricked up into his eyes and his voice caught.

Emily wasn't sure how she felt about seeing Mr Jessop again. He'd changed a bit, was thinner and more relaxed.

'You're looking just the same, Emily,' he told her. 'I'm glad you're alright. I was worried about the staff but there wasn't anything I could do. I just had to disappear. That seemed best for everyone. You see, I hadn't any money to carry on with after all the animals died. I couldn't have kept you all on.'

'We wanted to talk to you about Gordon.'

'Gordon?'

'Yes,' said Emily and then as she saw the name meant nothing to him, 'there was a baby we had for a few months not long before it all happened. The customer had gone away and I looked after it. Then he came back and took it away and you gave me a bonus.'

'That's right. It's coming back to me now. Funny little chap. Been treated as one of the family and was all dressed up.'

'Did it ever cross your mind,' said William, 'that he wasn't quite what you'd been told he was?'

'Yes,' he answered carefully. They both looked at him. 'It

crossed my mind that it was some kind of hybrid.'

'Between what and what?' William asked.

'Well, I didn't go into it but thinking back it could have been a chimp and an orang.'

'You didn't ever think,' Emily was asking now, 'that it might be a human baby someone was trying to keep hidden?'

'Great grief!'

'That's what I began to think. And Miss Wilkins even thought it was mine.' Emily laughed. 'She said you were too kind to us girls letting me bring my baby to work.'

'I only saw him twice. Once when he was brought in and then when he took him away.'

'Who brought him? Who took him away?' William probed.

Jessop gathered up his courage. 'It was a man called Forester I owed a favour to. He worked for the MOD, at their research institute near Salisbury.'

'Mum's Doctor?' Emily asked William.

'Could be. It must have been his child he was farming out.'

'How awful,' said Emily. 'Poor Gordon.'

'What did he do at this institute?'

'Primate research. That's how I knew him. He got me a contract.' It was out and Jessop felt lightened of part of his burdensome secret. But he was afraid to go further. He supposed that Sandra might have discussed things with Emily but he didn't want the Bardfields to think too badly of him. It was a long time ago. He had made Forester pay but that was partly because he disliked the man and felt that he was despised by him in return.

William and Emily decided that all this added nothing of value to Gordon's knowledge of his origins and that it was best kept to themselves. Whoever's child he was they hadn't wanted him and that was hard news enough. Mrs Bardfield agreed. She thought he'd been too tired the night he came to them to have overheard Emily's story about Jessop and in any case well was best left alone. 'After all in a manner of speaking he's been as much ours as anyone's. He can stop here along with us.'

'There were others,' he said one day to Emily, 'as well as you and William, weren't there?'

Errol had been killed by a car that didn't stop, she told him. Nina was working with her old friend Sandra near where they used to live and Jessie was working in France where she had gone as nurse to an English diplomat's children. She had last

177

written home that she had a French boyfriend and was thinking of settling there though she missed them all and longed sometimes to come back.

'Why doesn't she?'

'She'd never get another job because of being William's sister. Any more than I could.'

'What can I do, Em?' He was feeling so much better he had begun to be restless.

'I'll ask William.'

'You can help in the school, teaching some of the things you've learnt.'

Gor was happy. One evening as they sat out after supper before the music started, he began to sketch. He had found a whole roll of white paper in an empty house and had hoarded it carefully. Some he had made into a sketchpad. He roughed in a portrait of Mrs Bardfield; then Emily and William.

'That's very good, Gordon. Can you draw you?'

'I'm not worth drawing.' He scribbled quickly and there he was in cruel self-caricature.

His talent soon had takers. He was asked to make quick likenesses for fun and detailed portraits as keepsakes or presents.

'The committee wants to know if you think you could do bigger pictures that show different aspects of what we're doing,' William said one day.

'I could do some roughs and see what they think of them. I'd need some materials.' ·

'We'll get you some.'

The sketches became the basis for murals, some of which he drew for others to paint, others which were all his own.

Jessop had almost become one of the family too. He had looked at Gor with great interest when he had met him but had kept quiet about having seen him before as Emily had asked. 'We had a sad case today,' he said to her one evening. 'A woman who believes she had a child once and it was taken away. Her husband says they never had a child. She's lost him his job because of her outbreaks of mad behaviour but he's stuck by her.'

'He must love her,' Emily said.

'Yes,' said Jessop. It was an emotion he had never experienced. He supposed he never would, that it was left out of his make-up, like salt out of cooking and somehow never to be made up for no matter how much you tried later.

Gor had managed to ring Ann once with the simple news that he was alive but he had begun to feel a need to see her that grew stronger until it wouldn't be denied. 'Is anything worrying you?' William asked him, missing his usual smile.

'I want to go away for a day or two. There's someone I ought to go and see.'

'I'm sure that can be arranged,' William said.

But Emily was less happy. 'Suppose something happened to him out there on his own? For all we know Forester may have a polly search on for him.'

William made a quick decision. 'Gor, Em's worried about you going alone. Would you mind if I went with you? I could wait for you somewhere while you saw your friends.'

'I'd like you to come with me. I'd like you to meet them.' It would help him to fit the parts of his life together. Quick calls arranged a rendezvous with Empers at a time when they could visit Ann.

She had put the phone down, hoping he hadn't seen her slight disappointment that she wasn't to have him to herself but must share him with a new friend. Then she chastised herself mentally. He had to make his own life. She should be glad that he wanted to bring someone with him whom he wanted her to meet. She only hoped they would like each other for Gordon's sake.

William felt as if he was setting out on holiday as he and Gor climbed into the coach. He couldn't remember having one before. It was something he should look into perhaps: the need for holidays even in lives that could be said to be one long holiday. It was autumn. The harvesters had been at work and the long fields were stripped back to bare earth except where young soybushes still stood. William found the unfolding of slopes and brown shoulders soothing and yet stimulating as if his mind and body stretched and unwound with the eye that followed the curves to the horizon. He had been too long in the city.

They met Empers at Yeovil station, where Gor had last seen him. He was taller and just as thin. 'You look splendid,' he said as he shook Gor's hand and turned to shake William's. He had left Montgomery and was living with his uncle, whose heir he was, and cramming for exams. 'But I don't know what to do after,' he laughed as they walked the damp pavements. 'I could go into the agribusiness of course. My uncle's got a job for me

179

and he's keen but I'm not. What are you going to do?'

'Gordon's already teaching,' William put in quickly. 'Art mainly.'

'That's marvellous,' Empers said. 'He was always brilliant, you know, even at school.'

Gor was quiet when they boarded the coach again. 'He doesn't understand,' he said eventually.

'You can't expect him to. It's not his fault. It's all outside his experience. In a way you have to hope he never will, unless things change.'

Ann had been growing increasingly nervous as the time drew near. Suppose they couldn't talk any more; suppose she found this friend he was bringing unsympathetic and the meeting was made uneasy and stilted. She walked about the house making small adjustments to the sit of a cushion here and the hang of a picture there. Then she thought she would just pick a few flowers and so they found her.

'Ann!'

He came across the grass towards her, put his arms round her and kissed her cheek. He was taller than Ann now, taller than his friend who was hanging back a little, and she saw that he was grown-up. She put her arm through his and turned to meet his friend.

William could never quite remember after what any of them said. Nor did he understand at that moment what had happened to him. He was quite simply stunned. He heard a voice which was his, talking about Gor's painting and the murals. He knew that they had moved from the garden into the house but it was as if they walked in an enchanted landscape where all his senses were heightened and yet suspended. He hadn't expected her to be so beautiful. The Ann he had made in his mind out of the fragments Gor had given him hadn't prepared him for the reality at all.

She felt she might be making a fool of herself, talking too much, that she would appear merely rich and spoilt. She wanted Gor's friend to like her. William, 'sweet William' she surprised herself thinking. It was a tune she sometimes played. That was it. The blindfold god on her instrument smiled his polished rosewood smile up at her.

All too soon they had to go. 'You will ring me, won't you, and come any time you can, both of you, as long as we can arrange something? You won't just disappear, will you?'

180

It was William's turn to be silent on the coach. He felt sick, exhausted and overwrought. Perhaps it was the couple of glasses of wine Ann had given them.

'What was she like?' Emily asked.

'Beautiful. I hadn't expected that.'

Emily felt a pang of mingled envy and jealousy. She had everything and Emily had nothing and now she was taking William. Emily felt this even more strongly when William asked Gordon for a portrait of Ann done from memory. She suspected that as yet he didn't even know what was so laughably clear to her: that he had fallen in love.

'Are you alright, Em?' Jessop asked her. 'You look a bit tired.'

'Thanks,' said Emily sharply and Jessop who had never heard her use such a tone before realized that she must be very off-colour indeed. He cast around for something to divert her.

'By the way, an odd coincidence, that man I was telling you about the other day who'd lost his job because of his wife's illness, well he used to work in the primate section under Forester at the research institute years ago.'

'How long ago?'

'I didn't ask precisely. I will next time I see him.' At least he had caught her interest for a moment.

'Seventeen years about. Then they moved to Midsomer Norton where he finally lost his job about six years ago. Em, he says his wife first became ill because she was given a baby gorilla to foster and she began thinking it was her child. When he was moved it had to be left behind and she had a breakdown.'

'I want to talk to him,' said Emily. 'Will you take me to him, Stephen, please.'

The Knotts' house was immaculate because he kept it so, cleaning, decorating and cooking while Nancy watched him from her chair or stared out of a window. She'd been quieter since they'd been here because he could be with her all the time and though he never really broke through into the darkness of that undersea cave where she lived he was able to bring her snatches of the life above from time to time. Sometimes he kidded himself that one day he might come with a powerful beam to light it all up and coax her gently to the surface. 'We'll go into the garden if you don't mind,' he said. 'I don't talk about it in front of Nance in case it upsets her.' In truth he

181

didn't talk much about it at all. Shame and fear kept him quiet. He didn't know why he'd started to gab to Jessop. Perhaps he was just tired. Once he'd started he'd found it hard to stop. He'd regretted it as soon as the man came back with his questions, and now he'd brought in someone else. It had been his mistake: things were best kept to yourself and there was nothing anyone could do.

Emily felt his resentment and understood it. 'I'm sorry to bother you both. I just wanted to sort something out.' She found herself using an expression of her mother's to try to soothe him.

He found himself telling her the whole story. Even his own betrayal of Nancy, and his complicity in taking the little gorilla from her, he brought out at last after all these years and put into her hands, sensing that she would take it and the guilt that covered it and not thrust it back at him grown double with the added weight of her condemnation.

'You did the best you could, what you thought was right at the time.'

'I should have done what I knew she wanted: taken him with us and just gone. It would have been hard but it wouldn't have been worse than it has been. I was too worried about the wrong things. I see that now, but I couldn't see it then. And I blame myself for something else too.'

Emily looked at him, keeping the exchange between them flowing so that the vital current shouldn't be broken until everything was said.

'You may think I'm daft. I have to chance that. But there was his side, the kid's. I've never forgotten how he cried.'

'The kid?'

'He was supposed to be a gorilla, alright? Mary's baby. But there was always something wrong with him. I mean he was too human. I know they are. There's not much difference in some ways especially with the babies but even so... When I tried to tell him, Forester, he said it was a mutation and that's why it was so interesting. But you see that's why it harmed her so much, just because it was like a human kid she was losing.'

'Will, I'm frightened,' Emily said when she had finished retelling Knott's story to her brother. 'He even said the baby's name was Gordon. That was the name that was pinned to him when I undressed him. Perhaps Nancy Knott pinned it on him.'

'More likely Knott himself. Get Stephen to ask him, and ask him too if there were any records kept and where they might be. Not that they'll help much. If Forester substituted Gordon for a baby gorilla they won't tell us.'

'But why should he do such a thing?'

'Who knows? Maybe he wanted somewhere to hide a kid of his own, though I would have bet that if the mother had died Ann Forester would have been prepared to adopt it. On the other hand he might have got hold of another baby and been using it experimentally.'

'How?'

'Well, people take baby apes and bring them up as humans. Suppose he was doing two experiments: one like that and then the reverse, bringing a human up as an ape to compare results.'

'That's terrible.'

'I wonder if it's any worse than the other way round. I've never thought about it before but what we do is bring an ape up to be human and then throw him back into some form of ape world in a zoo or somewhere when the going gets rough. Did you ever think about it when you were working at Stephen's?'

'I tried not to. I shut it out. I just did my best for them while they were there because if they were in prison so in a way was I and if I complained or thought too much I'd lose my job and the money that we all needed. And Stephen was caught too, I suppose.' She suddenly saw the world as bound together in layers of suffering, an imprisoning mesh from which here a face looked out or there a hand grasped at the air outside and was drawn back.

'What about Forester? Is he caught?'

'I suppose he must be.' She wanted to say, 'And so are you now.' She had always thought of Will as strong and free since he had grown up but she remembered her fears for him when he was small and saw she had been deceiving herself. No one escaped entirely; no one could or perhaps even should. Aloud she asked instead: 'Why did he sent Gordon to school if he was bringing him up as an ape?'

'I don't know. Perhaps he wanted to measure their educational development.'

'Gordon was very late in talking. He had to have an operation before he could begin to talk at all.'

'Perhaps that was one of the effects of the experiment.'

'How could he do that to a human baby?'

183

'Some people see the line between the nons and animals as a bit blurred. What's the difference between a stupid human and a clever ape? That's the sort of riddle they ask themselves. It's all a matter of trying to prove their own superiority, that if they're the cleverest or the most hardworking, or whatever form their own hierarchy takes, then those below can be fitted into a descending order of virtue or usefulness until you tail off at the bottom with creatures who are so far down, so distant from the top as to be dismissible, of no account, another species at the mercy of the clever ones.'

Stephen reported that Knott had kept careful records and that if they still existed they would be at the Institute. He remembered quite well the name tag he had pinned to the baby's clothing. 'So that settles it,' Emily said. 'It was Gordon. What do we do, Will?'

William rang Ann. 'I want to talk to you alone. It's about Gordon.' He had no idea as he set out again on the coach that he was merely making himself an excuse.

'Do you think it would help him at all to know who his parents are?'

They were walking in the garden where autumn had taken a few more steps since his last visit and had laid a gauze over the lawn and the beds to filter the sunlight in a reminder of winter's coming darkness. 'Look,' she said, 'there's no finger on the sundial at all today, no shadow. If it could stay like that we wouldn't have to worry because there would be all the time in the world. How can I say? Whatever answer I give may be wrong.'

'When he first came to you what did your husband say about him?'

'That his parents had been killed and that Norman was an executor and guardian.'

'That would make sense.' He was being very careful not to suggest anything that might alarm her such as that Gordon might be her husband's child.

'Isn't it quite simple? Surely you can just ask the central register or whatever it's called. Can you do that?'

'Yes,' said William. He realized that although he knew a great deal about her she knew nothing about him. 'As a matter of fact I've done that already.'

'Well, then?'

184

'Gordon isn't on it. You see, Bardfield isn't his name. It's mine, my family's.'

'I don't understand.'

'Before he came to you Gordon was fostered out. It happens that it was my family, my mother, who looked after him and at some point he was given our name.'

'So when he met you in Bristol, or you met him, you recognized him?'

'Briefly, yes.' He laughed. 'It's all a bit complicated, I'm afraid.' There were things he didn't want to tell her yet.

Ann had decided that she wouldn't tell him about Norman's extraordinary outburst when he had said he would lock Gor up. It was somehow too humiliating, especially since he seemed to have forgotten it.

'Good riddance,' he had said when she had told him her one lie: that Gordon had never returned from Salisbury, but he watched the news and listened, she knew, for any mention of him, waiting.

Back on the coach again William felt once more that strange sickness coupled with a tension, a dizziness almost that by the time he reached home had turned to exhaustion. He found himself talking to Ann incessantly in his head, telling her things about Gor and the life they led in the city, explaining, questioning.

Ann discovered when he had gone that she couldn't get the tune out of her mind. In an effort to lay it she went and looked the song up, a mistake that merely reminded her of the words which became at once a circling refrain to all her other thoughts.

> 'Let me kiss off that falling tear,
> We only part to meet again...'

'I wish you wouldn't sing while you're doing other things,' Forester said. 'It makes it very hard to concentrate. What is it anyway?'

'Sorry. It's a folksong or rather something that became a folksong. I play it sometimes. You must have heard me.'

In the end it was Gor who made up William's mind by asking one evening. 'When I first came here Em said something about having known me before. What did she mean and what does it mean that I'm not on the computer? How can I find out who my parents were?'

'Forester must know if anyone does.'

'The Doctor?'

'He's the one who sent you to school and told everyone that your name was Gordon Bardfield and that your parents had been killed.'

Gor thought for a moment. 'Then I suppose I'll never know. I can't ask him because he'd lock me up on sight and he can't have told Ann or she would have told me.'

'There may be another way of finding out. It's a bit, perhaps very, risky.'

'How?'

'Well, if there are any records it's likely that Forester keeps them at the Institute where he works. We could either go and look at them one night if we could get in or we could try and get someone inside to copy them. There's a man living here who worked there at one time. He could draw us a plan and tell us about the kind of security. Then we could have a look and see how much it had changed before we decided what to do. I wouldn't mind a look inside there anyway. A lot of money goes into it. I'd like to know the kind of thing it's spent on.'

There was no need to confuse and upset Gor with the tales of his early fosterings, William decided. If they found the names of his parents among Forester's records he might tell him then. Knott was very helpful and his memory surprisingly precise.

'I think I should do very well with the map he's given me,' William told Gor.

'I'm coming too.'

William was about to protest but he changed his mind at the expression on Gor's face.

They left the coach at the nearest junction to Stonehenge with one or two other pilgrims. 'They'll think we're Stonies too,' William laughed. 'Let them get ahead.' He nodded towards a group of obvious cult members. 'We'll go across the downs.'

Not all the hills were cultivated. Some of them still showed green tops where tethered goats grazed whose flesh was an expensive delicacy. 'Do you remember when you got past the security beam into the fields?' William asked. But Gor had quite forgotten. William told him the story as they trudged, avoiding the protected areas with their warning notices. 'Everybody said it showed you were out of the ordinary when you helped Leroy, even though you were only a couple of months older than he was. Mum, of course, said you would have been cleverer not to get in there in the first place.' They both laughed at such a typical reaction. The sun going down at their backs walked their long shadows side by side in front of them.

'We need somewhere overlooking it,' William said, getting out his map again when they were nearly there. 'That little hill ahead should be the last. With any luck it'll give us what we want.'

As they lay looking down on the low buildings of the Institute Gor was aware of the standing stones they had left behind and felt a prickle at the back of his neck as if they were alive and might be watching them. He almost turned to see.

'That's the area we want. We'll have to wait until about midnight so you might as well get some sleep. If a chopper comes over we're just Stonies on our way home.' William turned on his side and closed his eyes but it was a long time before sleep came. Gor too lay wakeful thinking of his unknown parents. If he had the names he could look them up on a file and find out something about them. He supposed they were dead but if one of them was still alive he would have to think carefully before intruding into another life that had been going on so long without him. Perhaps it was a mistake even to try to find out and he should accept himself as he was now. On the other hand if the Doctor meant to pursue him all his life any piece of information might be useful. He was still a child in law and therefore at his guardian's mercy.

William looked at his watch when he woke. It was twenty-three thirty. The sky was immense above them and the stars seemed low and bright. Men had once thought them eternal. Now they knew that the stars died too. They had been up nearly among them and looked down on the coloured earth. They had walked and worked in space and on the moon and were poised to go beyond the solar system but in many ways they were still children breaking each other's toys and screaming for attention and possession. 'Gimme, it's mine and you can't play with it.'

Most of the lights had gone out below but the night was starlit enough for them with their adjusted vision to see by. Anyone coming out of one of the buildings wouldn't have their advantage.

'Let's go,' he said picking up the bag. They set off downhill and reached the perimeter wall. All seemed to be still as Knott

187

had described it. William unfolded a ladder that took them near enough to the top for him to bypass a section of the security system and drop on to the other side after Gor. They headed, bent low, for the primate quarters and paused against a wall to get their breath, both aware of caged presences, some watching them, some murmuring in their sleep behind glass. For a moment William had a wild desire to smash open the cages and let the dark figures loose into the night but he knew they would only be caught, that they wouldn't live out there alone in the human wild.

He pointed upwards and Gor climbed the ladder and on to the roof. Knott had remembered a skylight that might provide a way in. Shining a torch through, Gor could see the catch that had never been included in the security system. If that had changed sirens would go off as he prised at it. He took a breath, stuck a lump of tack on the pane to hold it and cut out a section. He put in his hand and worked at the catch. It turned and Gor felt the skylight loosen but no warning sounded. They were in.

Forester's office had been changed but since the doors were labelled that was soon solved. After a few abortive tries, William unlocked the one that bore his name with a master key and they stepped inside. The room was full of cabinets and there was a desk as well. There was no reason for them to disguise their visit if it meant wasting time. William gemmied open the first drawer. 'You look in the cabinets.'

They were neither of them quite sure what they were looking for, only that they expected to know it when they saw it. The cabinets contained an elaborate cross referencing system on all Forester's work since he had been at the Institute. Everything was meticulously labelled and filed so that when at the bottom of the third drawer William came upon a blank-faced file he knew instinctively that they had found what they were searching for. Flicking it open he saw the name printed as a solitary title on the first page. 'I've got it. Let's get out.'

The way back was easy. William unclipped the bypass circuit and dropped the ladder. Gor went down it and William followed. It was folded and stowed in Gor's backpack and they set off up the hill. Looking at his watch Gor realized that what had seemed an hour since they had come that way first was only twenty minutes. They walked on, elated with their easy success. They wanted to run and shout and slap each other on the shoulder.

In the dark they went a little astray and saw the great sarcens crouched against the sky like a circle of squatting stone apes. Gor understood why a cult had grown up around them. The Stonies believed that the henge was the work of extraterrestrials who had left it on a previous visit to earth as a sign that they would come again to rebuild their temple. Gor and Empers had gone in an educational party from Montgomery, and had been given the orthodox history which seemed almost as remarkable as any intervention from space in its harnessing of a primitive society to build such a bridge between earth and the heavens, Ann's garden sundial for giants.

They caught a night coach after a long wait that drained their euphoria, and dozed until it was time to stumble out at the city station and drag their feet home. A cruising policar ran alongside them for part of the way but didn't intercept. They passed through the barrier. 'There's no point in me going home to bed. I'll go straight to HQ,' William said, handing Gor his pack. 'See you later.'

He let himself quietly into the house and crept into the front room where he slept. Should he have a look now or leave it until he woke? He took out the file from William's pack and opened it at his name. He turned to the first page but it swam in front of him. He would have to read it carefully for there was no simple statement of parentage. It seemed to be a series of notes in diary form on some experiment. Suddenly it wasn't important to know, not important enough to keep him from sleep. He hardly had time to take his clothes off.

He woke early and sat on the side of his bed with the file on his knees. Turning more pages he came to a series of reports on development which led in their turn to printouts of his records from Montgomery. This was undoubtedly his file. He went back to the beginning with a growing sense of excitement and read through the puzzling opening. It took him a long time, for it covered the whole course of Mary's pregnancy. Then he turned back to the first page again.

Fear flooded up in him like bile. He went into the bathroom and retched and retched but nothing came. He sat on the edge of the bed and held himself in his own arms while he rocked and moaned a little. He must go, get away before anyone else was up. He stuffed the file into his backpack, added a few items that his eye lit on, opened the door and crept down the stairs into the damp morning that didn't weep with him but merely strengthened his desolation.

'Where's Gordon?' Emily asked when William came home.

'What do you mean?'

'Wasn't he with you?'

'He came back last night or rather this morning, didn't he? I left him to come home. I didn't think it was worth it. Perhaps he's still asleep. Have you looked?'

'No, we thought he was with you.'

William went into the front room. He saw the slept-in bed, a pair of socks on the floor, an open drawer, his own backpack.

'I think he's run away, Em. I've made a terrible mistake. I should have looked at the file with him but I was too tired to think straight.'

'What do you mean?'

'He must have found something in it about his parents that's upset him.'

'You don't think he's run away to find them?'

'Wouldn't he have told us? There wouldn't be any need to run off if that was all it was.'

'What could it have been?'

'I'll have to try to find him before he gets himself into trouble. I'll ask Ann. She's most likely to know where he might go, if indeed that isn't where he's gone.'

He sat in a chair while she rang Fanny and arranged her alibi and then input a message for Norman and left the green light on to show him it was there. Quickly she put a few things in a bag, looked round and was ready. She set the alarm system and opened the car door for William. Wherever Gor was they must find him quickly before anyone else did. They drove off into the late September twilight.

V
THE CROWNING
OF GOR

He needed to stop running and think but as soon as he did the horror would rise up and confront him. The horror was inside his head and couldn't be run from yet movement, action of any kind held it briefly at bay. If he stopped he might find there was no answer but death, to kill the monster that should never have been. Yet the instinct for survival that is in every individual organism still fought against that finality and kept him running.

He was in the forest now, loping along the rides. He had got off the coach as soon as there was a stop where he knew the trees were close by and he could lose himself among them because he could no longer bear the faces of his fellow travellers who weren't his fellows any more and, if they knew, would look at him with disgust, fear or ridicule.

Here there were still birds. They fluted overhead or ran from him chattering their alarm calls. Already autumn had fingered the beeches, thinning their green before the first cold beat it into copper. Exhaustion dragged at him. He had to stop, to lean against the rough ridged bole of an oak tree and let thought have him. He put his cheek against the bark and his harsh breathing became sobs that gradually died away.

The wind swayed the branches against each other with little rubbing creaks as if creatures were moving stealthily among them. There were animals in the forest: foxes, weasels, badgers, rabbits and mice. There might even be deer. He wasn't sure. The wild animals lived out their lives here away from men until the men came hunting them. He had never thought about the worlds within worlds of the remaining forests or woods before. He had never had to.

There was a kind of society here: an animal commonwealth rather than kingdom for there was no king among them. Even man wasn't king here but more a marauder from another world with power over life and death. Yet man was himself an animal, top dog, boss cat, and in the evolutionary hierarchy Gor stood between man and the rest. He was less than human; more than fox. Perhaps he should stay in the forest and live among the wild animals where he would be king like the one-eyed man in the country of the blind. Yet he yearned towards humankind. He had been imprinted with them since birth, had sucked in their values from the bottle Nancy stoppered his eager mouth with and now he was self-condemned by those values to his lowly status of sub-human.

They had made him unfit to be king even of the forest. Soon he would get hungry and his stomach would crave human foods. He couldn't digest bark, leaves and grass. It clamoured for soypie and fries, ice-cream and cups of coffine. He supposed he could try to live by hunting as the foxes and weasels did but he hadn't their skill and in any case he shrank from the blood of other animals on his hands. If he wasn't wholly human he needn't be like men in that. The rabbit and the deer who might have been his prey seemed so vulnerable to the part of him that was human that he longed to protect them from himself. There was something too that when he thought of them brought Ann and Emily into his mind and made him want to weep again. He wouldn't let the murdering human in him loose on them to break, and tear and crush their soft skins and flesh and poke fingers in the sea-anemone eyes.

He was less than the beasts for they were the products of their own nature while he was manmade, as synthetic as soypie. There had been no love or even lust in his conception except Forester's lust for himself and his own power. Human children conceived as he had been were desired for themselves and as symbols of love and immortality. What Forester lusted after was immortal fame and his creation was merely the vehicle for it. Gor was a thing, a construct and yet he breathed and suffered and his suffering was still not great enough for self murder.

Perhaps the Gordon file was a joke or a fantasy of Forester's which he had built around a child left in his charge because of that child's simian ugliness. Much as he wanted to believe in any idea that would give him back his full humanity, Gor found it impossible. Something in him whispered that the file was true.

What did Forester intend for him? To reclaim him and put him on show? To keep him among the apes in his prison to be experimented on, tested continually, without freedom or rights like the insane? It would drive him mad. He shrank from the thought of his half-brothers and half-sisters who had surrounded them at the Institute behind their glass walls. He had been educated to all the human disgust at the near and yet so far of the anthropoid. It crossed his mind that there might be others like himself, perhaps in other parts of the world. If Forester could do it, and had done it, why not others? Still he flinched at the thought of them as he knew others would shrink from him if they knew of his nature and existence.

As he had known it would, hunger began to ache in his belly, an emptiness accentuated by the tears and mucus he had swallowed and the constant flushing of the secretions of his fear and pain through his blood. He wanted to be dead but his body demanded food. He laughed out loud in his bitterness at the paradox.

What would they do when they found he was gone? What would they think, the friends he would never see again? They would know he had found something in the file but they would never guess what. If he destroyed it he could go back with some pretence about his parents that might have been enough to drive him away for a time yet left him fully human. Perhaps one day he would be able to do that but not now. His own knowledge was so fresh it would burst out of him. He would long so much for them to know and not turn from him that he would tell and see them turn away. The thought that he might one day go back, even under cover of a lie, gave him that fragment of hope that makes it possible to survive, to go on. He began to walk forward through the forest towards the north. He would find a highway and a coach that would carry him towards the midlands where there were cities like Birmingham more decayed than Bristol that he could lose himself in among the tattered human cast-offs who were still nearer to the stars than he was.

He came first to Swindon where he got a pirate going north that clattered and juddered a wandering route to Cheltenham.

It was too ancient to have any modern safety devices and travellers knew that they rode in it at their own risk, but looking at their faces Gor saw that like himself most of them were beyond caring for such refinements as compensation for a lost limb or life. At Cheltenham he changed coach, for the pirates were forbidden the main highways which were the preserve of the big companies. The appearance of the passengers, however, didn't alter and no ripple of excitement went through them as they neared the end of the journey, circling the grimed concrete maze of the ringway.

Now Gor knew how to work a city and he set off to find himself a roof against the night in one of the crumbling terraces. Here he stretched out on the floor with his knees doubled up against the hunger pangs and fell asleep. There was a heap of bedding in one corner but it was probably lousy and he preferred the hard discomfort to being eaten alive, though the fleas would probably scent his warm blood and seek him out while he slept anyway.

When he woke it was dark and he was very hungry indeed. He must get food somewhere but the journey had almost exhausted his small stock of cash. Gor turned over the possibilities in his mind. Since he wasn't human he was no longer bound by the laws and rules of conduct men laid down for each other and that he had absorbed at Montgomery. Now it was the laws of animal survival that he would follow. He needed money and something to eat. Leaving his refuge he went out into the street searching for an automart to investigate as a source of both.

He found two, which was better as it gave him in theory a choice though in reality they were so similar it hardly mattered which he took. Nevertheless he weighed them up carefully, buying some sandwiches in one and a drink in another which gave him an excuse to look around.

The checkout took either cash or account debit. If you keyed in the required amount and your bank number there was a pause while the till checked you and, if you had tried to cheat, it flashed up an angrily winking sign. 'You have no credit,' the sign announced to all the world. The conveyor belt wouldn't deliver your purchases until the till cleared them. The whole equipment was inside a reinforced glass cubicle. Any serious interference with it brought a grille down to seal the offender in the automart until the police arrived. Gor went back to his

196

house with his purchases to eat and plan.

He needed something to slice through the glass and fortunately he still had in his pack the cutter he had used at the Institute. Then he needed something to prevent the grille coming right down to floor level. He searched his own house and those nearby until he found three strange implements in a cupboard under the stairs, made of solid metal, brass and iron, one in the shape of a giant's flat spoon, another with two long hinged arms that met and the third that was an ornate handled rod. Gor couldn't begin to guess what they had been for but they suited his purpose exactly. He wrapped them in rags and practised carrying them up his sleeves, a device that should have worked but merely made him awkward and he was forced to pack them into a bag.

It was gone midnight when he let himself out and took up a vantage point to observe his chosen automart from a doorway. The machines inside winked at him with a mechanical insolence that dared him to take them on, cloaked as they were with their security system that left them tantalizingly open to the night although there were few walkers who might need their services.

Gor timed the passing of two policars and as soon as the second had been gone five minutes he unwrapped his tools and stepped forward. Two he placed in the upright grooves on either side of the doorway and jammed them into position with some pieces of wood from the same cupboard under the stairs. Next he made a swift series of purchases from the dispensers and carried them to the conveyor belt. As the first one passed into the glass cubicle for registration of its price code he took out his glass cutter and, pressing hard, removed an entire panel from the side. The machine continued to tot up the purchases while he made himself wait patiently. Then it rang up the total and demanded payment. He put forward a couple of dollar pieces. It opened its mouth drawer to receive and evaluate them and Gor struck, ramming the long rod into it and prising it back. Alarms began to ring but he went on stuffing money into his bag. Behind him he was aware of movement. The grille was coming down. He prayed his wedges would hold. Wrenching out the rod he turned and saw the grille resting on the top of them. There was just room for him to wriggle on his back underneath the bottom bar. Clutching the bag and the rod he fled up the street and flung himself into the darkness of a

197

doorway as the policar sirens wailed and screeched towards him, their sensors turning as they sought for him up and down the dark road.

Ann had suggested to William that Empers might know Gordon's whereabouts. She had rung him and arranged to meet.

'You can come to my uncle's place. I expect everyone will be out and we'll have it to ourselves.'

William had thought Ann's house big and handsome enough but Burrages overwhelmed him, first with its park and view across the Empson acres, then with its own nineteenth-century rust brick and tile ugly grandeur. In spite of its gothic ornamentation it gave an impression of gauntness and the inside seemed harsh and gloomy in the sunless autumn light that appeared to hang back at the long windows rather than suffuse the room where they sat.

There was a tasteless opulence about the furnishings too. He longed for a faded patch in the curtains, for a dint or scuff-mark in the sofa, for a sign of use and wear. Everything was too untouched as though it was renewed each year not from necessity but as a matter of form. The house made him feel tetchy. So did Ann's ease with Empers. He had to remind himself that they had known each other for years but however he reasoned with himself he felt excluded. Suddenly he realized that what he wanted more than anything was to touch her. Their hands had met over a glass and the sensation that had gone through his body told him what had happened to him, what Emily had seen at once. Now he was apprehensive. What did she feel? He didn't know.

He had nothing and was nothing. Confronted by the house and her ease with Empers he felt as strange as he might with a space visitor. How and on what neutral ground could the two nations they represented meet? Used to command in his own world, he felt weakened and diminished in hers. She would, could see nothing in him to evoke the response he wanted, that she had evoked in him. How could he even ask it?

Restlessly he got up and went to stare out of one of the long windows, across the terrace and a shallow valley to the rise cutting off the horizon. Though Sir Saunders made his living out of the agribusiness he didn't let it come to his door. His windows looked on grass and trees and the abandoned combings of grazing sheep, a landscape ordered from another age not the exotic colourings of the workaday or the stripped raw autumn earth.

William turned back to the others. 'So you haven't any idea where he might be either.'

Ann had looked at the set of his shoulders as he had stood with his back to them. She understood his reactions completely and wanted only to be alone to reassure him. She wasn't sure how she understood, from what reservoir of knowledge beyond her experience she drew understanding, unless it was she had detected the same conflict in Norman though his expression of it had been different, a hardening against pain rather than an increased vulnerability to it. She caught herself wanting to put back the fringe of mist-darkened fair hair in order to smooth the wrinkles out of the forehead underneath, knowing how it would feel with such physical precision she almost blushed.

'If he gets in touch with me I'll try to persuade him to come back or at least to give me some idea where he is, and let you know if you can tell me where to get hold of you.' Empers felt uneasy with this tense chap in dungarees.

'I'll give you a number where you can leave a message for me to phone you or perhaps better for Ann to,' William said and recited the number of his HQ section.

'Who shall I say the message is for?'

'Will Bardfield.'

'I thought Ann said your name was Bardfield; then I thought I must have misheard.'

'Gordon was fostered by my mother and given our name.' William explained once more.

'Does he know what his real name is?'

'He may do now. That's probably half the trouble.'

'And is this your family's number? I mean who will I get?'

'You'll get whoever is on duty. It's my section headquarters. My family doesn't have a phone. There aren't many private ones in Bristol.'

'You're in the army, then?'

'In a way.' William paused, embarrassed at having to explain further. 'Whoever's on duty may refer to me as the commander, I should perhaps say.'

'What did you mean,' Ann asked as they drove away, 'when you said that you were in the army "in a way"?'

'It's not what people usually mean by being "in the army".'
'I still don't understand. You're a commander, you said.'
He would have to tell her; there was no way out. 'I'm one of the two Bristol commanders for the UGs West.'
'UGs?'
'Urban Guerrillas.'
'Do you kill people?'
'No.'
'As a commander you can get other people to do that.'
'We don't kill people. The name was stuck on us by the media and the authorities early on and we've kept it, as well as the military flavour, partly because it does the other side no harm from our point of view to see us in that way since that seems to be all they respect.'
'If you're an army that doesn't kill, what do you do?'
'We organize and extend the no-go areas.'
'No-go?'
'It's an old term again that's stuck with us. They're more like independent autonomous communities within the cities, people organizing themselves into small societies to pool resources and help each other, rather than retreating into isolated units that end up killing themselves out of loneliness, shame and despair; re-making urban villages if you like, going back to the beginning.'
'Yes, I can understand that. But how is it wrong?'
'It's outside the national system; therefore it's in a sense illegal by its very nature. And we don't welcome people coming in and trying to interfere with what's happening.'
'People?'
'From time to time the army or the police come in to investigate or rather intimidate, particularly after there's been a riot.'
'But don't you cause the riots?'
'They're nothing to do with us. They're the opposite of everything we're trying to do because they let out constructive energy on bottle-throwing and thrashing around. And they give an excuse for the riot squads to be called out and both sides to wage a mock war, that helps maintain the status quo. You feel good after you've shouted and chucked a few stones, like having a drink or two and staggering home singing, 'We are the brave boys,' rather than helping serve a hundred meals in the cafeteria or teaching an adult retraining class. I'm sorry: there's no way of putting any of this that doesn't sound . . .' He

200

searched for the word.

'Priggish? Pi? Pretentious?'

'What's "pie"?'

'Oh, holy Joe, from pious I suppose.' Ann laughed.

William leant forward and switched on the radio, searching the band for news through the static of pop and commercial. 'The commander ought to keep in touch,' he laughed in his turn. They let the international items wash over them, followed by the trade figures and the latest round of price rises and exhortations from ministers. Then came the reports from around the country. William was listening for any mention of Bristol but all was quiet there. 'The Home Secretary warned today of increased penalties for armed robbery after the attack on an automart in Birmingham last night where the thief used an assortment of weapons to foil the security system and escaped with several days' uncleared takings. Police have issued a videograph of a man they wish to interview – taken by the security system closed circuit telly – aged about nineteen, of medium height, dark complexion.'

'How they blow these things up out of all proportion,' William said. 'It's just some kid beating up a machine. No one was hurt or they'd have said, yet it'll be made an excuse for more stringent laws and stiffer punishments that only cause resentment or apathy. What do they expect from unemployed kids when the automarts flash their temptations at them?'

'It couldn't be Gordon, could it?' Ann asked. 'I suddenly thought: he's probably run out of money by now.'

'The description almost fits. He could be taken for nineteen quite easily.'

'He's such a gentle person, though,' Ann said doubtfully. 'It all sounded so violent.'

'That's just to make it more impressive and exciting. Nobody was actually harmed. If we could get to a telly screen we'd know.'

'We could have dinner somewhere, a motel for instance. There'd be one there.'

William laughed. 'I'm not dressed for having dinner in a motel. I'm sorry. You could go in though. Drop me off and pick me up again later.'

'Don't be daft. How could I? We'll have to think of something else. Meanwhile, I'll head us towards Birmingham just in case.'

201

Gor hadn't seen his own picture staring furtively out at the nation in a grainy videograph. All day he had been holed up eating and sleeping off a deep exhaustion of mind and body. He felt rested when he woke in the evening but with his better physical state came a renewed anguish of spirit that drove him out, picking up the metal rod with its bright golden handle as he left the house.

Rounding a corner, his mind struggling with the 'Gordon' file and all it meant, he was confronted by a policar. The sensors sprayed across him and back. There was a second while he hesitated like a headlight-pinned rabbit before he turned and ran. Behind him the policar had begin to screech. They knew him, he was sure of it. He cursed the thoughtlessness that had exposed him on the streets. Ahead was a blank wall. Beyond it there might be somewhere to hide. Gor leapt up, got his hands on the top and swung himself over, dropped into a yard on the other side. The policar wailed past.

It was a factory yard and the other sides were higher with no footholds. The only way out was back over the wall or through the workshop which had a door on to the yard. Gor opened it a crack and peered in. The night shift robots were at work in the windowless box under a blue light. Somewhere a minder would be drowsing in front of his console, waiting for a warning buzz to alert him to a problem.

The robots weren't humanoid in shape but Gor still felt a shudder as he watched the unattended machines going about their tasks. They were making plastic mugs and stamping them with bright designs. It was hard to realize that no immediate ganglion of moist tissue was directing their movements. For a moment his whole grasp of reality wavered and he couldn't be sure whether he or one of them was the more human.

Gor stepped into the factory shop and began to walk through them. 'Hey you! What are you doing in there?'

He swung round reflexively. A man had come down a flight of stairs and was blocking his way out the way he had come. 'You're the one whose picture was on the telly.'

Gor turned and bolted towards the far end where there was a door into another shop. He must get out before the minder called the police. Shop after shop opened in front of him, each filled with busy machines extruding, slicing, welding and painting the cheap wares to fill the automart dispensers. At last he came to the end of them, threw himself at the final door and ejected into the dingy entrance hall. He tried a door which must lead to the street but the power seal was on.

Gor hefted the metal rod in his hand and smashed into the only window, an opaque oblong of netted glass. He struck swift and hard several times, his flesh cringing from contact with any jutting broken fragment. Then he clambered through. As he touched the pavement a policar rounded the corner. A mechanical voice called on him to stand still but he ran up the street weaving and ducking as the tranquillizer darts pinged past him. He dodged round the next corner out of their range and ran on. He must find a refuge somewhere. Ahead he saw the outline of a church set back in a paved yard behind a low wall.

He jumped the wall and ran round the building. The porch was dark and empty and the thick wooden door fast shut. He ran out again and round to the left. Hope was dying in him. There was a small round-headed door in the wall but it would be shut too. When the latch gave he was so unprepared he almost fell into the lit vestry.

Father Jeffries didn't find prayer easy and therefore he worked at it. He was better at visiting, and dispensing alms such as he could raise, old clothes, bowls of vegetable soup made by his housekeeper. He prayed three times a day, apart from services, religiously and aridly. No word, no comfort came to him. When he was young, he remembered, communion had coursed through his body to his very finger ends with a tingling power. His inner eye had been able to visualize it burning along the bloodstream. Now he saw nothing. He sometimes thought that the mystics in their dark nights had at least known anguish. He knew nothing. How could he when such envious thoughts were all that came to him, blocking grace? Yet they came because there was no grace for him. He treadled this wheel endlessly and there was no way off.

'Help me, please. I can't go any further.'

He recognized the face at once and saw the clenched poker that could dash out his brains if he refused. But it wasn't that that made him open a large chest, half filled with vestments, and take them out. 'Get in and keep absolutely quiet.' The boy, as he saw now he was, belying the videograph, folded himself in. Father Jeffries arranged the vestments over him and dropped the lid. 'Try to get your mouth near the keyhole and breath through that.' There was a faint shuffle in the chest, silenced by a hammering on the main door.

The priest switched on lights in the dark hall of the church, genuflected as he passed the altar and heard the slight swish of his cassock as he went down the aisle and turned to the south door.

Four policemen stood there. 'We're looking for an armed robber; you may have seen his picture on the telly. He broke into a factory a while ago and we've been chasing him until we lost him around here.'

'It's so very dark, it's hard to see. I was in the vestry when you knocked.'

'You'd have seen him if he'd come in here?'

'Oh,yes, yes. I'd have seen him.' He hadn't yet told a lie.

'He's a dangerous thug. Don't try to tackle him if you do see him. Call us. Goodnight, sir.'

'Goodnight.' He watched the policars wail away. 'You can come out now,' he said as he lifted the lid of the chest. The heap of vestments was pushed back. The intruder sat up. Father Jeffries considered that he might die in a minute. He felt no fear. It would solve the problem of prayer, of faith itself.

Gor heaved himself out of the chest and then his legs seemed to tremble and he found he was sitting on the edge. He rested his head in his hands, the poker sticking up vertically above the coarse black hair.

'You could put that down.'

'I mustn't forget it.' It had become something to hold onto.

The voice wasn't at all what Father Jeffries had expected. The first plea for help had come through the distortion of running hard and urgency. Now that he heard it speaking quietly and slowly, he realized that it was an 'educated' instrument as he preferred to express it, rather than use crude status terms. With faint shock he also realized that his own responses were being conditioned by it. He was inclined to believe that the boy wasn't a dangerous thug simply because of the way he spoke.

'If I could just sit here for a few minutes. . . Thank you for not giving me up.'

Father Jeffries didn't believe in chance. At the least, any happening gave one the opportunity for choice. The boy's coming to his door presented him with such a moment. 'I think

204

you should stay here tonight and rest. I'd like to talk to you.'

More than anything Gor ached to talk, to confess his original sin in being born, to plead that even so it wasn't his fault and to ask what should happen to him. The priestly figure in its cassock was familiar from the chaplain at Montgomery. Had he stayed on he would probably have been baptized and confirmed that year. He had a vision of Wednesday morning chapel which was a sung eucharist with blended boys' and mens' voices and longed to be held in the comfort and aspiration of it. 'I'd like to talk to someone but I don't know...'

'We'll go into the vicarage. You'll meet my housekeeper, Mrs Ellis. She's very discreet. I'll carry the poker, shall I; then she won't be worried.'

Gor handed it over. 'What did you say it was, sir?'

'This? It's a poker. Didn't you know?'

'I found it in a cupboard under the stairs in an empty house.'

'Yes, you would.'

'What was it for?'

'It was for making the fire burn brightly in the days when there were coal and wood fires. You thrust it in like this and the flames leapt up.' He made thrusting motions with it as if fencing.

'Good gracious, Father. What have you got there? A poker?'

'Yes, a poker. This is a young friend, Mrs Ellis, who's staying the night.'

'How do you do, ma'am,' Gor said falling into the Montgomery salute.

She nodded at him. She too had seen his picture, and she understood the poker. Equally she knew that the vicar would try to help him. He wasn't the first to arrive in strange circumstances and find temporary sanctuary. 'Supper's ready.'

'Good. Perhaps you'd like a wash. I'll show you the bathroom.'

The vicarage was dingily shabby as a broken but undiscarded slipper that bears the long impress of its wearer, but there was the comfort of hot water, soap and a clean towel in the bathroom.

'What's your name, by the way?'

'Gordon.'

'You sit there, Gordon. You'll excuse me while I say grace.'

Gordon bent his head. 'Can I give you some of Mrs Ellis's excellent marcaroni cheese?'

'Thank you.'

'She spoils me. Cooks in the old way. I eat better than in the finest restaurant. Where were you at school?'

'Montgomery, sir.'

'Mrs Ellis thinks you have "very nice manners". I'm afraid you've won her heart. I take it that you don't live in Birmingham?'

'No, sir.'

'Few people would choose to.'

'You do.'

'It's a kind of choice, I suppose, a daily choice to continue to stay here where I've been for, let me see, thirty-two years. Sometimes, often, I ask myself whether it is any longer a true choice or merely habit.'

Father Jeffries continued to meander the conversation through apple sponge and custard and on to coffee while he watched the boy unwind. 'We'll take our coffee into my study where there's a fire of sorts; not the kind to give your poker any exercise, I'm afraid.'

'Did you get into trouble at Montgomery and run away?'

'No.' He wanted so much to talk but he didn't know how to begin.

'Where do your parents live, Gordon?'

'I haven't any.' He put a hand over his eyes to hide the tears that he couldn't control and tried to fight them down. The priest let the silence hang until the boy was ready to speak again, knowing he would be forced to fill that silence with words, an old confessional trick he had learned from his first vicar when he had come to St Andrews as a green curate. 'I had to have the money to eat.'

'I understand that. I'm not blaming you. But you can't go on like it. You'll get caught. Somewhere someone will be missing you, be responsible for you and it would be better if you went back and faced whatever it is than tried to hold on here until the police catch up with you. Already everyone knows what you look like. It's only a matter of time. I'll help you all I can to get back to your friends or go wherever you can take up your life again. I'll go back to Montgomery with you and talk to your principal if that would help. I expect he's called something special. Montgomery has rather a military flavour, I believe.'

'I can't go back there. My guardian threatened to lock me up. If I tried to go to Montgomery he would catch me.'

'What did you do to make him say that?'

'I kissed his daughter.'

Father Jeffries smiled. 'That's a very venial sin.'

'It's different for me.' Again the priest leant on silence. 'I shouldn't have anything to do with anybody. I shouldn't be here at all. I'm not human.'

The boy had seemed quite rational but he was obviously deeply disturbed. Perhaps he was harbouring guilt for a road accident in which his parents had been killed and he hadn't. 'How did your parents die, Gordon?'

'I never had any. I'm made, made in a laboratory.'

Father Jeffries had never met a child born of a test tube mating. Perhaps there was always a psychological problem. Presumably it was alright where the child was born into a family and was merely, as it were, the product of an external mating between its parents. But where the woman had had a child by an unknown man that child might well wonder about its father. Then there was the more extreme case of a child implanted in a host mother. Some of his poorer women parishioners did this for a living, he knew. Suppose the real mother, if you could use such a term, didn't want the child after it was born? That would cause additional feelings of rejection. He sighed to himself. 'We know not what we do.' Aloud he said: 'Even though the meeting of two elements takes place in a laboratory God still presides over the fusion, the act of creation, still breathes a human soul into the child that is the result of that fusion.'

'Only if parents are human. Mine weren't.'

Father Jeffries cast around for the right words. Clearly there was a deep obsessional wound here. He must probe carefully. 'Sometimes when the mind is very distressed it invents explanations, fantasies like the stories of changelings.'

'I don't understand.'

'In the days when people believed in fairies, if a child was born that was a little different in some way, people believed that the fairies had taken the real child and substituted, changed it for, one of their own, the changeling, who often, they thought, had a knowing look as if it was too old for its years. There were no fairies of course but it provided an explanation for otherwise perhaps intolerable facts like sickness or deformity in a child. Aren't you doing rather the same thing: trying to find an explanation for not being wanted or for some

207

imagined lack in yourself, either physical or emotional?'
'I've seen the file. I have it here with me, in the house where
I was hiding. I can prove it to you.'
'Gordon, are you really willing to put this to the test?'
'Yes.'
Father Jeffries stood up. 'We will go to get it together. If you
went out alone you might be arrested. I'll find a cassock for you
and you can be a visiting ordinand, and I think, yes, a hat of
some kind.'

All the time they were dressing him up the priest expected
Gor to break down and admit that it was all a lie or rather a
fiction. When they reached the street he thought that the boy,
now suitably disguised, fed and rested, might break from him
and run off into the dark. He would be sorry but he wouldn't
inform the police. Someone somewhere might stretch out a
helping hand that would be more skilled, more effective than
his had been. They walked through the night streets together
until they reached one of the rotted and abandoned terraces.
Here, if he was a psychopath, the boy could easily kill him. He
was young and strong. Father Jeffries thought that he might
not resist or even try to avert it. Would that be a sin?

He was taken down a side entry and in through a back door.
He saw the heap of bedding. 'Why don't you bring all your
things?'

The boy opened a bag that had been hidden in a cupboard
and took out a file. 'You see. It's here, I didn't make it up.' He
opened it and pointed to the single word 'Gordon'.

'Let's read it at the vicarage.' Perhaps he would be able to
unravel whatever had caused the breakdown. Father Jeffries
looked round at the walls that were an atlas of mouldering con-
tinents and mildew seas. Families had lived here. Children had
played, shouted, slept; lovers had held each other under the
sheets and cried into each other's mouths; dog and cat had
jostled for the warmest bit of the rug. Now it housed only
Gordon's pain and his inadequacy. Where had they all gone,
the people he had known in these streets when he had first
come to St Andrews all those years ago? Epidemics, malnutri-
tion, despair had thinned them out to the point where the
population was collapsing in on itself like a dying star, a black
dwarf that might in the end be the city's only inhabitant, a
changeling indeed.

They reached the vicarage again without interruption. The

policar panned the two priestly figures and cruised away.

'I think you should get some rest. Leave the file with me to read and we'll talk about it in the morning. Try to sleep.'

An hour later he went back to the beginning for the third time to see if he could have been mistaken or if there was any evidence that the whole thing was a hoax but there was none and he had understood the facts perfectly. The progress of the first stages of the experiment was clearly and clinically recorded, including the first failure to impregnate Mary by artificial insemination.

The boy, the being, he no longer knew what to call him, asleep in his bed upstairs was only half human. The human mind had always conceived of such creatures; now it had conceived indeed and brought forth. There had been children of men and horses, the centaurs; of girl and bull, the minotaur. The classical gods had come to earth in animal shape and peopled the imagination with their offspring, and whatever man could imagine it seemed that he could and must do. He had made Gordon to live in a new limbo on the edge of hell. Man had played God.

The human part of him couldn't be saved because it was so mixed with the ape. He had put his own finger on the dilemma. To have a soul you must be man. However much the human in him craved it he could never be given communion, any more than Father Jeffries could see himself offering it to his mother Mary. The image of the chalice at her lips was too grotesque. Mentally his hand dashed it away.

Yet he coudn't condemn him to despair. Somehow he had to find words to help him live as he would have found words and gestures to soothe a distressed animal. He cursed the irresponsibility of the man who had made him and brought him up to be human. The error would have been less if Gordon had been kept in some special environment and never encouraged to think of himself as part of mankind.

He would have to be celibate. Even if he could propagate he mustn't. The terrible mistake mustn't be compounded unless of course it were to be with creatures from his mother's side where the offspring would be far less human and therefore pose no problem. He should never approach a girl and ask to be loved. And yet the palliative he had himself found to celibacy, to love God, was also closed to this being. Only a human soul could love God. The castration of an Abelard would be a kindness. Perversely men might wish to couple with apes but he knew instinctively that Gordon would be drawn only to humans. He must stop following the theological thread if he was to find the right words, and lean on compassion.

In the morning he looked across the table at the weary face and thought he could see the two components like a rippled image in the mirror of a lake. 'I've read it all through very carefully. The man who called himself your guardian, who was he?'

'He was the Doctor who made me.'

'I thought so. What is his name?'

'Norman Forester.'

Father Jeffries hesitated. He held one piece of information that he thought Gordon hadn't absorbed. Should he tell him? Would it make it worse or better? Perhaps in the end it was simply that truth was best and best taken now altogether.

'He is your father.'

Gor half rose and then sat down again. 'How do you know?'

'In both cases when an attempt was made to make Mary pregnant, a batch of sperm was used whose coding began with the initials N.F. Five and six. There had been other experiments, I expect. Come into my study. Now,' he said when they had taken the same places as last night, 'I have some very hard things to say to you. Can you bear them?'

'I'll try.'

'When you leave here you must go in the clothes you wore last night. Where you will go I don't know and perhaps it's better that I don't. If you decide to go on living among men you must try to forgive them because they are your brothers. Bitterness and anger would only drive you mad. Whether you tell anyone else your history is up to you. But you must resolve firmly that you can never marry or have children or indeed touch a woman in that way at all.' He thought: 'You should not take a boy of nine,' was it? 'And make him swear never to kiss the girls.' Aloud he went on, 'You see, a girl might fall in love with you, even if she knew your full story.' He could imagine only too easily that they might indeed, that Gordon would awaken the strongest mothering instinct in some women. 'But she wouldn't really understand what she was taking on, even if she thought she did.' It was the best he could do. Confronted by the reality of Gor and his pain he couldn't even hint at the true nature of the barrier. Where did the dividing line between man and animal lie? 'You must try to look at your suffering as part of your unique contribution to life.' He picked his way carefully, aware that his everyday vocabulary was full of knives that would cut sharp and deep. He must avoid any occasion for prayer or blessing. Father Jeffries had always found services where people brought their animals for benediction mawkish and theologically unsound in spite of St Francis. It was true that all creatures were by definition part of the creation but Gordon was probably not even that, unless you were to extend the concept to plastic artefacts or argue for the indivisibility of creation, even including the secondary creations not of nature but of man. Could he bless the human and mentally exclude the ape? He asked a blessing on apples and ears of corn and tins of soysteak at the harvest festival but he knew he couldn't make the sign above Gor's kneeling head or bring out the crucial words.

'How much money have you left?'

'Quite a lot.'

They had dressed him up again and put a prayer book in his bag with his own clothes and the poker. After he had gone Father Jeffries let himself into the church and lowered himself to his knees but Gor's face came constantly between him and the words in his head. It wasn't surprising perhaps that the silence seemed even more impenetrable than usual.

Ann and William had paused just before Birmingham. 'This is ridiculous,' she said, 'if we can't stop anywhere to eat or sleep because of your clothes.' She had never encountered the problem before.

'I'm sorry. Look, I've told you, you go in somewhere. I can sleep in the car.'

'That would be too awful. I couldn't. Where are people wearing what you're wearing supposed to go?'

'There are hostels if you've got an employed certificate.'

'Well, that excludes both of us.'

'If we go on into Birmingham I can get in touch with the UGs there.'

'Are there groups like yours in all the cities?'

'Most of them.'

'And you're all in touch with each other? It's a world within a world I didn't even know existed.'

Their camp in Birmingham was in the Ladywood district. The car stopped at the barrier. William got out and spoke to

211

the guards while Ann sat nervously and, she thought, conspicuously at the wheel. The barrier was lifted and she drove through. William directed her to the building that served as headquarters. They were taken through a hall and a corridor to a room whose door was guarded. As they entered a woman rose from behind a desk and came round. 'Will.' She put out a hand to shake his. 'Lovely to see you. What are you doing up here?'

'Looking for someone. Jenny, this is Ann Forester. Jenny Lloyd.' The two women shook hands. William explained their quest.

'I'll get his picture put on the video for you. Then you can see if it's the one you're looking for.'

'We'd be grateful. We need somewhere to stay tonight as well. Any suggestions?'

The one she would have liked to offer she knew wouldn't be accepted. She had tried before in as many ways as she could to make her interest clear to Will Bardfield, but he had turned it aside with a show of brotherliness that disarmed without hurting too much. She wondered if Ann Forester was succeeding where she had so often failed.

Ann found it physically painful to see Gordon's face distorted by the videograph. She put up a hand as if to ward off a blow and William was tempted to take it.

'Is that the person you've looking for?'

'Yes, that's Gordon.'

'How can we help?'

'If anyone sees him they could let us know. We want to make contact with him before anyone else does.'

'What's he done?'

'Nothing,' Ann said. 'He's just frightened, perhaps, and lonely.'

'He broke into an automart,' Jenny Lloyd said.

'He must have needed money and thought he had a right. . .' Ann felt that she was putting it badly. How could she convey so many years' knowledge of Gordon that made her sure it wasn't a vicious but rather a desperate act?

'He's my foster brother,' William said.

They ate at the cafeteria, sharing a table with Jenny Lloyd and some of her officers. There were no flowers or dancing.The city kept its old reputation for practicality. William was glad his own charge was more gentle. He thought Ann would like it better. When they were left alone at the table he said, 'They're much more under siege than we are. At home we have flowers on the tables and when the main meal is over for most people we have music. People sing and dance. I wish you could see it.'

'Who else is there at home?'

'My mother and my sister Emily. It was Em who first found Gordon in a way.' He told her the story and of the strange coincidence of finding the Knotts, his addition to Gordon's history and the taking of the file. Later they walked in a nearby park that was within the area of the camp where children were still out playing and older people sat and talked in a beer garden.

'That old lady looks just like Mrs Goulding,' Ann said, pointing at the middle one of a trio.

'Who's Mrs Goulding?'

She explained about her pensioners. They were paying each other the small coin of love, offering little tokens of themselves to see if they would be pocketed or returned. For a few minutes they stood by the stream and watched a late duck heading up towards a bowed bridge to sleep. At the door of Ann's room in the terrace which had been turned into a guest house William put out a hand and touched her shoulder.

'Perhaps there will be some news in the morning. Sleep well.'

But she couldn't. As soon as she was alone all the day's happenings began to unreel in her head. Something nagged at her. She came to William's story of his sister's first encounter with Gordon, of the baby she had been told was a little gorilla and of the even stranger tale of the Knotts. What precisely had Norman said to her when he had heard about Cressy and Gordon? She had dismissed it at the time as a fantasy but suppose it was true?

Ann sat on the hard clean bed and tried to fit the pieces together. Something in his file had seemed so terrible to Gordon that he had run from it. She thought back to Norman's first story of the orphan and the dead parents, of the name that was William's and his family's and realized that whatever the answer to Gordon's parentage she had been deliberately deceived and manipulated.

Norman had been involved with the infant since its birth. With a chilling shock she heard herself asking what had happened to Mary's baby and she remembered his almost angry response. Was it possible? Could such things be done? She knew some of Norman's work had to do with genetics, that Mary's pregnancy had been as the result of implantation. She got up and opened the door.

William had been lying fully dressed on his own narrow bed. He had been thinking about her so hard that when the knock came he would have been completely disconcerted to find someone else there but he saw at once that this wasn't an erotic visit. 'What is it? What's the matter?'

'I have to talk to you. I have to ask you something.'

'What is it?'

'Can you make a person out of a human and something else?'

'What do you mean?'

'Can you combine the sexual elements from two different species?'

'Like tigers and lions making tigrons you mean?'

'Yes.'

'I don't know enough about genetics to say positively. Why, Ann?'

'My husband once said that Gordon wasn't human, that he was only humanoid. I thought he'd made it up, that it was because of Gordon's looks and his own suppressed resentment, but suppose he was telling the truth?' Ann put her hands over her face.

He went towards her and took her in his arms, holding her while she shook under the battering of a stream of emotions.

'The boys at school called him Monkey.'

'Start from the beginning. Tell me everything you know.'

When she had finished he said, 'I think it's possible, and it's such a chain of circumstantial evidence that it has to be seriously considered.'

'Isn't there any genetic barrier to such things?'

'Usually, as far as I understand it, but with modern techniques of genetic engineering such barriers can probably be overcome. After all, we are cousins, many times removed by evolutionary changes but still related. That's why scientists bother to study the other primates.'

'He kissed Cressy. Suppose. . .'

'He didn't know. You can't blame him any more than you can blame a dog that makes up to a human.'

'I don't blame him. I blame Norman. He used us all and put us all at risk, emotional risk. We were all part of his exper-

214

iment.'

'If it's true.'

'I feel it; instinctively I know it's true.' She realized he still had his arms round her.

William had realized it too. Without thinking he kissed her hair, her cheek, her throat, her mouth. He felt her lips open and her arms tightening round him.

'I'd better go.'

'Try to sleep.'

'I'll try.'

Alone again both lay awake for a long time. Ann had wanted love. She felt herself soaking it up as if it was a dew shed on thirsty skin whose every pore was a small demanding mouth to carry it down to the roots of her being. Yet she was made fearful by the difficulties in their way. She felt instinctively that William would be as serious in love as she was but the difference in their ages worried her. She wasn't quite sure how much it was but she hoped that they inhabited the same decade. She was tempted to get up and look in the mirror above the washbasin. Had she any right to snatch at his love? Even as she asked she knew she no longer had any choice.

William in his narrow bed took her in his arms again, kissed her, felt her respond. If he breathed into the pillow he could still catch the scent of her on his own skin. Could she love him? Why should she? He drew her down into him with every breath until he was lulled to sleep.

'Your foster brother's been seen,' Jenny Lloyd reported in the morning. 'At least we're pretty sure it was him though he was dressed up like some kind of priest.'

'Where is he?'

'He was boarding a coach at the station.'

'Do you think anyone else saw him?'

'The pollys? I doubt it. They wouldn't be expecting him to leave and they don't have the wide cover we do.'

'Where was the coach going?' Ann asked.

She looked as if she hadn't got much sleep, Jenny Lloyd noted enviously. 'South.'

'Then he could be on his way home. Thanks, Jenny, and for putting us up.'

'Come and see us again soon.'

Gor left the coach at Cheltenham. He rang Ann's number but

there was no reply. He found a private coach going east and retraced the route he had come, back to Swindon. This time Forester answered his call. Gor felt the hairs rise all over his body. Disguising his voice he asked for Ann. 'She's away for a few days. Who shall I say rang?'

Gor mumbled something indistinct and put down the receiver. He went out into the station yard and found the stand for Salisbury. While he waited he kept his mind empty as if deep in the meditation his clothing might have suggested. He got off at the familiar stop as though he was simply arriving at what had come to be home for the holidays. He took the poker from his bag just outside the gate and left the bag in the hedge. Then he walked up the drive with the poker hidden down the side of his cassock, relying on his disguise to get him to the front door.

Forester was puzzled by the ring. Through the spyhole he saw the clerical figure that had turned its back to look down the drive towards the road. He opened the door.

Gor turned, thrust his foot in the gap and raised the poker. Forester backed away. Apes could be very volatile and potentially dangerous. Gor forced his way forward and suddenly lunging with the poker shattered the telephone receiver with a blow.

'Sit down.'

'Put that down, Gordon.'

'My name is Gor. Sit down.' Under the threat of the raised poker Forester sat.

Ann and William had reached Bristol in a couple of hours but there was no news of Gor.

'I have to go home,' Ann said. 'I have to try to find out the truth.'

'I'm coming with you. It occurs to me that Gordon may have gone there.'

Forester calculated his chances of reaching a door and outstripping Gor as nil. Younger, stronger and in better physical condition, the humanoid could beat him easily. His best plan was to try to establish dominance, relying on his combined human and primate superiority as the older and cleverer male.

Gor had had no clearly defined objective in confronting Forester. His actions had been instinctive. Part of him still hoped that Forester would declare the Gordon file a fiction and tell him the names of his real parents. He saw that the man was afraid of him now but his own fear of the Doctor was old and deep-seated.

'I have the Gordon file.'

'Then you know what you are and that you have no rights, no status and can be destroyed as easily as you were made.'

Gor's instinct was to smash the cold face in front of him but he resisted it. Even so Forester had crushed his last hope.

'Then I have nothing to lose by killing you.'

'What good would that do?'

'It would free me.'

Ann had parked the car outside the drive. 'I'm coming in with you,' William said. If Gor had been there before them who knew what they might find? William didn't want her to face it alone.

'Look.' Ann pointed. 'Isn't that a bag under the hedge?'

William carried it over to the car. 'It's Gordon's, the one we brought with us the other night. These are the clothes he was wearing. He must be inside. Is there some way we can get close without alarming them?'

'Come on.' She led him to a side gate in the garden wall.

'What did you intend to do with me?' Gor asked. He felt the chill of the man's personality numbing him.

'I shall show you to the world: my creation. Almost the perfect young man of status except that he is sub-human.'

'Your son.'

'You know that, do you? How did you find out?'

'The coding on the sperm.'

'I see. That was clever of you.'

'You are as much my father as Cressy's. Twice my father because you made me.'

'But Ann isn't your mother and that makes all the difference to your make-up. Sperm and ova are just different kinds of cells. They might as well be dividing amoeba except that they fuse instead of separating. Outside the bodies that make them, in the culture dish, that's all they are.'

'No. That's not true. You can't separate things like that. You put two cells together but that wasn't the end of it. By that act you made a person.'

'I made a thing, an artefact.'

Gor felt himself trembling with anger and grief. 'Even my mother was a person. You made her a thing, a vehicle for your own pride and vanity.'

217

'Lesser creatures are there to be used by higher, by those clever enough to do it. Anyway Mary wouldn't have minded having my child though she didn't care for the operations or for the result. Your loving ape mother would have soon done for you. Maternity wasn't her strong point.'

'What happened to her?'

'She died or rather was terminated a few years later. It's in the file. She was very clever but foul-tempered. At least you won't pass her temperament on.'

'What does that mean?'

'I've never done a sperm count on you but I expect to find you're sterile. Hybrids usually are.'

Gor let out a scream of misery and lifted the poker high. All control was gone. His grief was too great.

'No, Gordon, no!' Ann cried, running into the room.

He turned towards them, his face distorted.

'It's alright, Gordon. He can't hurt you any more,' William said, coming forward. 'He's done all the harm he can.'

'You heard. You heard.'

Ann went close to him. 'It doesn't matter.' She put out a hand and touched him quite deliberately, seeing behind the adult the ugly child she had first brought back from Montgomery, waiting anxiously in the hall with his bag and Empers,ugly until he had smiled.

'Rather in the nick of time like the US cavalry,' Forester said uncertainly, watching William and Ann. 'I don't think we've met.'

'William Bardfield.'

'I see. You know the story?'

'All of it.'

'William, would you take Gordon upstairs? I expect he'd like to wash his face. I'll be up in a minute to pack.'

'He doesn't need to wash,' Forester said. 'He's broken the phone but I'm sure the three of us can manage him.'

There was a moment's silence. Gor was too exhausted to look up. If they intended to betray him in a human conspiracy there was nothing he could do. He no longer had the strength to care.

'You don't seem to understand,' William said. 'Gordon has the file. He's free of you. There's no evidence that he exists except himself. Without the file no one would believe you.'

'You can't mean to let him loose in human society.'

218

'Why not? You did. And anyway he will be with us. You made him my foster brother. That hasn't changed. Come on, Gordon. Show me the way upstairs.'

'What are you going to do?' Forester asked Ann.

'I shall go to Fanny and Charles.'

'When will you be back?'

'I am leaving you.'

'Is he your lover?'

'I am leaving you because of what you are and what you did.'

'You're being emotional.'

'No. For the first time in my life I am strong enough to do what I know is right.'

'You'll be back. You need my authority.'

'You don't understand even now.' She would cry later at the humiliation he had inflicted on her, at how he had used her, Gordon and Cressy, at his bloodless deception.

She drove Gor and William into Salisbury. 'Give me your phone number,' William said, afraid of losing her.

'Don't worry.'

'You won't go away?'

'No.' She gave him Fanny's number for comfort. 'Ring me tomorrow to let me know how you both are.'

They climbed into the Bristol coach. Gor closed his eyes and leant his head back. William looked down from the window. He thought that if he was to be told at that moment that he would never see her again he wouldn't want to go on living.

Ann buzzed at Fanny's door. 'This time I'm really staying with you. I've left Norman.'

'Sit down and tell me all about it,' Fanny said with relish.

It was Emily who first noticed the soldiers or rather they noticed her. She was on her way to the hospital. Lately she had taken to helping out there in the afternoons. In a way it was like being back at Jessop's.

'Where you going?'

She looked at their faces through the riot helmets. They had been drinking. 'To the hospital.'

'Got something wrong with you?'

'No.'

'Not yet. I'll give you something to see the doctor about.' Oh God, Emily thought, this isn't happening.

'You hold her.'

She fought them but against two trained young men she had no chance. Inside her was a great sadness that this was how it should be after all her dreams.

Jessop couldn't have said why he set out to meet her that day. Perhaps it was the autumn weather making him restless. At the strip of grass beyond the grounds he saw the three figures in the distance, understood them though he didn't know who the woman was, shouted and started to run.

'Christ, drop it,' said the one who was holding her. 'Let's get out.'

'I never bloody got in. She was as tight as a duck's arse,' his mate said as they began to run.

Emily lay where they had dropped her. Jessop went down on one knee. 'Em, Em, I didn't realize it was you. Are you alright?'

'I don't know.'

'Oh Em, if anything happened to you I don't know what I'd do.' Even as he said it he thought it sounded like something from a cheap song.

'We have to get back to the camp and tell them about those soldiers. I wish William was here.'

'Can you get up?'

'I think so.' She struggled up and leant against him. 'I feel a bit wobbly.'

He put his arm round her.

William noticed the extra activity as they walked from the coach station, and quickened his pace. When they reached the camp they found it, already alerted by Emily and Jessop, preparing for action. Riot shields and helmets were being issued. Everyone was glad to see them. 'You stay with me,' William told Gor as they collected their own armour.

'What is it? What's happening?' The excitement had overcome his exhaustion.

'From time to time they send in the soldiers to destroy the camp. We have to contain them so they do as little damage as possible.'

William seemed able to be everywhere at once, deploying his volunteers. The whole area had to be cordoned since no one knew from which side the attack would come.

They came in three prongs, sirens wailing, and crashed through the barriers only to be met with a human wall. The soldiers jumped from their cars and advanced behind their shields. No blood must be shed which might give unease to the decent citizens who would see the conflict later in the comfort of their homes. It was a modern tourney. Phalanx met phalanx and shoved. The line held.

The soldiers withdrew. 'Batons!' shouted an officer. They drew their riot sticks: 'Charge!' They rushed forward.

'Out shields,' William ordered at the last minute. The line of curved tortoiseshells leapt forward two-handed forcing the batons up or down. Here and there a young soldier lost his temper and beat on a helmet with his stick. The officer drew them off.

There was a sound of shouting from one wing. 'Come on,' said William. 'It sounds as if they've broken.' He spoke into his walkie-talkie, calling up the reserves. Then he ran, Gor close behind him, in the direction of the shouting. 'Be careful with that,' he had said when Gor had insisted on bringing the poker. 'There mustn't be any injuries.'

They ran towards the cafeteria. A young soldier came hurrying along with a little crowd of women after him who cut him off, ringed him with their shields and jostled him back the way he had come until he began to run, and they opened their circle and let him out. All around them the same tactics were repeated to drive back those who had broken through.

One quicker than the rest ran on towards the cafeteria with a flamegun cocked in his hand. William and Gor set out after him but William was a commander not an athlete and the soldier, followed by Gor, soon left him behind. Gor gained on him fast and as they reached the open-air tables he was only a few steps behind. The soldier raised the gun to let a stream of flame run up the nearest wall. Gor took two steps and with his poker held like a foil sent the gun spinning away. A group of women appeared, led he could see through her helmet by Mrs Bardfield. They rounded up and turned the soldier. One twitched off his helmet and that was enough to set him running.

Gor meanwhile had turned his attention to the fire and immediately organized a bucket chain from the kitchen until a hose was brought up and the last small flames beaten down by a jet of water.

Sirens began to wail all round and a cheer went up. 'That's it for this time,' William said. 'Now we'll clear up.'

The news would carry a report of troops called in to quell

221

riots, of burning and looting. He must ring Ann and let her know they were alright.

They sat for probably the last time that year at the outdoor tables in a mood of euphoria compounded of their victory and more to drink than usual. William noticed that Stephen and Emily were holding hands. There was music, dancing and laughter. His mother suddenly got up from their table and went over to the band. They stopped their playing at the end of the tune and put down their instruments.

'Help me up,' said Mrs Bardfield, climbing onto a table. There were shouts and clapping. 'Mates,' she called. 'Sometimes when we have a little do like we had this afternoon, just a little do, nothing special. . .' There was more laughter. 'Sometimes,' she went on, 'when someone's been specially brave or clever we have a little presentation. Well today I think you'll agree with me that someone was Gordon, our Gor.'

'Yes, yes,' came the cries to more clapping.

'We wouldn't be sitting out here now enjoying ourselves if it hadn't been for him and I want you to show your appreciation while I thank him in the usual way.'

William realized it had all been planned when he saw the circlet of flowers. They had been sitting almost drowsy after the action of the last few days. Gor was aware that his pain had retreated deep inside him, overlaid by the excitement and Ann and William's acceptance of him.

'Go on, Gor. You've got to put up with it. It gives everyone a sense of occasion,' William said. He pushed the unwilling boy forward until he was standing below Mrs Bardfield, still clutching the poker for support. She bent forward and placed the circlet on his head. William hoped she wouldn't fall off and spoil the effect. She twirled Gor round so that he was facing the other tables.

'There you are everybody: our King of the day.'

Gor blushed and raised the poker in a kind of salute. One day, William thought, he might be a commander. I wish Ann could see him now. He held the image of her close against him.

'Kiss me, Stephen,' Emily said firmly.